"WHAT IS THE PROBLEM?"

"Problem?" Jacey gulped at the squeak in her voice.

Oh, there was a problem all right. But she couldn't very well tell Stryker that *she* wasn't the one who was supposed to marry him. *She* hadn't written those letters he was so fond of bringing up. She could scarce imagine his reaction if she told him she was a fraud masquerading in her twin sister's place. Or the money that he had sent to pay off the contract had been spent long ago. Instead, she smiled up at him.

"There isn't a problem," she lied through her even white teeth.

"There better not be." He looked down at her for a moment and added in a low voice, "I need you."

Jacey gasped aloud at the words and the blatantly sensual images they evoked.

Oh, dear heavens, the man had just told her he *needed* her.

Heat pooled in her stomach, then swept lower. Her eyes widened at the strange sensations she had never felt before in her life.

"You aren't thinking of backing out of our bargain, are you?" he demanded, his low, silky-smooth voice suddenly turning harsh.

Jacey swallowed and drew in a deep breath. The way he had added a certain emphasis to the word *bargain* worried her. He was talking about the marriage contract between him and her — wasn't he?

STRYKER'S
BRIDE

Joyce Adams

Zebra Books
Kensington Publishing Corp.

http://www.zebrabooks.com

ZEBRA BOOKS are published by

Kensington Publishing Corp.
850 Third Avenue
New York, NY 10022

Zebra, the Z logo and Splendor Reg. U.S. Pat. & TM Off.

First Printing: May, 2000
10 9 8 7 6 5 4 3 2 1

Printed in the United States of America

Chapter One

1876

Jacey Forester barely held back the strangled scream. She stared at the papers in her hands, wishing them away. If she had anything to do with it, they would go up in smoke. But they remained, every word legal and binding. She reread the shocking words.

Mail order bride!

This couldn't be possible. It had to be a nightmare. Or someone's poor idea of a joke. She shoved one hand into her curls, dislodging several pins, then tucked a disheveled blond tendril behind her ear.

She stared down at the papers again, still too stunned and angry to believe what she saw. In her hands she held a contract for a mail order bride with *her* name on it! As well as her flowing signature. She could scarce believe it.

Jacqueline Forester. The name practically shouted itself out loud.

This had to be Jeanette's handiwork. As she studied the papers closer, she recognized her twin sister's handwriting by the small swirl above the *i*. Her quick temper soared. When she got her hands on Jeanette, she would strangle her. Absolutely, definitely.

She dared not think what would have happened if she hadn't needed to borrow a pair of blue gloves for tonight and rummaged through her sister's bureau. Otherwise she might never have found the marriage contract.

Until it was too late.

The very words sent a shudder through her. She wasn't adverse to marriage, but she secretly dreamed of a love match with a man who could be her equal. Or stronger.

A mail order bride didn't sit well with her at all. She refused to be any man's mail order anything! She had to put an end to the ridiculous marriage bargain before it proceeded one bit further.

She would get Jeanette for this latest mess.

She would confront her twin the moment Jeanette returned from the best milliner shop in Baltimore. She simply had to return the contract money and cancel the entire transaction. There was no way on this earth that Jacey was going to become anybody's mail order bride.

Absolutely not!

She stormed out of the bedroom, kicking at the flounced ruffle of her green-and-white-striped skirt when it got in her way. For a moment, she wished it was her sister's dainty ankles. Finding it impossible to hold in what was on her mind, she dashed down the stairs. She would be prepared and waiting in the hall for her twin's arrival—albeit impatiently. Jeanette wasn't wheedling out of explaining the forged marriage contract.

And canceling it!

Jacey stopped at a point in the hall halfway between the doors and checked in both directions. She released a small sigh of relief. At least her meddling cousin Earl was nowhere to be seen. He was the last person she wanted around her at the moment. He would insist on interfering and only make matters worse.

It had scarcely been a week since Uncle Harvey left Earl in charge, and everything had gone to the devil!

She paced several steps and whirled around only to retrace her steps. She had a perfect vantage sight of both doors to await Jeanette's arrival, if she could only stand still. No one could sneak past her waiting here. Plopping both hands on her hips, she tightened her fingers around the contract, crumpling it in her hand, and waited.

As the minutes ticked by, her temper inched ever upward. Quick to anger, quick to forgive was how her parents had described her long ago. Disgustingly it still held true; she wouldn't be able to retain her anger at her twin for long. However, Jeanette wasn't sweet-talking her way out of this muddle.

Endless minutes later, Jacey heard the front door swing open and click closed. Sure enough, Jeanette entered and sauntered across the room toward the stairs. A new hatbox dangled from her hand.

"Jeanette," Jacey greeted her instantly, stepping forward into the sitting room. "We need to talk."

Her twin jerked to a halt, then looked around as if searching for an escape route.

"Now," Jacey demanded through clenched teeth.

"I . . . I'll . . . just put my purchases upstairs first." Jeanette started past. "You've got to see my new bonnet. Why, it's the latest—"

Jacey grabbed her twin's arm and half dragged her into the library. "No, you're not going anywhere until we talk."

Jeanette froze and blanched, her cheeks turning paper white; then she blushed with guilt. Her twin never could hide any trace of guilt.

Right now, Jacey knew her sister was as guilty as sin on a Saturday night. It was written in her eyes. Their color was practically the only visible difference between the twins: Jeanette's a calming, pale blue, Jacey's a fiery sapphire blue.

"Jeanette, what is this?" She pushed the contract under her twin's nose.

Jeanette's eyes widened, and she stepped back as if the papers burned her. "I . . . I can explain."

"Explain."

"Ah, let's go outside and talk?"

Jacey shook her head. "We're not going anywhere until I have answers."

"You're angry."

"You're right I am," she shouted, forgetting about her good intention not to yell.

"I didn't mean any harm. It sounded fun at first. If you insist, we'll just send him a letter that the marriage is off."

"It's not that simple."

"Well, I'm not marrying him. I'm in love with Franklin. At least I think I am. We're eloping."

Jacey ignored the dramatic announcement. Franklin Prescott was the latest in a string of anticipated "elopements" for her twin, none of which ever materialized before she changed her mind and found another beau.

"Jeanette—"

"Really, Jacey. Don't worry. We'll just tell him I've changed my mind."

"And return his money."

"The money?" Jeanette's voice cracked.

Jacey released a sigh of frustration. "The payment money you received from him." She tapped the papers and pointed to the sum. "You do still have the money, don't you?"

A decided sense of unease came over her as Jeanette

turned away and chewed on one fingertip. She couldn't have spent it, could she? Jacey glanced down at the new hatbox and recalled the new gown her twin had brought home the day before yesterday. The unease grew to a tangible fear. Hadn't there been a new riding outfit last week? And before that. . . .

"Jeanette? Tell me you have the money."

The young woman remained silent. Jacey's heart sank in her chest, and her temper returned.

"Jeanette." Jacey demanded an answer.

"I didn't mean to spend it all—"

"All? You spent it all?"

A delicate shrug was the only answer she received.

"Jeanette, you could go to jail for this—"

"Oh, pooh. That's ridiculous. What's he going to do clear from Texas?"

Jacey closed her eyes and bit back an unladylike oath. "You could be arrested for fraud. This is a legal contract." She waved the papers at her twin.

Jeanette merely pushed them away with a sniff. "It's not legal. I didn't sign my own name."

This time Jacey groaned out loud. "No, you signed *my* name." She caught her sister by the shoulders, forcing them face-to-face. "We could both go to jail for this."

"Oh, no," Jeanette wailed, comprehension dawning. "But, I thought if I signed your name—"

"You thought wrong."

"What are we going to do? Uncle Harvey—"

"Will be furious. And likely disown us for true this time." Jacey swallowed down the flutter in her stomach. Their guardian had never wanted to take on the care of the twins after their parents' death, the sight of girls reminding him that his beloved wife died in the same accident as their parents.

Thank goodness Uncle Harvey had traipsed off on a

business trip and wasn't due back for a month. Surely, they could figure a way out of this latest mess by then. But it didn't look promising at the moment.

Jeanette began to sniffle, and Jacey knew tears were not far behind. As usual, she felt her anger weakening at her twin's distress.

"Let's go upstairs and make plans." She caught up her sister's new hatbox in one hand and started out into the hallway. She knew her twin would follow the fancy new bonnet anywhere.

The sound of a loud fist on the front door stopped Jacey in midstep. She flattened herself against the wall and peered down the hall.

Her cousin hurried to the door, smoothing his brown hair with his hands. He had a face that bordered on handsome, but leaned toward petulant. He paused a second to check his appearance in the mirror, then continued to the door.

At the sight of meddling cousin Earl greeting two of Baltimore's uniformed police, Jacey nearly dropped the hatbox. She ducked back, colliding with Jeanette.

Trouble was calling; she knew it for certain. A familiar sense of dread rose up in her chest.

What else has Jeanette done now?

Her last shred of hope of keeping herself and her twin out of more trouble while Uncle Harvey was away on business vanished quicker than the marriage contract money. To make matters worse, Earl swung the door open and greeted the police with warmth. Jacey wanted to choke him for the smug certainty she heard in his voice.

Without taking time to think, she grabbed her sister by the hand and pulled her into the library, leaving the wood door partially ajar. She didn't want to miss a word of what was transpiring.

"What do *they* want?" Jeanette asked. Her voice quivered, a sure sign of a guilty conscience.

"Why don't you tell me?" Jacey whispered back.

Thank heavens she hadn't walked out into the sitting room yet. Maybe there was still time to figure a way out of this latest bout of trouble.

Setting the new hatbox on the floor, she whirled on her twin. "Jeanette, what have you done now?" she demanded in a whisper.

"Me? They can't be here for me."

A guilty flush colored her twin's cheeks before she turned her face away. Jacey could have sworn she heard her add, *Yet.*

Jacey's stomach tightened into a cold knot of dread. "Jeanette!"

The firmly whispered order didn't do a whit of good. Her twin remained silent and stiff-backed. Jacey wanted to throw something, preferably the new hatbox, hat and all. Instead, she pressed her ear against the crack of the partially closed door and eavesdropped without a bit of shame. After all, their futures could be at stake, she reasoned.

She barely kept her patience in check through the boring pleasantries exchanged between the men and her cousin. How much longer before they got to the point of their visit? Earl's self-satisfied voice decreed that he was enjoying this entirely too much. She released a pent-up breath of pure irritation, then tucked a wayward curl behind her ear and strained to hear the conversation.

What did the men want?

At the sound of *her* name, she nearly gasped aloud. They couldn't be here for her!

"What charges?" Earl asked.

Charges! Jacey leaned even closer to the door.

"Theft," a man answered.

She barely stopped herself from barging into the sitting

room to demand an explanation. Her a thief? Of all the ridiculous—

"Mr. Canefield is quite upset about the matter," the man continued.

She just bet Gregory Canefield was upset. She had sent him packing last night, nursing a solid slap to his cheek after he had presumed to take unwelcome liberties with her. No man dared to. . . .

"The stolen heirloom belonged to his grandmother. The necklace was discovered missing after . . ."

Missing? He had clasped it around her neck last night just before he had. . . .

And now he dared to claim she had stolen it!

Why that lying, good for nothing. Jacey raised one hand to finger the silver and diamond locket hanging around her neck. He had presented the necklace to her as a gift last night. Now he had the audacity to say she had stolen it?

She balled her hands into fists. She would confront him, and when she finished with him, he would beg her to keep the necklace. But she couldn't approach anyone, not without the danger of being arrested.

When Uncle Harvey got finished with Mr. Canefield, he would. . . .

Oh, no. She covered her mouth with her hands. Her uncle wasn't scheduled to return home for another month, and she couldn't count on her cousin Earl to step forward like a gentleman. She would be locked away in jail long before then, and her cousin would help turn the key. She leaned against the door to catch Earl's next words.

"Of course I'll cooperate with you." A hint of pleased satisfaction edged his voice. "I will bring her round to you the moment she returns home."

The devil he would. If her cousin thought for one moment she would meekly trot off to jail, he had another thought coming. She had never done anything meekly in her entire life. And she wasn't about to start now.

"I was on my way to the office. I'll walk you gentlemen out," Earl offered in a condescending tone that grated on Jacey's nerves. "And I'll let you know the moment the girl returns."

She balled her hands into fists, wanting to strike him. Earl would like nothing better than to see her and Jeanette out of the way so he could inherit the entire family business. He had always resented their presence.

She forced herself to remain still until she heard footsteps pass in the hallway and the front door slam shut behind the men. Straining, she listened for any giveaway sounds outside the library.

"Jacey, what are—"

"Shh!"

She eased the door open and peered around the corner. No one in sight. Cautiously, she tiptoed into the hall, then motioned for Jeanette to follow her upstairs. For once, her twin followed without balking.

Jacey led the way to Jeanette's room and pulled her twin inside. Dropping the hatbox on the bed, she paced back and forth, deep in thought. An idea formed and took root. She knew her plan was rash, but she didn't have the time to formulate a better one.

Whirling to face her twin, Jacey put her hands on her hips in a determined stance. Jeanette waited for her to speak.

"We've got to leave town for a little while," Jacey said. "Until this can all be straightened out."

"I knew you could fix it." Jeanette clapped her hands, but stopped when Jacey shushed her.

"I can't right now," Jacey admitted. "That's why we have to slip away for a while. How much of the money do you have left?"

Jeanette's face fell. "Only a little." Suddenly her expression brightened. "But I still have the train ticket to Texas," she announced.

Jacey smiled with relief. "Good, then, we'll go to Texas and explain—"

"No! I am not going to the wilds of Texas. Besides, there is only one ticket. I told you I'm eloping."

"No, you're not."

Jeanette nodded her head vigorously. "Yes, I am."

Jacey saw the determination in her twin's eyes and nearly groaned her frustration. Her sister needed someone to take care of her, but right now she didn't have the time or patience to cajole her into seeing reason. "Jeanette—"

"Don't you see? It's perfect. You can use the ticket and go to Texas. And I will elope."

Jacey's mouth dropped open at the pronouncement before she snapped it shut. "No. Absolutely not."

"Well, I'm not going to Texas."

"If you don't want to go to jail—"

Jeanette crossed her arms in defiance. "It's your name on the contract," she pointed out.

Jacey closed her eyes and bit back the words she wanted to say.

"Come on. Please?" her twin pleaded. "You don't have to marry him." She clapped her hands together suddenly. "I have it. Go and delay the wedding. That way if I change my mind about Franklin, I can join you in Texas, and I'll marry this Logan Stryker. If I like him."

Trust her fickle sister to think of that solution.

"You can keep an eye on my Texan fiancé until I decide between the two men," Jeanette said with a delighted giggle.

"That's the most ridiculous thing I've—"

"Would *you* rather go to jail? I heard our cousin Earl. You're wanted for theft."

"I didn't take that necklace," Jacey denied through clenched teeth.

"Of course you didn't." Jeanette waved her hand in the air as if swatting an insect; then as if thinking of something more distressing, she dropped onto the bed. "But who is going to believe either one of us? We'll likely both end up behind bars," she wailed.

Jacey opened her mouth to answer, then shut it. Jeanette was right. Jacey herself was in danger of being arrested. And if one of them didn't show up in Texas, they might well both go to jail.

Jacey had only two choices—jail or marriage to a man she had never met.

Never one to pass up an obvious opportunity, she accepted the ticket as the only way for the two of them to escape the law and jail. Surely it would be a simple feat to take her twin's place and delay the wedding.

"Start packing," Jacey ordered, with a new confidence to her voice. "I'll go to Texas. But you are going to Great-aunt Cordelia's." She held up her hand at the defiant look on her sister's face. "It's either her or Texas."

Jacey knew the old woman wouldn't be too pleased at an unexpected visit, but she would keep Jeanette safe and controlled until this situation was resolved.

"But, what about Franklin?" Jeanette wailed.

"Take him to visit Aunt Cordelia, too. And wire me when you get there."

"Remember, Logan Stryker is my fiancé." Her twin stuck out her lower lip in a pout, then grudgingly agreed to visit their great-aunt.

Jacey smiled wryly. Jeanette had nothing to worry about; Jacey had never been in the habit of stealing her sister's beaus. She would take the train ticket and go to Texas, but she had no intention of going through with a wedding to Logan Stryker.

No, absolutely not.

Stryker leaned back in his chair and rubbed at the tension settled in the back of his neck. He glanced around his office and at the door emblazoned with the word *Marshal* with a sense of pride. No one was taking this away from him. Determination tightened his muscles.

Rubbing his neck a second time didn't do any good; the knot there remained tight and hard. The tension between him and the banker Bertram Raines was the problem, and it threatened to worsen each day.

The arrival of his mail order bride should pacify the jealous banker. He hoped. He was betting everything on it working.

It wasn't as if his marriage would be based on love or anything close to the foolish emotion he no longer believed existed. It was purely a business deal. His stomach knotted, and he frowned.

He just wanted the marriage over and done with—while he still had a job and a ranch. If some of the town husbands with overinterested wives had their way, he wouldn't have either his job or his ranch. He didn't need anyone to tell him his vices; he knew what he was and accepted it. Why couldn't they let him live his life his way?

The door emblazoned *Marshal* opened, and in sauntered Madeline Raines.

The very married *Mrs.* Madeline Raines.

Stryker resisted the urge to shove her right back out the wood-and-glass door and slam it loudly behind her. The beautiful, bored woman was nothing but continual trouble to him. Pure and simple.

Madeline crossed to the desk in a vision of pink muslin and a cloud of lavender fragrance—a sure sign the beautiful redhead was on the prowl. Holding out both hands, she leaned forward and rested her palms on his shoulders.

His gut clenched at the display of feminine lushness her decolletage presented when she bent closer to him. He wasn't immune to womanly charms of the type she offered, not by a long shot. While he could be a sinner or saint, he chose the middle ground and eyed her with an inscrutable look.

"Aren't you happy to see me, Stryker?" she asked in a suggestive purr of invitation.

"No," he answered, pushing his chair back from the desk while disengaging her hands. He rose to his feet and faced her squarely.

He would prefer to put even more distance between himself and the banker's too-amorous wife. Over the past year, she had become more and more determined to seduce him. While he admitted to being tempted on more than one occasion, she wasn't worth losing his ranch, and that would be the cost.

Her husband held the deed to his ranch and had threatened to foreclose on more than one occasion. If Bertram Raines thought he had encouraged her attentions in any way, the banker would find a way, legal or not, to make good on his threat this time. Balding, paunchy Bertram would never accept that his wife had pursued Stryker, and not the other way around.

A man besotted with a beautiful woman would believe anything she told him, Stryker thought in disgust. Hadn't he, himself, been that foolish once?

Never again.

Madeline sauntered around the desk, trailing her fingertips across the scarred wood surface. Her bottom lip stuck out in an appealing pout.

"Why, Stryker, we both know you're only resisting because of Bertram—"

"You're a married woman, or do I need to remind you of that fact?" he answered.

She laid her hand on his forearm. "You don't have to be so mean to me. You know that he—"

The door burst open, banging against the wall.

"Get your hands off my wife," Bertram Raines ordered. He drew in a gasp of air as he surged through the doorway, sweeping his bowler hat from his head.

"Aw, hell," Stryker muttered.

"I said—"

"I'm not touching your wife," Stryker answered.

"Don't you start with your lies. I know what I saw with my own eyes." Bertram shook his fist.

Stryker looked at the pitiful little man in disgust. He didn't need this. Not today of all days. He was fast getting fed up with the banker's unreasonable jealousy over a woman Stryker didn't want.

"Listen, Raines—"

The shorter man stepped forward, still shaking his fist. Stryker barely stopped himself from punching the man in his florid face. Only remembering the fact that Raines held the deed to the ranch saved the disagreeable man from nursing a sore jaw.

Even the marshal's enemies gave him grudging respect, but not Bertram Raines. The banker was a fool in love and possessed less sense than a turkey in a rainstorm. Stryker faced his accuser, carefully revealing none of those feelings. His frozen, immobile face reflected no emotion at all.

"If ... I ... I," Raines stammered a moment under Stryker's steady gaze. "If I catch you touching my wife again, I'll see you gone!" he shouted at last. With this he shoved his bowler hat on his bald head, grabbed his wife by the hand, and led her away.

Madeline looked back, smiled and sent him an airy wave before she stepped through the doorway.

Stryker watched the door slam and shook his head. The devil take both of them. Soon his problem with the banker would be solved. A wry grin tugged at his mouth. One day he would take great relish in informing Bertram Raines all about his little wife's deceptions.

Crossing back to the desk, he sank into the chair and propped his feet on the old desk's surface. He reached into the drawer and withdrew a tintype and studied it.

His bride-to-be.

She couldn't get here too soon for his peace of mind. Still, one question nagged at him.

Would she keep the secret bargain they had struck?

She had to. He would see to it.

Chapter Two

Jacey shifted on the uncomfortable seat, resisting the impulse to rub her aching posterior. The journey that had started out an adventure had turned tedious after the first day. She had begun to wonder if this interminable train ride would ever end.

Thank goodness her stop was next. The last thing she needed was more time to think. Suddenly nervous, she checked that her tiny blue satin and feather bonnet sat securely on her curls, then changed her mind and resettled it at a saucy angle to boost her flagging confidence before brushing a spot of dust from her blue traveling gown.

As the train slowed, approaching the town of Braddock, curiosity overcame her. Jacey rubbed at the dust-laden pane of glass with her lace-edged handkerchief, then leaned closer and peered out the window. In spite of her dismay at actually being halfway across the country from both her beloved twin and Baltimore, she felt a flare of excitement.

What an adventure!

She eagerly awaited her first glimpse of the western town of Braddock.

And my intended husband.

Jeanette's husband, she immediately corrected the errant thought, reminding herself he rightfully belonged to her twin. While there wasn't going to be any wedding, she admitted to a certain amount of curiosity about what the man looked like. It was only natural, she assured herself.

In truth, curiosity ate at her, and she focused her wandering attention back out the window. A row of short, stocky buildings passed by, and she stared at them in amazement. She looked closer at the town, and shock hit her. The streets were dirt!

She saw not a single cobblestone or paved street in the entire town. Jeanette had been right to call this the wilds of Texas.

The train jerked to a halt, and Jacey grabbed for a handhold to keep her from tumbling to the floor. Holding onto the seat, she attempted to steady herself, and failed. The next instant she tumbled onto the floor, her bonnet hanging over her forehead and a feather dangling in front of her nose. She blew out her breath with a muttered oath, and the feather danced merrily back and forth in front of her eyes.

"Dust. This is all Jeanette's fault," she grumbled as she pushed herself up.

She was determined to be back in her seat before the conductor appeared. Being picked up off the dirty floor would be the final indignity. She had already ruined her gloves with the persistent dust on the train and had to toss them. Now her gown was likely a mess.

She heard the telltale sound of fabric ripping and looked down to see a two-inch split in the side of her fancy traveling gown. She brushed off the layer of dust covering her hem, then gave up and edged up her dress to wipe her dusty palms on her petticoat. At least no one would see the stains there.

Resettling her blue bonnet on her curls with the feather facing sideways instead of over her nose, she turned back to peer out the window. A crowd of people awaited the train. It looked like the entire populace of the town had turned out. She swallowed down the sudden trepidation. In truth, she was certain they were awaiting Logan Stryker's new bride. Her stomach tightened into a knot at a new thought.

Which one is Logan Stryker?

Jacey searched the crowd, studying each man.

Searching.

Wondering.

Worrying.

She felt her cheeks flush and tried to recall what Jeanette had told her about him. Actually it hadn't been much. Her twin had been unusually quiet on the subject, almost evasive. Something about that fact bothered her. Come to think of it, her sister had left out a lot of pertinent details.

Jacey nibbled her lower lip in an old habit of nervousness she thought she had long outgrown. The conductor hadn't called for her yet, so she gave in to curious temptation and peered out the window again for a better look.

The crowd of people filled the wooden platform, and Jacey swallowed down her sudden nervousness. It seemed as if a sea of faces peered up at the train. Waiting. At one side of the crowd of onlookers stood a band with their dented, but shiny, instruments poised and waiting. Oh, heavens, even the town band had shown up for her arrival.

She spotted a tall, leanly muscled man standing apart from the crowd by several feet, and her heart jumped in her chest. He stood with a take-on-the-world stance, his

dark Stetson shadowing his face. Her lips parted as she
studied him. He was clearly a law unto himself. Heaven
help her if he was Logan Stryker!

She forced her gaze away from him and noticed a portly
man wearing a bowler hat heading up the crowd on the
platform. When he waved at her, she gave him a tentative
wave in return. He waved again, clearly quite pleased at
her arrival. Was this man Stryker?

A flutter of relief rushed over her, followed quickly by
disappointment. The middle-aged man removed his black
bowler hat and bowed to her, the sunlight glinting off his
balding head. The gentlemanly gesture settled the utmost
question on her mind—before her surely stood Jeanette's
"intended."

A twinge of something stronger than disappointment
struck Jacey unexpectedly. She forcibly shook off the ridiculous feeling. The friendly little man would do fine. His
age didn't matter a whit. This marriage wasn't real, and it
certainly wasn't going to take place under any circum-
stances anyway.

She most assuredly intended to delay the wedding.
Indefinitely. She wasn't about to marry a man rightfully
belonging to her sister. However, she couldn't hold off
the questions about the man himself.

Jacey drew in a deep, calming breath to prepare herself
for the crowd awaiting her on the wooden platform. She
thought back to the man who had waved in greeting. Surely
this older gentleman wouldn't be hard to handle. It would
be a simple enough task to hold off his attentions and
postpone the wedding without raising his ire.

She would be charming, but firm. Definitely within her
abilities. She had absolutely nothing to worry about, she
assured herself, suddenly brimming with self-confidence.
She imagined he would be understanding. It wouldn't

present a problem to change his mind about wanting a wedding.

When the tall, skinny conductor appeared with her valise, Jacey met him with an assured smile, feeling more in control than she had felt in hours.

"Ma'am, this here's Braddock." He smiled at her in return. "It's a right fine town. You're going to like it."

She refrained from informing him she wouldn't be staying in his fine town. At least not for long, she hoped.

"Thank you."

She tried to hide the remaining twinge of uneasiness that returned and insisted on troubling her usual optimism.

"It seems all of Braddock is here for your arrival," he pointed out.

She suspected that very thing, but didn't know what she should say, so she merely smiled again. Was it customary for all of the townspeople to greet the train? Something told her it wasn't.

As if her smile had encouraged him, the conductor continued, "I know Marshal Stryker has been looking forward to this day. As are several of the town husbands." He chuckled at his private joke.

Jacey's mind stumbled on one word.

Marshal?

She froze in midstep, unable to move even in the slightest. Her entire concentration focused on the new fact presented to her. Marshal Stryker, the man had said.

Oh, darn it all. She tightened her fingers around her blue reticule.

Logan Stryker was a lawman?

Could her luck turn any worse? Here she was running from theft charges, hiding from the law for the first time in her life, and who does her intended bridegroom turn out to be but a lawman. She stifled her groan of frustration.

Whatever was she going to do now? A dark cloud of

gloom settled over her, but it didn't remain for more than a few deep breaths. A sudden thought struck her.

Her sunny optimism came to the fore. What better place for her to hide than right under the nose of the law? What better place, indeed. She smiled and stepped forward to meet her bridegroom-to-be.

Logan Stryker stood at the bottom of the train steps and watched for his mail order bride. As the minutes crept past, he wondered what could be taking her so long to depart the train.

A sinking feeling hit his gut. She hadn't up and changed her mind and remained in Baltimore, had she?

She couldn't.

He needed her.

"Can you see her yet?" asked an older brunette lady coming to stand at his right side. She caught his arm, holding on tightly in her obvious excitement.

"No, Rosalyn, not yet," he assured her.

"Well, where is she?" A blond woman walked forward to join them. She prompted, "Is she on the train?"

"I don't know, Linda." He barely stopped from gritting his teeth. The same question persisted in his own mind.

Perhaps this was insanity. However, the idea of a mail order bride to appease the jealous town husbands had seemed like the perfect idea earlier when the two town matrons had devised the plan. Now he wasn't so certain.

Rosalyn patted his arm as if sensing his thoughts. "Don't you worry none. We helped you pick her out of the replies to the ad. And you know this is the right thing to do," she pointed out.

"The only thing to do," Linda added for emphasis. "With a wife at your side, the husbands will stop thinking of you as such a womanizer." She whispered the last.

"I don't give a . . . care what they think," Stryker stated.

"Of course not, but we don't want you to lose that nice ranch of yours," Rosalyn said.

Stryker closed his eyes a moment against their combined assurances. The two women made a formidable team. He held back the threatening sigh of frustration. The two town matrons insisted on mothering him against his protests. In fact, they never listened to a thing he said.

He knew he was too soft with them, but he couldn't for the life of him hurt their feelings. Excusing himself, he stepped away from them and walked toward the train. A flicker of movement at the top of the train steps drew his full attention. A young woman appeared, dressed in a deep blue gown, and his breath fled in a rush. He immediately recognized the woman from the tintype kept in his desk drawer.

His mail order bride.

She couldn't look more out of place. A tiny blue bonnet of lace and feathers sat perched saucily on her blond curls. The soft tendrils framing her face were sun-streaked as if kissed by sunlight and slightly mussed. He took note of the fashionable blue gown that hugged her curves, the impractical bustle drawing all male eyes, including his, to her delightful backside.

She tilted her chin at a defiant angle, and he realized she was fire and ice combined, with a spark of passion shining from eyes that hinted at what lay below the outwardly calm, cool surface. Most definitely an irresistible combination. He took a step forward without even realizing he had moved.

She paused on the top step and looked around as if searching for someone. As her eyes met his, Stryker felt as though he had taken a sucker punch to the gut. From the top of the fancy bonnet on her golden curls to the toes of her slippers, she spelled pure trouble. Stryker sensed it in an instant.

Instinctively he sized her up—petite, stubborn, with a mind of her own that gave forth a subtle challenge. He couldn't refuse the gauntlet she threw down.

He stared at her, held in place for the space of a long heartbeat by the look of determination in her blue eyes. He broke the contact with an effort of will. At closer inspection, he noticed the slightly bedraggled state of her fancy dress. He detected a faint aura of vulnerability beneath her outward show of calm, and something in him responded. Her fair skin looked like the softest silk with the hint of peaches in her cheeks. He had the sudden impulse to brush his thumb across her smooth face.

Something in her reached out and touched something deep within him. Stryker instinctively took a step backward. It felt as if she had laid a hand over his heart.

He hadn't counted on this. He wasn't supposed to feel anything. Not for her. Not for any woman ever again. Would she keep their secret bargain?

Then she stepped down the stairs with small, dainty steps, and there wasn't time for further speculation or thought. A flash of delicate stocking caught his full attention as her ankle peeked out from the side slit in her gown. She had the prettiest turn of ankle he had ever seen before. He strode forward to meet his bride with a new eagerness.

Jacey stopped, unable to take another step. For the life of her she couldn't take her eyes off the man approaching her. He had pushed his black hat back on his head, and the dark, unruly hair falling across his forehead begged for someone to run their fingers through it. Her fingers almost itched to feel the thick, springy hair.

No, she almost shook her head in instinctive denial

before she caught herself. She wouldn't be touching this
man. He possessed an intensity that practically reached
out and touched her. Not merely touched.

Stroked.

Cajoled.

Charmed.

And tempted her more than she had ever been tempted
in her life.

This man wasn't the intended bridegroom-to-be. No,
absolutely not. She refused to even entertain such a
thought.

She tore her gaze away and searched for the safety of
the portly, balding man she had seen from the train window, but she couldn't find him in the crowd. Why wasn't
he stepping forward? Most surely her intended was the
balding, easy to manage man she had spotted earlier.
Wasn't he?

She swallowed down the growing sense of uneasiness
building in her. Her stomach knotted into a lump of tension she couldn't manage to dislodge. As if forced to, she
returned her gaze to the tall man who moved with a sure-
ness of purpose.

Even though she had stopped in place, the most handsome man she had ever seen in her entire life continued
to come straight toward her. Her heart sped up, and she
could practically hear its beating.

She stared at the man coming to a stop before her. He
wore dark pants and a white shirt that emphasized every
bit of his masculinity. Beneath his shirt, he possessed the
kind of broad chest that invited a woman to lay her head
on it. A gun belt strapped narrow hips, and the leather
thong tied to his thigh drew attention to his long, muscular
legs. Jacey swallowed. Once. Twice.

He took another purposeful step, drawing even with her,
and her heart dove to her stomach. Then he reached up

and took her hand in his, and her heart raced to her toes. His hand was hard and calloused against hers. She gulped and simply stared at him, utterly speechless for the first time in her entire life.

"Miss Forester?"

His voice was velvety soft and measured. For the life of her all she could manage to do was nod.

"I'm Logan Stryker from the letters."

Oh, heavens. He *was* Logan Stryker. She felt the shock all the way to her toes.

What letters? She nearly voiced the question out loud. Another item her twin neglected to mention. The increasingly familiar twinge of unease settled over her again. What else was Jeanette hiding? And what had been mentioned in those letters?

His long, work-roughened fingers warmed her hand, pulling her full attention back to him. She told herself she really should remove her hand from his hold. It was quite improper. And she would—in a minute.

So this was the bridegroom. Oh, heaven help her.

Logan Stryker was six feet of raw power, encased in sexy good looks. And he made her heart race in her chest. No man had ever caused that to happen before.

Standing on the lowest step of the train, she was nearly eye to eye with him. She stared up at him like a dumbstruck fool. Dark eyes with an enticing quality to them, half-brooding, half-tempting, met her appraisal. He seemed to peer into her very soul. Would he see through her? She had never been very adept at deception; her natural-born honesty got in the way too often.

He gently tugged on her hand, and she stepped down to the platform. He was even more intimidating now with the top of her head scarcely reaching to his chest, but at least she didn't have to meet his piercing gaze.

"Don't be afraid," he leaned down and whispered.

His breath tickled her neck, and she barely stopped herself from taking a step. For the life of her, she didn't know if it would have been a sensible step away from him or a dangerous step closer.

She raised her chin in sudden irritation at herself. What was happening to her? She had never behaved like such a ninny in her life. And she wasn't about to start now. Not over a man. Not even this man.

"I'm not afraid," she answered, proud that her voice didn't waver in the slightest.

"Of course not," he whispered back in reassurance.

For a moment she wanted to strike him.

Suddenly, she was handed a pretty bouquet of flowers by two older women, one dark-haired, one blond. Their smiles showed a hint of pride and an I-told-you-so quality that puzzled her. Before she could wonder at it or thank them, a man dressed in a dark suit stepped in front of her and faced her almost as if to block her way. He clasped his hands in front of his chest and nodded solemnly.

Jacey opened her mouth to comment on his rudeness when the band suddenly broke into song. She winced as the second off-key note pierced her ears. The band stopped, then started up again with more enthusiasm than talent. The notes collided into each other, then in a minute settled into a recognizable pattern of music that struck near terror into her heart.

The makeshift band played the wedding song.

Jacey looked around at the townspeople, hoping to spot a woman in a wedding gown. Instead, everyone in the crowd was staring at her!

She took in the music, the dark-suited man standing in front of her, and the flowers she held before her. She began to tremble, and Stryker reached out and covered one of her hands with his. Full realization struck her, and she gulped back her instant denial.

Oh, no. This couldn't be happening.

Once again her tendency to rush in without heeding the consequences had landed her in trouble. She was attending her own wedding! Ready or not. And she definitely was not ready!

Jacey clutched Stryker's arm in near panic to stop him and make him listen. But when he took her right hand in his, all power of speech fled along with her reasoning. All she could do was stare up into his handsome face, which looked like it was cut from granite.

He glanced down at her askance. His look from those dark, velvety eyes softened, and she knew she was in danger of sinking, of drowning in his dark depths.

Jacey swallowed, breaking the spell enveloping the two of them. Then suddenly panic set in. She couldn't go through with this. Desperate, she grasped at the first idea to spring into her mind that might delay the marriage.

There was only one thing she could do now. She didn't stop to think of the consequences, or to look for a fault in her plan. She simply acted.

With only a moment of hesitation, she slipped her hand from the warmth of Stryker's hold, then released a soft moan and daintily raised her hand to her forehead. Checking first for any barriers, she let her body go limp and faked a ladylike swoon.

She attempted to brace herself for the impact of her body hitting the ground. She ordered herself not to wince and to hold back any betraying sound. After all, a bruise or two was a small price to pay for preventing the too-hasty marriage.

The worst possible thing in the world happened next.

Stryker stepped forward with lightning quickness and caught her in his arms. Swinging her limp body upward, he held her against his broad chest.

Jacey barely caught back her yelp of protest. This wasn't supposed to happen!

He was much too close. She could hear the even beat of his heart against her ear where he had tucked her head against his broad chest.

This wasn't supposed to happen. The thought repeated itself over and over in her mind.

She had meant only to postpone the wedding, not end up in Stryker's arms—although, she had to admit, his strong, muscular arms suddenly felt like the place she most wanted to be and belong.

"Attention, folks!" an unfamiliar voice shouted.

Jacey nearly jerked in Stryker's arms. Absolutely the last thing she should do.

She forced herself to lie still and try to make out who was talking. All she could tell was that the speaker was a man.

The stranger shouted to be heard above the murmurs of the crowd. "Attention. It seems the wedding will have to be delayed a mite."

Jacey gave a silent sigh of relief. Her ploy had worked. In the process of congratulating herself on her acting ability, she nearly choked at the next words spoken.

"Come back here tomorrow. The wedding will be held at noon tomorrow."

Chapter Three

Tomorrow?

Jacey nearly sat straight up in Stryker's arms before she stopped herself. Shock coursed through her, temporarily pushing out every other thought and feeling, even the pleasurable warmth of Stryker's muscular chest.

The wedding will be at noon tomorrow. The words she had heard raced through her mind. It couldn't be, she denied.

Maybe she had misunderstood.

Maybe she had been mistaken.

Maybe the words had been about someone else, she pleaded desperately.

No, she knew she had heard correctly. The words had been spoken too clearly to misconstrue. At noon tomorrow. She gulped, nearly blinking her eyes open in her distress. She couldn't be getting married tomorrow. Not at noon or any other time.

She was not marrying him. She wasn't!

She had to think of some way to avoid a wedding with

the man holding her. At the thought, she once again took note of the strong arms carrying her so effortlessly. She noticed how his wide chest made a perfect pillow for her head. His heartbeat beneath her ear sounded like the best lullaby she could dare to imagine.

Jacey didn't know how much longer she could force her body to lie still. Being carried so close in Stryker's arms was becoming sweet torture to her senses.

She resisted the temptation to snuggle closer to Stryker. Whatever had come over her? She had never once experienced this unreasonable temptation or the feelings that came with it. She had to put a stop to this insanity. She had to make him put her down.

Her throat tightened at the sudden realization of the danger in the slightest giveaway movement. If she moved or spoke, Stryker would know she was faking. He would likely turn right around and carry her back to the where they had started, and the wedding would proceed as planned immediately!

She swallowed the protest on the tip of her tongue, which threatened to choke her, and forced herself to remain quiet and unmoving against his chest. She couldn't voice any disagreement in the slightest about Stryker carrying her wherever he chose.

Her heart skipped a beat. One question stirred past the sensations filling her. Where in heaven was Logan Stryker taking her and what did he plan to do next?

The same question haunted Stryker. He gazed down at his bride-to-be and nearly missed a step.

What was he going to do about her?

The last thing he had expected was for her to faint at his feet before the ceremony. He paused a moment and stared at the woman in his arms. She was nothing like the woman depicted in her letters. Nothing like he had been led to expect.

And neither was his reaction to her!

He studied her with the freedom offered by her swoon. She looked different somehow from the picture he had carried of her in his mind these weeks past. She was beautiful, perhaps more so than in the tintype. Her eyes were a darker blue, almost the color of a sapphire stone in a beautiful setting. There appeared also to be a depth to her that he hadn't expected. It struck something in him.

He tried to deny it. But he failed.

He shifted her slight weight and thought he saw her eyelids flutter. Bending his head lower, he whispered, "Jacey?"

No answer.

"Jacey, can you hear me?"

She remained quiet and still in his arms. He shifted his embrace ever so slightly around her. The realization struck him that she was quite a pleasant armful. Unconsciously he tightened his hold on her, trying to control the discomforting feelings she evoked in him.

"Stryker," Rosalyn called out, stopping him. "Where are you taking her?"

He answered automatically, "To my place."

Rosalyn and Linda caught up with him, both speaking at the same time.

"But you can't."

"No."

He stiffened beneath the disapproval in their voices. They were the only people whose opinions mattered at all to him. He didn't want to hurt their feelings, but he wanted to get Jacey out of the crowd.

"I am taking Jacey to my place. Now," he gritted the words out through clenched teeth.

Jacey tensed, refraining from jumping out of his arms like a cat whose tail had been caught beneath a rocking chair. His place? Not likely. And only over her dead body.

She would not allow him or the townspeople to force a marriage because she had been compromised.

Suddenly she had no doubt that if she willingly accompanied this man home, she would be thoroughly compromised. Her lips lifted the tiniest bit in a smile.

No, she jerked her imagination away from the tantalizing image of their two bodies entwined. Why, she had never in her life entertained such thoughts. Shame flooded through her, and she hoped it hadn't colored her cheeks with the giveaway pink of a blush.

"Stryker, think of what you're saying," Linda admonished him.

"The poor girl would be ruined," Rosalyn pointed out. "And it wouldn't do your reputation any good either."

Only the shocked expressions on the two women's faces prevented him from noticing the slight movement in his arms. The women were right, as usual. He couldn't risk Jacey's reputation, not when he needed her. He didn't give a care about his own reputation; it couldn't get much worse.

"All right," he gave in. "Where am I taking her?"

"Why, to our place, of course."

"Of course," he gritted out the agreement.

There was no use standing here arguing with the two women, not to mention holding Jacey in his arms for all the town to see. Not that she was a burden, he mused. In fact, she felt quite right in his arms. From the corner of his eye he saw the very married Madeline Raines turn on her heel and stomp off. A smile crossed his face at the sight. It seemed his mail order bride was already doing some good.

Continuing to smile, he held Jacey a little closer and headed toward the boardinghouse owned by his two friends. For a moment he almost wished it was a longer distance away to the house; then he grumbled at himself for his foolish thoughts. Anyone would think he wanted to be carrying his mail order bride off somewhere.

He stared down into her face and took in the faintly flushed cheeks and the lashes forming dark crescents against her soft skin. She was a beauty. Something unknown tempted him to brush his lips over hers to see if she would waken like in a child's fairy tale.

He shook off the thought. What was it about this woman that had him behaving like a smitten boy?

He should be worrying about her health instead of letting her fascinate him. His gut tightened at the possibility of her being ill. How long could the wedding be postponed before trouble erupted over it in the town?

He feared not very long. He needed her well and healthy. And married to him.

He refused to risk his ranch for her or anything else.

Worry etching his features, he strode faster to the boardinghouse. The sooner he could turn her care over to Rosalyn and Linda, the better. They would know what to do with her, because for the life of him, he didn't know what to do with the tempting, gently curved woman who fit so well in his arms.

As he reached the boardinghouse, someone pushed the door open for him. He didn't even notice, intent on striding through the familiar house to the sitting room. Once there, he eased Jacey down onto the sofa.

"Here, use this." Someone pushed a small vial into his hand.

Stryker glanced at the vial only long enough to ascertain it contained smelling salts. Then he plunged it directly against Jacey's nose.

The most dreadful smelling thing Jacey had ever encountered assailed her senses. She breathed in, and the action brought tears to her eyes. Before she stopped to think, she shoved at the foul-smelling object and sat upright.

"What are you . . ." her words trailed off, and she almost added *oops*.

She had given herself away, but there was no way she could have lain still with the horrible smelling salts pressed against her nose. She waved her hand in front of her face, attempting to draw in a breath of clear air.

"How are you feeling, dear?" a woman asked her.

Jacey gave a wan smile in answer.

"Jacey?" Stryker bent down on one knee and leaned closer to her.

Too close. She thought she might swoon for real this time.

"Are you all right?" he asked.

Disappointment swept over her at his question. She didn't dare think on what she had anticipated him doing. "I . . ."

How was she supposed to answer him? She was perfectly fine, but she couldn't very well tell him that. She would just have to fake a delicate constitution from the train journey.

"I'm tired," she lied, feeling the distinct pinch of guilt. "The trip—"

Stryker leaned closer, brushing a calloused hand over her forehead and smoothing a strand of hair away from her eyes. Jacey swallowed her words, her heart instantly speeding at his gentle touch.

"Excuse us," a woman's voice cut in. "But I'm sure Jacey needs to rest up some. We'll just go into the kitchen and let you two say your good-byes."

Jacey didn't miss the wink the two women shared before they slipped out of the room like two coconspirators. They were obviously trying to give the supposed lovers time alone. The very thought brought a blush to her cheeks.

As if he had come to the same conclusion, Stryker jerked to his feet and took a step away from the sofa. "They're right. You need to rest."

He turned on his boot heel as if suddenly uncomfortable. Jacey watched him stride to the door with distance-eating steps.

"Good-bye," she whispered without realizing it.

He stopped and looked back at her. A smile tugged at his lips. "I'll see you tomorrow, Jacey. At the wedding at noon," he added in a lower voice.

His voice tantalized her, softly stroking her senses. Then his words penetrated her dulled mind.

He was talking about their wedding!

"No," she gasped out before she thought about what she was saying.

Across the room, Stryker stiffened, his back now ramrod straight. She could feel his anger bridging the distance separating them. Oh, dear heavens, she had made a mess of it this time.

He turned around slowly to face her. His impenetrable gaze pierced her, holding her frozen. She felt as if she had been pinned in place.

"No?" he asked.

"I . . . I . . ." she stammered, scrambling for the words to dig herself out of the situation she had landed herself into. "I mean I'm not certain I'm ready to get married so quickly."

She paused, at a loss for more words that wouldn't be an outright lie. Something told her he would see straight through a falsehood right now.

"Then, why did you come here?"

She stood, taken aback at his forcefully spoken question.

"Uh, I came to marry you." She swallowed her next breath at the blatant lie she had just told.

For an instant she expected some action to give her

away. It was dreadful being so naturally honest; she actually felt a pang at the falsehood she had told him.

"But I think we need to get to know something about each other first," she rushed to add, her words nearly tumbling out in her haste.

He stared at her, surprise written on his handsome face. Jacey couldn't think what she had said that could be so startling. Didn't most couples get to know each other before the wedding? Wasn't that the purpose of a courtship?

"I thought that was why we corresponded first. For months," he gritted the words out.

"Corresponded?"

He nodded sharply. "The letters."

Jacey opened her mouth to ask what letters, then just as quickly snapped her mouth closed on the giveaway question. To ask it would betray her deception.

"Of course, the letters." She waved her hand in the air as if dismissing them. "How could they have slipped my mind? I must be tired."

"Yes, the letters. *Everything* was settled between us in them. Wasn't it?" His hard-edged voice clearly dared her to deny the fact.

Jacey forced her lips into a smile. "Of course." She purposely made her voice light.

The next time she saw Jeanette, the girl had a lot of explaining to do. Jacey would strangle her for certain. Whatever had been in those letters? What she wouldn't give right now to know their contents. Something told her they contained more than the usual get-acquainted chitchat.

"Then what is the problem?" Stryker's stance was as tense as a wire pulled too tight.

"Problem?" Jacey gulped at the squeak in her voice.

Oh, there was a problem all right. But she couldn't very

well tell Stryker that *she* wasn't the one who was supposed to marry him. *She* hadn't written those letters he was so fond of bringing up. She could scarce imagine his reaction if she told him she was a fraud masquerading in her twin sister's place. Or that the money he had sent to pay off the contract had been spent long ago. Instead, she smiled up at him.

"There isn't a problem," she lied through her even white teeth.

"There better not be." He looked down at her for a moment and added in a low voice, "I need you."

Jacey gasped aloud at the words and the blatantly sensual images they evoked.

Oh, dear heavens, the man had just told her he *needed* her.

Heat pooled in her stomach, then swept lower. Her eyes widened at the strange sensations she had never felt before in her life.

"You aren't thinking of backing out of our bargain, are you?" he demanded, his low, silky-smooth voice suddenly turning harsh.

Jacey swallowed and drew in a deep breath. The way he had added a certain emphasis to the word *bargain* worried her. He was talking about the marriage contract between them ... wasn't he?

A nagging voice in the back of her mind told her there was more going on here than she had been led to believe. Dare she ask him about the bargain?

One glance up into the shuttered expression on his face told her firmly not to push him by asking. Not now.

She decided on impulse to play it light. "Are we having our first fight already?"

She used every bit of her acting ability to force her lips into the tempting pout she had witnessed her twin accomplish without a tad of effort. Jacey thought her own performance must be sadly lacking in comparison.

However, she was proven wrong when Stryker's face softened. He took a step closer, and his movement sent her heart plummeting to her stomach. She forced herself to stand her ground. Something told her if she dared give in to the impulse to retreat, he would pursue her with relish.

"No," he answered, his voice dropping lower as he stepped even closer. The silky quality that caused her to blush was back in his words again.

Jacey resisted the little voice in the back of her mind that told her to step back, turn on her heel, and run. She wanted to step closer, and felt like the proverbial moth drawn to the candle's flame. However, she knew the flame of Logan Stryker could most assuredly burn her to bits. She raised her chin in a spurt of defiance.

Stryker stared down at her a moment, their gazes locking almost like two combatants in a battle.

"Just be ready for that wedding tomorrow. Noon." He turned and strode out of the room without saying another word. His boots echoed on the wood floor.

Jacey didn't know whether to be relieved or angry. For the briefest moment, instead of leaving her, she had thought he was going to pull her into his arms and kiss her!

Well, she most certainly would not have let him. Would she?

That persistent little voice told her that her denial would prove to be as futile as her argument with him had been.

She touched her fingertips to her lips and allowed herself to imagine what his kiss would have felt like. Powerful, she was sure of it. Demanding, too. Stryker appeared to be a man who took what he wanted, likely without asking.

For some strange reason that thought sent a thrill of excitement coursing through her.

She wasn't falling for him, was she?

The question jolted through her, replacing all other feelings. She couldn't be falling for a man like him. He was too strong, too forceful, too intimidating.

And entirely too tempting.

She straightened her back, pushing such shameful things out of her mind. Logan Stryker wasn't hers to fall for, she reminded herself. He was promised to her twin sister. And there wasn't going to be a wedding come tomorrow or any other day. Not between Jacey and the marshal.

She would make certain of it!

But precisely how to do that, she wasn't at all certain. She had less than a day to devise a plan. She closed her eyes and groaned. However was she going to stop tomorrow's planned wedding?

By early the next morning, Jacey had spent a mostly sleepless night devising plan after unworkable plan. By the time daylight streamed through the window, she had run out of ideas.

The wedding was mere hours away!

A light knock at her door nearly caused her to fall out of bed in her nervousness. She scrambled to scoot over on the soft feather mattress.

Could it be Stryker already?

"Who is it?" she called out, her voice wavering.

"It's just us, dear."

Jacey recognized the women's voices as the two owners of the boardinghouse who had introduced themselves yesterday evening. She sighed in relief. At least she didn't have to face Logan Stryker yet.

"Come in." She tried to make her voice sound weak and shaken.

The door swung open, and the two women crossed to the bed, concern written on both their faces.

"Oh, you poor dear. You're still not feeling a bit well, are you?" Rosalyn asked.

Jacey jumped at the opportunity. "No, I . . . I'm not." She bit her lip, feeling like a fraud deceiving these two likable women, who had opened their home to her. She couldn't keep faking a delicate illness much longer.

"What you need is something to relax you," Linda stated. "A cup of our special tea."

"Yes, it will perk you right up, dear."

"If you don't mind, I think I'd like to bathe and get dressed first."

"Oh, dear child, you look like you truly need a cup of that tea," Linda insisted.

"Linda," Rosalyn admonished her.

"I only meant that she looks so pale. It would put some color in her cheeks."

Jacey hid her smile of satisfaction behind her hand. Hopefully she looked suitably weak. Too weak for a wedding today.

"A bath would be lovely," she said with a smile.

"Oh, of course. You must want to wash away that train dust."

"We'll have a bath drawn in no time."

The women swept away a folding screen in the corner to reveal the welcome sight of a large, claw-footed bathtub. Jacey sighed in pleasure.

"Would you like some rose water added to the water?"

Jacey gazed at the tub in longing and muttered, "Oh, yes. Thank you."

In no time her bath was readied, and Jacey relaxed in

the fragrant water. Hopefully she could deal better with Stryker if she were more relaxed.

Instead his presence remained solidly in her mind, haunting her every move as she bathed. The brush of the washcloth against her skin reminded her of the soft touch of his hand against hers. The increased beating of her heart recalled the sound of his heartbeat against her ear when he had carried her in his strong hold.

The bath water, which had seemed pleasantly warm at first, now felt too hot. The wisps of steam brought to mind the soft feel of Stryker's breath against her cheek.

Frustrated with the path of her thoughts, Jacey realized the lovely bath was doing nothing to relax her. She stood, suddenly in a hurry to dry off and dress. The water lapping softly against her skin was too reminiscent of the way Stryker's voice lapped at her resolve.

Jacey dressed quickly in a gown of cream-and-white stripes, eager to put the bath and its disturbing images behind her. She had chosen this particular gown purposely because it made her look more delicate, just what she needed today if she had the tiniest chance of convincing people she wasn't up to a wedding. Yet.

She had just finished putting her hair up when the sound of a fist pounding on the front door nearly made her drop her hairbrush.

As she laid it on the dressing table, she noticed that her hand trembled. She hated the betraying state of her nerves. Why, she had never suffered an attack of the nerves in her entire life.

Jacey had a feeling she knew who was pounding on the door. Stryker. It had to be him. Somehow she knew with absolute certainty in spite of the hope she was wrong.

She crossed to the door, opened it, and tiptoed into the hall. She would let Rosalyn and Linda see to the door, but she wanted to know if it was Stryker or not. Leaning forward, she listened to the murmur of conversation from downstairs.

"What do you mean she's ill?" Stryker demanded in a near shout that Jacey could clearly hear from the upstairs hallway.

"Stryker."

"She can't be sick," he said in a lower voice.

"How dare you say such a thing," someone told him in an irritated voice.

Jacey wanted to repeat the same admonition to him herself. How dare he, indeed.

She could be sick if she wanted to. As a matter of fact, she truly didn't feel so well. Her hands insisted on trembling.

"Stryker, don't disturb her."

He was coming upstairs!

Jacey whirled around and raced for her room. She left the door partially ajar on her way, not daring to risk him hearing the telltale click of it closing. She flung herself onto the bed, smoothed out her skirt, and leaned back against the headboard.

Fastening her gaze on the partially closed door, she held her breath. A moment later the door swung inward, and there he stood. He paused a moment, almost as if hesitating, but she sensed uncertainty wasn't in his nature.

"Jacey," he called out quietly.

The sound of her name from his lips had the effect of a feather skittering along bare skin. She shivered in delight and met his questioning gaze with a smile.

"Good morning." She couldn't think of anything else to add. She didn't dare ask if the wedding was still on.

"Morning." He sent her a smile that bordered on tender.

Jacey knew her nervousness showed, and there wasn't a thing she could do to ease it or hide it. He was far too perceptive. She watched as a frown replaced his smile.

He crossed straight to her with a strength of speed that secretly thrilled her. He discarded his black hat on a nearby chair.

"How are you feeling?" he asked, coming to a stop at the side of the bed. "Are you still ill?"

Concern etched lines into his face. She stared at him, her pulse speeding up at his sudden nearness. He really was quite handsome, she thought.

"Jacey?"

He bent over her, and she remained perfectly still. Was he going to kiss her in greeting? Instead, he laid the back of his hand against her forehead. Unexpected disappointment flooded through her, along with a small burst of anger. That wasn't what she wanted him to do. She didn't want to be treated like a sick child with a fever.

She bit her lower lip in vexation. Stryker drew his hand down from her forehead, along her cheek, and smoothed his thumb over her lower lip. The roughness of his skin caused a tingle within her. She was tempted to place a kiss against his thumb. Oh, how she wanted to give in to the impulse, but she simply mustn't.

As if reading her mind, he dragged his thumb ever so slowly back and forth across her lip. A low moan eased past her lips, encouraging him in a way as old as time.

Stryker leaned lower, drawing closer. And closer.

Jacey stared up into his dark eyes and watched in wonder as they softened, gentled, darkened. They held her as surely as if he had reached out and gripped her tightly. She was mesmerized, unable to move away even if she had wanted to. But moving away was the furthest thing from her mind. She leaned closer to him, drawn into the warm cocoon slowly but surely enveloping the two of them.

Stryker slid his hand lower, trailing his roughened fingertips over her chin and along the column of her neck. Jacey's pulse jumped beneath his thumb. He slid his hand down her collarbone to her shoulder. Wherever his fingers grazed, a flick of flame followed in their wake.

Jacey didn't even know if she was breathing, the pleasure was so intense from his mere touch. She had never been so thoroughly seduced by a man's eyes and the light touch of his hand.

The flame increased in strength as he eased his thumb across her breast, then slid his hand along its fullness and back up to her shoulder. When his palm came to rest against her back, he drew her to him with the lightest of pressures. Jacey came willingly, unable to deny him.

Lowering his head, he stared at her lips a brief moment, and Jacey thought her heart would stop if he didn't continue. As time seemed to stand still, he closed the gap between them with a deliberate move, taking her lips in a kiss that she felt all the way to her toes.

Chapter Four

Stryker's lips were warm and tasted of coffee, dark and strong. Jacey slid her hands around the back of Stryker's neck. And held on. Sensations newly experienced flooded through her.

Warmth.

Passion.

Heat.

When he slanted his mouth more firmly over hers and increased the pressure of his lips on hers, she thought surely she had died and gone to paradise.

She had never been kissed like this before!

As he eased her back against the headboard, she nestled her fingertips in the thick, dark hair at his nape. He leaned closer, his muscular chest covering her, nearly blocking out the rest of the room. She moaned against his lips.

As if the sound drew him on, encouraging him, he deepened the kiss. When she thought that surely he had stolen her breath, he slid his mouth across her lips, kissing the corner of her mouth, her cheek, her chin. Jacey could scarcely draw in a breath for the sensations flowing through her.

His lips returned to hers, begging her surrender. All thought left her as she gave herself up to the magical pleasure of his kiss.

A discreet cough from the open doorway broke the spell surrounding them. Stryker pulled away from her, putting an end to the kiss and anything that might have followed. He forced himself to release Jacey and dropped his hands to his sides.

"We brought your tea, dear. We'll leave it here on the washstand."

Once glance at the two older women left him in no doubt they had witnessed plenty.

He knew he should have closed the door.

No, he never should have kissed Jacey in the beginning, he told himself.

Stryker pushed back with a supreme effort of will. Kissing Jacey had been a mistake. He risked a glance at her and immediately regretted it. Her golden hair was mussed from his touch, and he recalled the lush curls had felt like silken threads between his fingers. He dragged his gaze downward away from her love-tousled curls. Her lips were swollen from his kisses, and they offered an invitation he found nearly irresistible.

He stiffened with self-control, then stood and stepped away from the bed where she lay, and from temptation. If he dared to look at Jacey again, he knew he would never be able to walk out the door and down the stairs.

And he *had* to walk out of the house and not look back.

He had made a desperate error in giving in to the temptation to kiss Jacey. Now that he'd tasted her sweetness, it would be harder than ever to keep his hands off her.

The wedding couldn't take place quick enough for him.

He needed her. The marriage and their bargain would proceed as planned. Nothing would get in the way.

He resisted the urge to touch his lips with his fingers like a smitten schoolboy. He could still feel the softness of Jacey's lips against his. He tightened his hand into a fist, resolved to not turn back and pull her into his arms once again.

She had tasted sweet, so sweet.

He swallowed down the forbidden desire. There would be no turning back. It was the taste of the forbidden tempting him, he told himself, not the woman herself. Although a man would be a fool, indeed, not to be tempted by her.

He admitted the truth. He was no fool.

Grabbing up his hat from the nearby chair, he jammed it on his head, not thinking to give his usual care to his Stetson. Then he walked out of the room without a word to either Jacey or his two friends standing outside the doorway.

Jacey watched him until he was out of her sight. He moved with such strength of purpose. The same way he had kissed her, she thought.

She touched her lips, lightly rubbing her fingertips across their swollen fullness. If she concentrated, she could still feel the pressure of his mouth against hers. Stryker's kiss had been powerful, and wonderful, and demanding.

And the biggest mistake of her life.

She tingled from head to toe from his mere kiss. She touched her fingers to her lips again; then realizing what she was doing, she chided herself. It wasn't as if this had been her first kiss. She lowered her hand to her lap in indignation. It was ridiculous to react this way. She had been kissed before. Many times.

But never like this.

Raising her hand to her lips, she caught herself and jerked her hand away. There was no reason for her to act this way. It wasn't as if she was some insipid, smitten miss. The kiss had been a terrible mistake.

She still couldn't go through with the marriage contract. Whatever was she going to do?

She absolutely couldn't risk further contact with Logan Stryker. Her lips tingled again, reminding her of the warmth of his lips against hers.

"Oh, no," she muttered.

Belatedly, Jacey threw an embarrassed glance to the doorway, but her two hostesses were nowhere to be seen. They must have left in Stryker's wake. She sighed in relief. She didn't know how she would face them after what they had interrupted between her and Stryker. Much less what he might have told them about her.

The thought of her situation jolted her back to reality. She couldn't stay here. She hadn't a hope of stalling Stryker on the wedding now with her so-called delicate constitution. *Or of refusing him either,* a little voice in the back of her mind whispered.

Shaken at the truth, she jumped off the bed. Panic set in, settling deep in her stomach and tying her insides into knots. She couldn't continue to remain here, not in his friends' boardinghouse, and not in Braddock. She couldn't marry him like he would expect.

She had to be on the next train out of here. Whirling around, she dashed across the room to the bureau where Linda and Rosalyn had insisted on unpacking her clothes after issuing their invitation for her to stay with them until the wedding. Yanking open a drawer, she grabbed up a bundle of her underthings and raced to toss them on the foot of the bed.

At the sight of the rumpled bed, she skidded to a halt. Memories of Stryker's passionate kisses skimmed over her, and she blushed so much her cheeks burned. Oh, what had she done?

She had allowed Stryker to kiss her. Not merely allowed, but she had relished in his kisses. She swallowed down her shame. And her guilt. He was her sister's fiancé—not hers. There was absolutely nothing going on between her and Stryker. She had to tell herself that three times before her breathing returned to any semblance of normal.

Turning on her heel in determination, Jacey walked back to the bureau and scooped up the contents of the second drawer. She retraced her steps to the bed, this time keeping her eyes averted from the mussed condition of the covers.

Guilt rushed over her, leaving her shaken. Never before had she trespassed on her twin's man. The courtesy hadn't been reciprocated by Jeanette, though. What her twin sister wanted, she took. That didn't matter; Jacey had her own code of honor she refused to break.

She clenched her hands into fists, then forced herself to straighten her tense fingers. This upheaval was ridiculous. She had never fought for a man before, and she wasn't about to start now. She would *not* fight her sister over any man.

Not even Logan Stryker.

"How long does it take you to read a wanted poster?" a lazy voice asked from across the desk.

Stryker glanced up from the papers in his hand to see his friend, Brett Mason, standing in front of him. He had been so absorbed thinking about his mail order bride that he hadn't even known anyone had walked into the office.

Fine state for a lawman to be in, he thought in derision. He hadn't been himself since he had kissed Jacey today.

He had been staring at the poster without reading the words for at least ten minutes. Embarrassed and angry with himself, he shoved the papers to the side of his desk as if he had finished with them.

Brett chuckled and sank down into a chair without being asked. "Well, now I finally know the truth behind your mail order bride."

Stryker snapped his head up. "Brett," he warned softly.

"I'd been wondering why you didn't chose a town girl to marry when you got so all fired ready to settle down." His friend rubbed his palm over his blond beard and grinned.

"I had my reasons." Stryker picked up the papers again and pretended to read them, hoping his friend would take the hint and leave it alone.

The last person he wanted to discuss right now was Jacey Forester. The feel of her soft lips against his was still too fresh in his mind and persisted in occupying his thoughts far too much.

Brett slapped his hands down on the desk, catching Stryker's full attention. "You're in love with her."

Stryker jerked back as if he had been hit. He stiffened in his chair and sent his friend a quelling glance that warned him off.

"No, you're wrong."

"Am not."

"Brett, believe me, you're wrong on this." Stryker's voice carried absolute conviction.

His friend's grin disappeared, and he leaned forward. "Then, tell me, why are you marrying her? And especially why so fast?"

"I have to."

Brett's brows furrowed before his eyes widened. "She's not pregnant, is she?"

"No!" Stryker fired the denial out. "I just met her yesterday."

Brett held up his hands in a gesture of surrender. "All

right. But why are you so set on marrying her? If you don't even know her?"

Stryker rubbed the ache that had settled at the back of his neck. He had held off telling the truth to anyone. Only Rosalyn and Linda knew the facts behind his search for a mail order bride. It had all been their idea.

"I need her," was his only response.

Brett's glance clearly demanded more of an answer than those brief words. Stryker knew his friend had settled in like a dog with a bone too juicy to give up. It was time he shared the truth with his closest friend.

"Bertram Raines and a couple of the other men in town are pushing to get my badge." He stated the plain fact without explanations.

"I always said your charm would land you in trouble." He chuckled, then sobered. "You can't be serious."

Stryker nodded sharply. "Raines is also threatening to foreclose on my ranch if—"

Brett's muffled oath cut through the office. "If that fool would rein in his wife—" He stopped and cleared his throat. "Madeline has always been nothing but trouble."

Stryker's noncommittal shrug silenced any further words from his friend.

"Marriage will work better than anything else."

"But why a mail order bride?"

"Because we made a bargain. And come today at noon, we're getting married."

At a knock on her door, Jacey nearly dropped the clothes in her arms. She whirled around, tripping over her hem in her haste. Instead of the tall, handsome form of Logan Stryker, she saw Linda standing in the doorway.

"Jacey? What are you doing?"

She swallowed down her panic and raised her chin. "I'm leaving."

"Dear—"

Jacey shook her head. "I'm sorry. This . . . this isn't going to work out."

"Oh, dear." Linda turned to the door and shouted, "Rosalyn! Go get Stryker."

"No!" Jacey called out, but was too late to stop her.

The door to Stryker's office swung open, then bounced against the wall from the force of the movement. He jerked around, dropping his hand to his hip and drawing his gun.

He faced the intruder, gun leveled at the center of the doorway.

"Stryker!" Rosalyn chided in a shaken voice.

Sighing, he let the tension slide from his shoulders and slipped his revolver back into his holster. "Sorry, Rosalyn," he apologized in a low, gentle voice intended to calm.

"Well, you should be." She patted a hand to her chest. "You nearly scared me out of a year's life." She waved one hand back and forth in front of her face.

He smiled at her dramatics. It assured him that she was fine.

"Here I come to tell you something important, and you pull a gun on me."

"What is it?"

"I'm not sure I should tell you now." She smoothed a hand down her skirt.

"Rosalyn."

She looked away from him, making him wait for her answer.

"Rosalyn," he repeated.

At last she turned to face him. "I thought you should know Jacey is packing."

"Packing?"

She nodded abruptly. "Packing. As in leaving town."

"Aw, hell."

Stryker grabbed his hat and shoved it carelessly on his head. Without giving Rosalyn a thought, he strode out the door, not even bothering to shut it behind him.

"She can't leave town," he muttered to himself.

He strode down the street with long strides, ignoring the startled glances his unaccustomed hurried pace drew from the townspeople. He didn't even care. Only one thing mattered—reaching Jacey and stopping her.

There was no way she was leaving Braddock without marrying him first.

Jacey knew she was running out of time.

She snapped her valise closed and threw a worried glance at the door. She wanted to be gone from the boarding-house before Rosalyn returned with Stryker. Long gone.

One last look around the bedroom assured her she was ready. She would send for the rest of her things later. She felt like a common criminal on the run. A little voice in the back of her mind reminded her how close to the truth the thought had struck.

Not only was she on the run, but she was running away—from Stryker.

Jacey laid her fingers over her lips, for a brief moment remembering the pleasure of his kiss. She closed her eyes and drew in a deep breath. Opening her eyes, she faced the truth—she couldn't stay. She couldn't risk it happening again. He had breached her defenses too easily once. She couldn't chance that happening ever again.

Not with Stryker.

If she hurried, she could catch the train that ran through town on Tuesdays, Wednesdays, and Fridays. She didn't care about the destination, just as long as it wasn't Braddock, Texas.

Resolute, she caught up her valise and practically tiptoed across the bedroom to the door. Pausing a moment to soothe her guilty conscience, she tightened her grip on the bag, raised her chin for courage, and walked down the hallway.

A dangerously soft voice stopped her in midstep. "Going somewhere?"

Stryker.

She yelped in surprise and whirled around to face him. Her valise crashed into the wall, and she dropped the bag. It hit the floor with a loud *thump.*

He stood straight and tall, his legs shoulder width apart. He waited, about five feet away from her. How had he gotten here so fast? And how had he sneaked up behind her?

As if reading her mind, he stated, "There's a back door. You should try it sometime."

Jacey licked her suddenly dry lips. She couldn't think of a thing to say in response. His dark gaze trapped hers as surely as if she had been caught by a snare.

He was the one to break the eye contact. He looked from her to the valise at her feet and back to her.

"I asked if you were going somewhere." His dark eyes hardened with the words.

Jacey licked her lips again. There was nothing left but to admit the truth.

"I . . . I'm leaving." Her voice wavered, making the words soft and nearly indistinct.

"What?" he fired back.

Jacey gritted her teeth and repeated her announcement. "I said I'm leaving."

"Where are you going?"

"Away from here. I can't marry you."

"You will."

She swallowed down her sudden case of nerves. Lifting her hands, she said in a sincere voice, "I'm sorry. I . . . it won't work. I've changed my mind."

"No."

"A lady can change her mind," she stated with a distinct raising of her chin in defiance.

"If anybody's going to change their mind, it will be me. Do you understand?" He advanced on her, until he stood less than a step away.

Jacey's temper crept upward with each word Stryker spoke. Who did he think he was? No one talked to her that way or in that tone of voice.

Planting her hands on her hips, she tilted her head back and met his angry gaze. "Oh, I understand all right. I just don't care."

"Lady, you better care."

She picked up her valise and tossed her head in disdain. "I'm leaving. Get out of my way."

"No."

She raised her eyebrows at him, then promptly ignored his anger and turned away. She took only one step before he stopped her.

Catching her by the arm, Stryker turned her back around to face him. Jacey gave his hand a disdainful look, then raised her gaze to meet his. Their eyes locked, shutting out everything else around them.

He released her arm and took a step, closing the distance between them, never taking his eyes from hers. Her heart quickened, and she forced herself to hide her reaction.

"Jacey." His low voice stroked her senses. "Don't go. I need you."

Her heart tripped and tumbled to her toes at his words. She stared up at him, unable to say a single word.

As the silence stretched out, the softening she had seen in his eyes disappeared, and his face hardened.

"If you get on that train, I'll arrest you," he stated in crisp, clear words.

"Arrest?" It was the only word she could push past her frozen lips.

Stryker nodded his head sharply once.

"You wouldn't," she challenged past the edge of fear creeping in on her confidence.

He leaned closer, staring hard into her face. "Try me."

Jacey could merely stare up at him. His wide stance told her clearly that he intended to follow through on his threat.

She had no doubt that if she took a step away from him, he would put her in jail.

Chapter Five

One look into Stryker's eyes and Jacey could almost feel the icy cold metal of the handcuffs touching her skin and hear the snap of their lock around her wrists. She knew he was serious in his threat.

Deadly serious.

"On what charges?" she forced herself to demand through stiff lips.

She would never show her fear to him. She had learned from her cousin it was a mistake to ever give someone that leverage against her.

"Fraud. Remember the marriage contract?"

Her eyes widened before she could prevent it.

"And anything else I can find," Stryker added, without a pause.

The mail order marriage contract flashed before her mind, and once again she saw the amount of money spelled out. Holding in the betraying sound of guilt that threatened, she wondered how she could have forgotten about the contract and the money her twin had already spent.

Jacey wanted to kick herself. Or preferably her twin, Jeanette. There was no way the money in her reticule would satisfy the debt and keep her out of jail if she fled.

"You win, I'll stay."

With a burst of anger, Jacey caught up her valise. Head held high, she walked as wide a path around Stryker as she could manage in the upstairs hallway, then continued down the hall and into her bedroom. She slammed the door closed, then locked it with a decisive click she knew he could hear.

Leaning against the door, she waited to see if he would follow her and pound on the solid wood barrier. When he didn't, she felt a flash of disappointment, then irritation with herself.

Embarrassed by her foolish reactions to the man, she fumed the entire time she unpacked her bag and replaced her clothes in the bureau. She stopped and listened at every slight sound. With each garment she put away, her temper inched upward. She had always hated being forced to do anything!

"He may force me to stay," she whispered aloud, "but he can't force me to marry him."

He had had the nerve to tell her she couldn't change *her* mind, and that he could change his, hah!

Then, she would simply have to convince him to change his mind.

Whirling about, she stomped over to the window and peered out. Not interested in the view presented by the town's main street, she flounced across the room and plopped down on the foot of the bed. Dropping her chin in her hand, she worried over the problem in her mind.

Logan Stryker would be completely unsuitable as a husband for her. Not that she had any intention whatsoever of marrying him anyway, she reminded herself. He was stubborn, and unreasonable, and demanding. She listed his faults, ticking them off on her fingertips. He was insufferable, she added. And he was . . .

He was the most tempting man she had ever met in her entire life.

She jerked herself up. Her thoughts were getting out of hand. She wouldn't think about him. He was completely unsuitable, she reminded herself.

Suddenly a smile lit up her face and her spirits. She had her answer. She would convince him how unsuitable she would be as a wife for him. She would show him just how citified she could be when she wanted. Her smile widened at the possibilities. This could prove to be fun. Oh, she would wipe that self-satisfied smile off his handsome face, just see if she didn't.

She had a surprise or two in store for the self-assured Marshal Logan Stryker.

Minutes later, Jacey closed the bedroom door behind her and strolled down the hall. She paused to tilt her cream-colored bonnet with its profusion of ostrich plumes to just the right angle for a fine Eastern lady. Swinging her velvet reticule with each step, she sauntered down the stairs to tell the friendly owners of the boardinghouse she was going shopping for some "necessities."

A quarter hour later, Jacey added a batch of delicate lavender lace to the growing stack of frippery on the counter of the mercantile store. She intended to add lace and frivolous trimmings to any of her gowns that could possibly be considered practical. She would show Logan Stryker just how impractical she could be when she set her mind to it. The anticipation of Stryker's reaction to a lace-edged parasol brought a devious smile to her face.

Oh, this would well prove to be enjoyable, indeed.

The store owner watched her with what she surmised to

be growing concern. She was sorely tempted to assure him she had sufficient funds in her reticule to pay for her purchases. As he studied her progress, she wondered at his odd expression, but rapidly brushed it aside as she spied another batch of lace. As she took off after the prized trimming, the proprietor's cough halted her.

"Ma'am?" He cleared his throat. "Do you know what time it is?" he asked her with a nervous catch in his voice.

Jacey blinked at the unusual question, then turned around to face him. "I'm sorry, no I don't. I seem to have left my watch pinned to another gown." She shrugged and turned back to her quest.

"Ma'am." Once again he stopped her with a nervous cough.

"Yes?" She turned back to him with ingrained politeness, but tapped her foot.

"Ma'am, it's well after eleven."

If he knew what time it was, why had he asked her? She held down her spurt of temper. Uncertain what to make of his remark, she merely smiled and nodded. "Thank you."

With this out of the way, she headed across the store again. Another nervous cough made her flinch this time. Maybe if she just ignored him, he would—

"Ma'am—"

"What?" she snapped, whirling around in a swirl of petticoats and rising temper.

"It's getting late."

She stared at him, questioning his sanity for a moment. Late? The sun shone brightly outside the storefront, and it was still morning.

"I was planning on closing the store soon. Didn't want to be late for the festivities and such."

She frowned, irritated at having to rush her purchases.

Especially when she had devised such a wonderful plan for Stryker.

"I'll hurry," she said, not attempting to hide her irritation at his rudeness.

"You'd better if you plan to be on time." He ended with an abrupt clearing of his throat. "We're all looking mighty forward to Stryker's wedding. I was planning on taking my wife Clara along to watch."

Stryker's wedding. My wedding.

She had forgotten all about the pending threat of the marriage taking place today, too caught up in her latest plan guaranteed to delay the wedding to think about its immediacy. Maybe she had subconsciously scooted it from her mind.

"Ma'am, you aren't planning on missing your wedding, are you?"

The question caught her off guard, and she frantically searched for a way to answer him that wouldn't be an outright lie.

Waving her hand in the air as if to dismiss the very idea, she responded, "What a foolish thought."

He sighed, visibly relieved by her answer. "Right you are, ma'am. A single lady would be a fool not to marry Marshal Stryker."

Jacey laughed with the store owner at his remark. Truth be told, she had been a fool to come here in her twin's place to begin with, but she had to see this out to the end, which mostly assuredly would not include a wedding.

Another disturbing thought prodded her. The store owner seemed awfully anxious to attend the wedding. In fact, suspiciously anxious. He had also mentioned everyone looking forward to *Stryker's wedding*. Something niggled at the back of her mind. As she recalled, the train conductor had also told her how the town was eager for the wedding to take place.

Why were the townspeople in such an all-fired hurry to witness the wedding between her and Stryker? It seemed as if they couldn't wait for him to get properly married.

She pondered on what reasons could possibly be behind such anticipation. None of the solutions boded good for her. Now, why would the townspeople be so pleased to see one of their leading unattached males wed? She sensed this was more than merely a case of the people being happy for him. It seemed almost as if the citizens were happy for themselves to see him wed good and proper.

A new idea struck her, and a smile tipped her lips, then spread into a mischievous grin of self-congratulation. She had the solution to her own upcoming wedding dilemma. She would simply insist on being "properly" married herself. And for that, she needed a "proper" wedding dress.

In fact, she needed a special dress. One that took *time* to make up. She entertained the idea of demanding a dress from back east, but feared perhaps that would be pushing Stryker's patience a little too far. Still, she could insist upon making the one special dress in her life herself, couldn't she? And therefore delay the wedding longer.

Oh, yes. Absolutely.

Spying a bolt of rich white cloth, she scooped it up with a smile. She didn't pause to wonder why such a fine fabric existed for sale in a small mercantile store; she simply carried it to the counter and made her purchases.

"I'll see you at the wedding, ma'am, and congratulations. You take good care of Marshal Stryker, you hear."

Oh, Jacey would take care of him all right.

She said her farewell to the owner and strolled out the door with both her scheme and purchases in hand. She had more than one surprise in store for Logan Stryker.

* * *

"I tell you something's wrong."

Jacey froze in the act of shutting the front door. The remark sent a chill of apprehension racing down her spine. Somehow she knew with certainty the words she had overheard coming from the next room were about her.

"Jacey's hiding something, I'm sure of it."

"What are we going to do?"

Jacey recognized the voices of Rosalyn and Linda, and she knew she was the topic of their conversation.

"You don't suppose she found out the truth about Stryker, do you?"

"She couldn't possibly have."

What truth? Jacey wondered.

Her curiosity raced as she laid down her purchases on a nearby chair, then tiptoed across the room so as not to miss one single word of the conversation. She had absolutely no compunction about eavesdropping on her hostesses. Not when they were talking about her.

"Then, do you think she's changed her mind about marrying him?"

"Oh, no! That would be horrible."

Why? Jacey leaned closer to the door, hoping to receive an answer.

"Think about what it would do to poor Stryker."

Poor Stryker?

"He'd be devastated. We can't let this happen."

"What are we going to do?"

"Well, we will have to change her mind back. We'll make her see how wonderful he is."

"Yes, we have to get him to kiss her again."

Jacey's cheeks heated at the remembrance of how good it had felt to be kissed by Stryker and to be held in his arms. Oh, no, the ladies didn't have to convince her of that.

"How could she not see that about him? The girl's got

eyes, doesn't she? If I were ten years younger, I'd be after him myself."

"Thirty years younger."

"Twenty-five." This was said with a huff.

"Well, then, maybe something else is wrong."

"I think she's just gotten scared of wedding him."

"Could that be it?"

"Well, they have only met."

"Humm."

"I know that look of yours. What are you planning?"

"I think we need to give them a little nudge. Why don't we—"

A sharp knock at the door sent Jacey scurrying across the room and racing up several steps. She had no intention of getting caught eavesdropping.

Another knock halted her on the next step. She turned around and tried to walk down the stairs with as much casual nonchalance as she could muster.

She swung open the door and faced a tall, redheaded woman she had never seen before.

"May I—"

"You're Jacey Forester, aren't you?"

"Yes."

"I'm Madeline Raines." She paused.

Jacey had the distinct impression she was expected to know the name. "Are you a friend of Rosalyn and Linda?"

"Not likely."

With raised brows, the woman swept past her into the room, then whirled to face her. "I'm a *friend* of Logan Stryker," she announced with emphasis.

Jacey nearly bit her tongue to stop the question from slipping out. She would not give this woman the satisfaction of asking about their friendship.

When Jacey didn't rise to the bait, Madeline strolled

across the room. She turned around and ran her hands down her waist and over her hips.

"We're very good friends." She paused to let the meaning of her words sink in.

Jacey merely smiled politely. This wasn't the first time she had encountered a spiteful, jealous woman. She knew the surest way to irritate her would be to remain silent and refuse to show any interest whatsoever.

"Aren't you curious about this?" Madeline's voice sharpened.

Jacey smiled for real this time. "Not really. I have nothing to worry about."

The other woman tossed her head, then focused her attention on the purchases on the chair. Jacey followed her gaze, wondering what had caught her interest.

"That's my fabric." Madeline pointed to the bolt lying on the nearby chair. "You stole it from me."

"I did not." Jacey was getting tired of being accused of theft. "I purchased it at the mercantile—"

"It's mine."

Jacey's temper prodded her to say, "Not anymore, it isn't."

"Whatever would you use such fine material for?"

"My wedding gown."

"You don't have a prayer of stopping him, you know."

"Stopping him?"

The woman tossed her head and flicked an unseen speck of dust from her abundant bodice before she acknowledged the question. She raised her head and batted her eyes in a gesture meant to be coy. "Why, from seeing me, of course."

Jacey stared at the woman a moment, taking in what she had said.

"He's mine," Madeline's voice took on a higher pitch. Jacey had the unreasonable urge to grab the woman by the arm and bodily throw her out the door. Before she could act on it, she heard footsteps behind her and turned to see her two hostesses approaching.

Rosalyn suddenly stepped forward. "Good day, Mrs. Raines."

The unwelcome visitor barely acknowledged the greeting.

"Did you come to offer your congratulations?" Linda asked.

Jacey couldn't fail to notice the catlike smile accompanying the question, or the indignant stiffening of Madeline's spine in response.

"No, I did not. I came to warn her—"

Rosalyn stepped forward. "I think it's time you returned home to your husband, don't you?" She pointedly opened the front door.

"I was just leaving," Madeline announced with haughty outrage.

"Good," Linda added.

Secretly Jacey couldn't agree with her more.

The door shut behind their visitor, and the two women turned their full attention to Jacey.

"Don't you worry about her," Linda rushed to tell her. "She's nothing to Stryker."

Jacey sensed a sudden sharp prick of what felt remarkably like jealousy, but that was ridiculous. She wasn't jealous. In fact, she didn't care in the slightest whom he chose to see. It wasn't as if they were involved—

No, they were engaged, a little voice reminded her.

She seized on the perfect opportunity offered her. She would pretend jealousy to postpone today's wedding. Lowering her head, she sniffed delicately and blinked several times, hoping to inspire the sheen of tears.

"I . . . I . . . can't possibly marry him now."

"Jacey, dear, you can't be serious."

"It's only in Madeline's imagination."

Jacey shook her head as if totally dejected. She let her shoulders slump forward and hung her head to sniff again.

Someone patted her shoulder in obvious sympathy.

"There, there, dear girl. It will be all right, you'll see. Stryker—"

"I don't want to see him." She sniffed again.

"You'll feel different in an hour, dear. No one can stay angry with Stryker."

"I don't even know him," Jacey wailed. "I can't marry him like this. And I don't have a proper dress yet."

"We'll fix that."

Jacey snapped her head up. She hadn't counted on the women offering to help. The dress would be done in no time. At least too soon to cause a significant delay.

"Oh, I couldn't ask you to—"

Rosalyn waved her hand to cut her off. "We insist."

Jacey opened her mouth, but was stopped before she could utter another protest.

"It will be our pleasure, dear. Now, why don't you go upstairs and lie down. You don't want him to see you've been crying. We'll talk to Stryker when he comes."

A flutter of relief surged in Jacey's stomach. She wouldn't have to face him yet.

"Thank you both." She laced her fingers together in a gesture of uncertainty. "Will he understand about the delay? I . . . I scarcely know him at all."

"He's very understanding," Linda assured.

Were they talking about the same man? Jacey wondered.

"Yes, and it will give you two time to get to know each other better."

Jacey caught the wink Rosalyn sent Linda. Something about it bothered her immensely. She might well need to watch herself around these two seemingly nice women. They were surely up to something.

"I think I will go lie down," she told them, needing to get away to think.

Crossing to the chair, she scooped up her purchases and started up the stairs. She had scarcely reached the top step when another knock sounded at the front door. It sent her racing for her bedroom. Let the two women handle Stryker for now. She needed to make some new plans. And she still hadn't found out why people were so anxious to marry off Stryker. That fact worried her.

If she had remained downstairs longer or dared eavesdrop again, she would have worried far more.

"What do you think?" Linda whispered.

"I think we'd better encourage her to room with us. That way we can keep an eye on her," Rosalyn answered in a lowered voice.

"Definitely."

"We can't have her leaving town, can we?"

"Absolutely not."

Another knock sounded at the door.

"Now, who is going to tell Stryker the news?" Rosalyn looked pointedly at the door.

Linda jumped to her feet, heading for the back. "You tell him, and I'll go cancel the wedding."

Jacey spun away from the sitting room window, then raised her chin and faced Stryker. Everything about his stance broadcast his anger from his legs braced shoulder width apart to his clenched fist.

She had known she wouldn't be able to put the confrontation off for long, but she had hoped to delay it until the next day. She needed more time to plan her strategy to convince him of her unsuitability as his prospective wife. But Stryker had demanded to see her this very afternoon. So she had insisted on meeting him in this room.

He spoke first, before she could utter a sound. "What do you think you're doing canceling the wedding?"

At the cold anger in his words, Jacey realized she had been mistaken. Stryker wasn't merely angry; he was furious.

"For your information, Linda canceled the arrangements." She faced him squarely, refusing to be deterred by his angry stance, then added, "After I made my refusal clear."

"Then it will take place tomorrow."

She forced a show of bravery and braced her hands on her hips. "I'm telling you no."

"What do you mean no?" Stryker's voice rose at the last in exasperation.

"I'm not marrying you tomorrow. And that's final."

At the hardening in his eyes, she purposely added, "I insist we wait a little longer after what I learned today."

"And what is that?"

"I am not marrying you until you get rid of your mistress," she announced with a dramatic toss of her head.

"What mistress?"

"Madeline Raines." Jacey gave a delicate sniff, then dabbed at her eyes with a lace kerchief.

"Aw, hell," Stryker muttered. He rubbed the back of his neck.

"I realized I don't truly know you. In spite of the letters," she rushed to add.

"Then, let me rectify that."

Before she realized what he meant, he pulled her into his arms and lowered his mouth to hers.

Chapter Six

Stryker's kiss consumed her. Jacey's head swam, and she felt as if she were being carried away by a swift-moving current. She knew she was rapidly drowning in the passionate demand of his lips.

She was supposed to be angry with him, she reminded herself, though the admonition didn't do her a whit of good. She was supposed to be convincing him how unsuitable she would be as his wife. This was hardly the way to go about that. If anything, relinquishing herself to his embrace would accomplish the opposite. It surely showed her they fit together perfectly. How could it not show him the same?

She raised her hands, intending to push him away, but found her arms had a mind of their own, sliding up his broad chest and around his neck instead. Well, she would certainly change that! In a minute . . . or two . . . or. . . .

As Stryker slanted his mouth more firmly over hers, she forgot all about resisting. Besides, pushing him away was the last thing on earth she wanted to do. Not when the strong cords of his shoulder muscles tempted her touch. She slipped her hands inside the fabric of his shirt and kneaded the sinewy strength beneath her fingers, reveling in the feel of his skin against her palms.

Jacey leaned closer, wanting to be even nearer to him and the wondrous warmth he made her feel. Stryker obliged her, wrapping her more tightly into his embrace. He made her feel womanly and desired. Their bodies pressed together, and though nothing but their clothing separated them, she resented the barrier it represented.

Stryker shifted his weight, sliding his leg between hers. When Jacey gasped at the unfamiliar intimacy, he deepened the kiss, stealing away her next breath. She couldn't have uttered a protest, even if she had wanted to, but protesting never entered her mind.

Something deep inside her urged to get closer, some unknown sensation crying out for release. All she knew was that he had the power to make her forget everything but him.

The realization scared her, shaking her to her very core. She could so easily lose herself in this man, be overcome by his strength and intensity, let it swallow her up. She tensed in his embrace, unsure of herself and what she wanted.

Stryker felt her tension, and bit by bit his ardor cooled. Reluctantly he slowly ended the kiss, sucking at her lips one last moment before easing back to look at her. He was prepared to demand an answer to her uncertainty, but one glance at her face stopped him.

Her eyes lay closed, her lashes dark against the soft skin of her cheekbones. Her lips had turned the color of a freshly bloomed rose and were temptingly swollen from the kisses they had shared. He gazed down at her as her eyelids fluttered open, meeting her blue eyes, and he recognized that they were darkened with the heat generated between them.

As she parted her lips and stared up at him, he knew he would agree to the marriage postponement if she asked again. He knew he would say yes to about anything she asked of him right now.

The realization shook him, jarring him back to the bitter past with brutal honesty. Hadn't he learned from his past mistake what happened when a man gave a woman that kind of power over him? She used it against him, getting what she wanted, then leaving him a fool.

Upset with himself for giving in to temptation and nearly losing control, he set Jacey away from him. He would never give her the satisfaction of holding that power over him. She blinked, her eyes beguiling and questioning. He forced himself to ignore the unspoken plea in her gaze. To give in to it, in to her, would be foolish. And he would never be that kind of fool again.

Not for any woman.

Infusing his voice with a coolness he was still far from feeling, he said, "I believe we can both say we know each other better now."

The flash of pain in Jacey's eyes was nearly his undoing, but he held himself firm and stepped back from her, letting his arms drop to his sides. She made him recall the sweet city-bred lady of their letters. She raised her chin with a dignity he had to admire. Then, without warning, his meek, sweet bride-to-be slapped him hard across the cheek.

He reeled with the shock of her action. This wasn't the amiable woman he had been corresponding with for long weeks. Who was this spirited creature who could stir his blood to passion then temper in the space of a moment's time?

"Get out," she ordered, her voice clear and as frosty as a winter morning.

He stared in disbelief. His fiancée had more courage than he had expected. Not a hint of fear or regret for what she had done showed in her expression. She surprised him further by stepping back from him, her head held high with pride and outraged indignation. He realized he didn't know her at all. Just who was he marrying?

This was not the woman from the letters.

At least, this wasn't how she had led him to believe she behaved and thought. The meek city lady in the letters would never slap a man, he was certain of it. He decided then and there he needed to learn all he could about his intended bride-to-be, and he had better do it before the wedding. A voice in the back of his mind prodded, *How many more surprises does this woman hold?*

They faced each other, her anger tangible between them, so unlike what he had thought she was capable of showing. It both confused and irritated him.

And intrigued him.

"Our bargain—" he began.

Jacey stiffened, her back straightening until he thought it might snap.

She spoke in clear, precise tones. "You can take your bargain, and your wedding, and yourself and please leave. Immediately."

Not waiting to see if he followed her order, she spun away from him and out of his reach. Without even a glance back, she crossed to the stairs and ascended them with injured pride and dignity in each step. Damned if he didn't have to admire her for it. Not to mention admiring the sassy sway of her bustle that drew his eyes to her backside.

He stood there, watching until she turned right and entered her bedroom. Something he couldn't define urged him to follow her up the stairs and into her room. He took a step, then hesitated. He wasn't about to follow her around like a lap dog, begging for forgiveness.

Jacey slammed the door behind her, the sound echoing in the room. She knew full well it would be heard downstairs by Stryker. Turning, she leaned her back against the door. Her breath came in short gasps. She hadn't been this angry since she had found the marriage contract.

If Logan Stryker thought for one moment he could kiss her nearly senseless, then have the audacity to insult her, he had another thought coming. She refused to tolerate that behavior, and she would be certain to inform him of the fact the next time she saw him. She ignored the tingle the thought of seeing him again brought to her stomach. Instead, she concentrated on her anger.

His words still stung her pride. She absolutely refused to acknowledge that they had injured her heart. No, her heart was safe from him. The taunt he had thrown at her pricked her, stinging again.

Know each other better, indeed.

She had had every right to slap him for such an insult after the kiss. Her palm still stung from the contact, and she rubbed her hands up and down her arms. She was glad she had slapped him, she told herself. He deserved it.

Spotting the bolt of white fabric for her supposed wedding dress, she crossed to where it leaned against the wall. A sudden impulse made her kick the bolt solidly with her foot. Pain shot into her toes, but it was nothing compared to the pain in her heart.

How had she gotten into such a mess? And how was she to get out of it without losing her heart?

Stryker strode from the sitting room into the kitchen of the boardinghouse. As suspected, both Rosalyn and Linda stood waiting inside the door. He didn't have to wonder how long they had been eavesdropping on the scene between him and Jacey. Nothing went on in the town without one or the other of the women knowing the details.

"The wedding's off," Rosalyn stated.

"I'm not surprised," Linda muttered under her breath.

Stryker chose to ignore the remark.

"Not for long," he insisted. "We made a bargain, and she'll keep it."

"If you want that wedding so bad, you need to court her, Stryker." Rosalyn poured him a cup of coffee and motioned him to a chair at the worn kitchen table.

"What?"

"Court. You do know what that is, don't you, dear?" Linda leaned forward and patted his arm.

Stryker balled one hand into a fist. "I don't need to court anybody. It's all been arranged. We are getting married."

"You will be if you court her."

He closed his eyes a moment against the absurdity of the conversation. The arrangements had already been made before his mail order bride arrived. Now he needed to *court* her?

"Madeline Raines paid a surprise visit on Jacey today," Rosalyn announced.

"I heard. And I may kill her," he said in a strangled voice.

"What you should do is start wooing your bride-to-be."

"And stay away from Mrs. Raines."

He sent both women a quelling glance. "I don't need to court—"

"Stryker, the poor girl has come all the way out here, far from home and friends. She needs to know you'll take care of her."

"She knows," he assured with a hint of derision in his voice. *And it's costing me plenty.*

"How?"

"I explained it all in the letters."

"Oh, dear. You can't tell a woman something like that in letters," Rosalyn said.

"No, you have to show her. You have to woo her," Linda added.

"Court her," they said together.

Stryker realized he was truly caught between a rock and a hard place. He couldn't reveal the entire truth about the marriage. The two women would never understand. Or agree.

"How do you suggest I start?" he asked, not even trying to keep the edge of sarcasm out of his question.

Either the women missed it or chose to ignore it.

"With a buggy ride—"

"Oh, yes. It's so romantic."

Stryker gritted his teeth. "I don't have time to spend gallivanting off around the countryside, leaving my job."

"You have a deputy. And if you don't do something about Jacey, you're going to lose her, and then you'll lose your job as our marshal."

"And your ranch."

They were right, but the fact didn't please him any. He decided to give in and court his reluctant fiancée. What could it hurt? It would have the added advantage of showing the town his so-called feelings for his bride-to-be. Then no one could question the unexplainable delay in the wedding ceremony.

He would play along, and pretend to be enamored of his little fiancée. A memory of their kiss crept into his mind, and he shifted in the chair, then cleared his throat. He wished the recollection of Jacey's lips and its disturbing effects could be cleared away as easily. She had fit so perfectly in his arms, as if she belonged there.

Shifting again, he forced a smile and asked, "What time do you ladies suggest I pick her up tomorrow?"

"I think around one would be fine."

It would be fine, he thought, as long as he kept his hands off Jacey. Something he was finding harder and harder to do.

One o'clock the next afternoon found Stryker knocking at the front door of the boardinghouse. A horse and buggy stood hitched to the post, patiently waiting for his fiancée.

Stryker was fast running out of patience himself. He had taken plenty of ribbing when he had rented the horse and buggy at the livery, then received more than his share of waves and shouted questions as he drove the buggy down the main street of town to the boardinghouse. Well, if he wanted the townspeople to know he was going courting, he couldn't have done a better job of broadcasting the fact, even had he stood in the center of town and shouted the news himself.

He had half expected Mr. Raines to applaud as he drove by the bank. To Stryker's dismay, Jake, the owner of the mercantile, had clapped from the door of his store, loud enough for his young wife Clara to hear from upstairs, which had likely been his intention.

Stryker's mood worsened as he stood at the door, waiting. He couldn't believe the lengths he had been forced to go to for a fiancée he had already well compensated to marry him. Not to mention that she would cost him even more in the future. He shook his head in disbelief. She had been well paid, and now wanted flowers and buggy rides as well.

"Aw hell," he muttered.

The scent of flowers wafted up from the bouquet of brightly colored wildflowers he held tightly in his hand. The flowers had been a last moment impulse. He wasn't sure if they were for Jacey or to pacify his two insistent friends at the boardinghouse. Subconsciously a part of him voted for Jacey's favor.

Here he was marrying a woman to keep half the town's females at bay, and the lady in question wanted courting and wooing. Disbelief and anger at his foolishness warred within him.

The moment Jacey opened the door, all anger dissolved. She was vision of sweet loveliness in a lace-edged lavender gown that brought out the vibrant blue of her eyes. He noted the frivolous bustle and smiled. He was beginning to like the way it drew his attention to the seductive sway of her hips when she walked.

She looked up at him, almost shyly, appearing uncertain around him, even hesitant. He mentally shook himself; the woman who had slapped him so soundly wasn't the hesitant type.

"Afternoon," he said, remembering to tip his hat to her in a gentlemanly gesture. If he didn't know better, he would swear Jacey blushed.

"Good afternoon," she said softly.

Today she was the picture of the woman in the letters. Ladylike, sweet, quiet. Something about that fact bothered him. Tremendously.

"Did Linda and Rosalyn talk to you?" he asked, wanting make sure the courting idea wasn't misunderstood. He didn't want her getting any ideas.

She smiled and nodded. "Oh, yes. They spent the morning talking about you. They extolled your virtues in great detail."

"I don't have any virtues."

She realized he meant the harsh words. Whatever had happened to hurt him so badly in the past? She wondered for a moment if it had been in the letters, but knew with certainty he would never reveal his feelings in writing. Or in any other way. At least not casually or easily.

Logan Stryker was a hard man.

The thought brought a surge of unexplained tenderness in her. Reaching out, she laid her hand on his forearm, wanting to offer comfort in some small way.

He eased his arm away, sliding free of her hand. Then he held out the flowers to her.

"I thought you might like these," he stated for lack of anything better to say. He didn't add that the beautiful flowers had made him think of her.

"Here, I'll take those and put them in some water," Rosalyn offered, reaching out to take the wildflowers from Jacey's hands. "You two enjoy yourselves."

Someone eased her out the door and closed it behind her and Stryker. Jacey bit back a laugh. The two women were doing their best to push Stryker's case—and nearly shove her at him as well.

"I think that means it's time for us to go." Stryker chuckled and nudged his hat back with his thumb.

The sound of his low, throaty laugh did strange things to Jacey's stomach. She resisted the urge to rub her hand over her abdomen to settle the turmoil, for she knew it wouldn't do any good. The unsettled feeling didn't come from something she had eaten.

"I'm ready," she offered, suddenly nervous, then glanced away from him. "Where are we going?"

"I want to show you something."

"What?"

"It's a surprise."

"Oh." She kept her face turned away and busied her hands with the strings of the small bag dangling from her wrist.

Stryker wanted to reach out and turn her face to his. Her nervous actions and the aura of vulnerability about her today bothered him. It pricked his conscience, but he assured himself she was only playing a game with him, attempting to make him feel guilty for yesterday. Anger edged upward in him. She knew exactly the way things stood between them. Wasn't that what he was paying her for?

As the silence stretched uncomfortably, Jacey glanced back at him and said with a hint of excitement showing through her seeming nervousness, "I've never ridden in a buggy before."

"Consider it an addition to our bargain."

He couldn't say why he had snapped the words at her. Maybe because he knew she was trying to bend him to her will. Maybe because she looked so pretty and tempting the way she was looking up at him with her big blue eyes shining.

Especially when he knew he shouldn't touch her. Couldn't touch her. None of this was real.

At his sharp words, the light disappeared from her eyes, and she stared at him blankly. It sent an uneasy itch to the back of his neck. He resisted the urge to scratch it. His temper grew even more at her unexpected action. What was she trying to pull on him?

"Don't tell me that slipped your mind, too?" he challenged her.

She looked as if he had slapped her for a moment, then raised her chin in that gesture of pride he was beginning to recognize only too well.

"Of course not," she answered with startling briskness.

"Well, let's get going before the whole town comes to see us off."

Jacey stiffened at his remark. He didn't have to act like escorting her on a ride was such a chore. This hadn't been her idea.

She frowned at him, then swept past him on her way to the buggy. He had to rush to catch up with her. Just what he needed—the townspeople seeing her prancing off from him. It wasn't the picture he wanted to portray.

No, they needed to look like two people courting. He inwardly cringed. He hated being forced into anything, and this courting business grated. He refused to acknowledge that being with Jacey when he knew he had to keep his hands off her was what really bothered him.

At the side of the buggy, Jacey stopped and waited with her nose in the air. He gritted his teeth, then tried to prepare himself for the feel of her when he would lift her onto the buggy seat.

No amount of determination could have kept his body from reacting to the sweet feel of her body against his. She smelled of roses and temptation. He held her for a moment too long before he set her slipper-clad feet onto the floor of the buggy. Feeling his resolve weakening, he suddenly released her and walked around to the other side. He cursed his two interfering friends for the idea of an intimate buggy ride.

Jacey could feel the tension emanating from Stryker. Was he also feeling the effects that the contact of their bodies had evoked. Her skin had heated from his mere touch, and even now the warmth remained. She tried to hold herself stiffly away from him, half-angry with him and half-afraid of her body's reaction if he touched her again.

The buggy bounced over the bumps in the road, jostling her and frequently throwing her against Stryker. The experience was nothing like the genteel carriage rides she was accustomed to back home in Baltimore. She could barely keep herself upright.

She tried holding herself steady with one hand on the seat and leaning away from him. It didn't do a whit of good. At every bump, she brushed against him. As the wheels hit another rut, the force dislodged her hold on the seat and threw her into his shoulder. Finally, he clasped one arm around her and held her close.

He looked down at her and stated matter-of-factly, "So you don't fall out."

He followed it with a smile that she felt all the way to her toes. Her breath caught in her throat, and all she could do was nod at him. Embarrassment colored her cheeks, bringing a chuckle from deep in his chest. This time her heart skipped a beat, then sped up as if to make up for it. Heaven help her, his arm around her felt good.

The air was fresh and clean, the sun shone brightly, but Jacey scarcely registered any of it. She missed the trees, and grass, and abundance of colorful wildflowers around them. All she was conscious of was Stryker's warm body pressed close to hers. She barely noticed when he slowed the buggy.

Unexpectedly Stryker turned to her and asked, "So what do you think of the ranch?"

He gestured to the land splayed out before them, and her stomach lurched at the one word *ranch*.

"Ranch?" Jacey asked, dismay edging her voice.

"Well, we're on the outskirts, but this land is part of the Rocking S spread," he explained with obvious pride.

Jacey's stomach rolled again as she wondered what this had to do with their ride. She had a nervous feeling about this. She couldn't help it; she wrinkled her nose.

"I don't care much for ranches, but thank you for pointing it out to me."

Stryker stiffened beside her, until she could feel the tension emanating from him. She wondered what she had said wrong.

"Let me get this straight, you don't *care* for ranches?"

"Well, no." Jacey lifted a shoulder in a delicate shrug. Here was an opportunity to show him her unsuitability for Texas and all that went with it. "Actually, I'm more a city girl. I would hate a ranch. Cows, cow manure, and pecking chickens. And everything that goes with it. Give me a nice house in town any day."

She was secretly thanking her lucky stars that he owned a house in town. Both Rosalyn and Linda had informed her with glee that he stayed in town to be close to the jail. For an instant she wondered what his home looked like.

He pulled back on the reins and drew the buggy to a stop. "I'd hoped you'd like my ranch."

His ranch!

Jacey had made a terrible blunder. Those darn letters. Surely he had discussed his ranch in them. When she got hold of her twin, she would kill her for certain. No wonder Jeanette had left out this particular detail. If she had revealed the fact Stryker owned a ranch of all things, Jacey would never have agreed to the masquerade. Now she had double reasons to postpone the wedding. She had no intention of living on a ranch!

She could feel Stryker staring at her, and a flush of color rose to her cheeks. What was she going to tell him about her lapse in memory?

Unable to come up with anything better, she decided to play it light. She forced a bubble of laughter and caught his hand with hers. The jolt she felt between them was nearly her undoing.

Immediately she released his hand and waved hers in the air as if dismissing his concern and the demand in his voice. "I feel so silly. It slipped my mind about the ranch is all, and you surprised me. But I'm sure your ranch is likable and"—she paused a moment, then on impulse added the insulting word—"nice."

Nice? She had called his ranch nice? His spread was big. It took hard work. And she called it *nice*.

Stryker stared hard at her a moment. The flash of anger and disappointment at her feelings regarding his ranch cooled and evaporated. What was he thinking? She wasn't supposed to like ranching. Her reaction fit in perfectly with his plan, so there wasn't any reason to feel disappointment. However, he was puzzled by her remark.

"Jacey, why are you lying?"

She froze, unable to even breath for a moment. Oh, dear heavens, he knew!

For an instant she couldn't find her voice. She stared at him, waiting for the damning words to come from him, but he remained silent, waiting for her answer.

"Lie?" she asked in a weak voice.

"You're never going to like ranching, but that's all right. It's already been settled between us."

She nearly sighed in relief. He hadn't caught on to the masquerade. He was talking about something else entirely, but what?

"Remember I already know all about you," he added.

That was what he thought. The woman he thought he knew was her sister, and she felt anger and hurt at the realization. Jacey knew with absolute certainty he didn't know *her* at all. Any more than she knew him.

She could tick off on her fingertips the few facts she knew about him. He owned a ranch, held a job as marshal, and needed to get married awfully bad.

And he kissed like no one she had ever met before.

Stryker flicked the reins and sent the horse and buggy forward again. She glanced at him from lowered lashes, wondering what was behind the handsome man.

"Ready to see my ranch?" he asked.

Jacey knew it wasn't a request she could refuse. "Of course," she lied in a forced voice.

"We'll save the house for another day," he informed her as he drew up beside a fenced area.

As she pondered her relief at not being shown his bedroom today, he came around to her side of the buggy and caught her waist in his grasp. His hands nearly spanned her waist, and she marveled at the strength in his hold. As he lifted her down, she couldn't suppress the thrill that swept through her.

For a brief moment, Jacey wished to see that bedroom.

Then her feet touched the ground, and Stryker released her. The moment between them was lost. Secretly she mourned it, but then chided herself.

He stepped back, almost as if reading her wayward thoughts, or having some of his own. She resisted the urging of the little voice in the back of her mind to step forward and close the distance between them again.

"I"—he paused.

Jacey held her breath for his next words.

"Need to go check with Hank on something."

"Oh," she said in disappointment.

He gestured to the area around them. "Make yourself at home. I'll be right back."

When she didn't respond, he asked, "Will you be all right?"

She stiffened at his question. "Of course. I assure you I can entertain myself for a few minutes."

Gone was the meekness and vulnerability that had bothered him. In its place returned a spirit and determination that challenged him. The latter disturbed him even more with its innate attraction.

Stryker nodded to her and forced himself to turn and walk away. He knew if he waited one more minute, he would sweep her up into his arms. And he couldn't allow that to happen.

Jacey watched him stride off with his distance-eating steps. She told herself she was glad he had walked away from her, but had to resist the desire to call him back. She was acting like a silly, smitten girl. And that wasn't like her in the slightest. Irritated with herself, she whirled about and practically stomped over to a gate. Unfastening it, she strolled into the grassy area. She had decided to take a walk, hoping the fresh air would restore her senses.

As she strolled along, Stryker continued to consume her thoughts. She kicked up a clod of dirt, then another. Intent on venting some of her anger at herself, she didn't pay any attention to her surroundings.

Suddenly an unfamiliar sound behind her penetrated her distraction. Slowly she turned around and came face-to-face with the biggest bull she had ever seen. He was a dingy white and towered nearly five feet high. His horns angled out and seemed to be pointing straight at her. For endless seconds, she and the animal stared at each other; then he took a huge step toward her.

Jacey gulped as the terror rose in her. She took one careful step backward, then another. The bull followed.

She couldn't seem to take her eyes from the animal. She had never seen anything so big before. Or so ugly. A huge hump rose up just behind his neck. He stared at her, then blew out his breath.

Screaming in terror, she whirled, caught up her skirts in both hands and ran for her life.

Chapter Seven

Stryker spun around at Jacey's scream. A chill of pure fear ran through him at the sound of terror in her voice. He had never felt this kind of fear in his life.

As he spotted her running hell bent for leather toward him, he ran to meet her.

"What's wrong—"

Before he got another word out, she flung herself at him. He caught her, but the force sent them both tumbling to the ground. They landed with Jacey lying atop Stryker in the dirt.

She screamed again, then buried her face in his shoulder. Stryker looked up to see the Brahma bull trotting toward them. The huge animal lumbered to a halt, then leaned down and sniffed Jacey's shoulder.

She screamed, and Stryker burst into laughter.

"Jacey, darling, meet Bo," he said with an uncharacteristic lightness in his voice.

She buried her face deeper into the safe haven of his

shoulder. Instinctively, he tightened his arms around her body.

"Jacey, Bo is a tame bull. He won't hurt you."

She raised her head only enough to see Stryker's chin. "Tame?"

"As a kitten."

The bull snorted over them, and Jacey shuddered, then returned to her hiding place against Stryker's shoulder.

"Well, almost as tame as a kitten." He gave a soft chuckle, but it caught in his throat.

Jacey's breath warmed his shoulder, heating the skin beneath his shirt. He shifted uneasily, and she turned her head into his neck. As she exhaled, her moist breath fanned his neck. He tried resisting the temptation, but his body seemed to have developed a mind of its own.

Stryker stiffened, feeling himself grow hard against the lush softness of her body pressing down on his. He cleared his throat, determined to ignore the siren call of temptation.

He concentrated on telling her about the bull. "Bo is a Brahma bull, imported by the last owner. Old Bo came with the ranch when I bought the spread two years ago."

As she remained silent, he felt her tremble against him in reaction to her scare. He ran his hands up and down her back to soothe her.

"Honey, nothing's going to hurt you here."

In spite of his assurance, she still shivered. He tightened his hold on her, wanting to show her she was safe. She snuggled closer against him, and his own body responded.

"Ah, Jacey." He cleared his throat, trying to dislodge the obstruction settling there.

She turned her head to his, and her lips brushed his neck. Her lips were warm and soft. And too tempting. It was his undoing.

Stryker turned his head to meet the invitation of her

lips. His mouth took hers in a breath-robbing kiss that blocked out all thought. Only feeling remained. Her lips tasted sweeter than the richest honey. He sipped at them, slowly savoring each taste of her, stretching out the pleasure.

Jacey returned his passion, her breath quickening at each kiss. She slid her hands upward to feel the strong muscles of his chest, then the power of his biceps. If anyone could keep her safe, this man could.

Sighing her surrender, she relinquished any doubts and returned his kiss with a fervor she didn't know she possessed. His hands on her back warmed her skin through the material of her gown, branding her as his as surely as if he had used a heated branding iron.

Her blood seemed to sing through her veins with the pure pleasure from his touch and the taste of his mouth on hers. As he ran his tongue across her lips, parting them, she moaned a soft sound of encouragement. He thrust his tongue into her mouth, and she gasped in surprise. He took advantage to plunder her mouth until she clung tightly to his shoulders with both hands. Such wondrous sensations were new to Jacey. As he ran his hands up her back, tingles of pleasure followed in their wake. He paused when his fingers grazed the column of her neck, and she moaned against his mouth. He stole the sound away.

Stryker's blood heated at the soft sounds she made. He grew rock hard beneath her. Sliding his hands upward, he cupped her chin, rubbing his calloused thumbs across her silken skin. She was so soft, so sweet, so enticing.

As she squirmed atop him, he shifted his body to more readily accommodate hers. A rock dug into the middle of his back, and he winced. The sharp pain brought him back to reality in an instant.

He groaned in silent denial. Here he was ready to take Jacey on the ground like a rutting animal. Disgust at himself swept through him, bringing irritation on its heels. He eased Jacey off him and to the side with less gentleness than he had intended. When she cried out in surprise, he felt like an even worse heel.

"I'm sorry—" he began.

She stopped him with an icy, withering glance, then pushed herself to her feet. Watching her brush off her skirt, he had the feeling that she was attempting to remove all traces of his touch as well as the clinging dust.

"Jacey, I—"

Whirling about, she faced him, sending him a scathing look when he stood. Her eyes snapped with indignation. He swallowed down both his apology and his explanation. The devil take her if she chose to be this way.

Jacey raised her chin in what he recognized as haughty contempt. He clenched his teeth until his jaw hurt.

"Don't ever touch me again." She enunciated each word with absolute disdain.

Shame, anger, and pain warred in her until she wanted to scream out her frustration at him, but she held her tongue. How dare he kiss her senseless and then go and apologize to her! Apologize! She had never been so insulted in her life.

What was he sorry about? That he had kissed her? That she had responded so wantonly? Or had he been disappointed?

She forced herself to turn away from him before he could see the sudden glimmer of tears reflected in her eyes. What was it to her if he didn't like her kisses? Nothing. Absolutely nothing, she told herself.

Liar, her conscience accused.

Well, it didn't matter, she argued with herself. She wasn't marrying him. And she wasn't about to let him touch her ever again.

Head held high with determination, she walked away

from him with as much dignity as she could muster. She would never let him know how much his callous apology had hurt her.

"I'm ready to go back to town now." She tossed the information over her shoulder, righteous indignation coloring every word. It was the only way she could speak without her voice wavering.

If she hurried, she might be able to climb into the buggy before he reached her side. She wasn't certain what she would do if he touched her while helping her into the buggy; she would either slap his handsome face or kiss him until they were both senseless.

She successfully reached the buggy first, then watched in growing irritation as Stryker dusted his hat off with a slap to his leg and walked with even, measured steps to the horse and buggy.

He seemed to take an unreasonable amount of time untying the horse and walking around to his side of the buggy before he climbed aboard. Jacey braced herself for his anger at her actions, but he remained stoic and silent.

She wanted to shout, rant, or yell at him for his silence, but forced herself to hold her tongue. She would never let him suspect the effect his words had on her. She set her mind to forgetting all about the attraction that blazed up between them every time he kissed her. If she didn't think about it, then it would disappear.

Not even when a certain hot place froze over, her conscience whispered. The nagging only served to boost her temper.

He could take his marriage contract and burn it with his hot kisses for all she cared. Nothing could make her go through with the wedding. She wouldn't marry him now if he got down on his knees and begged her. Resolutely, she turned her head away from his strong profile and pretended an interest she didn't feel in the passing scenery.

* * *

Stryker watched Jacey from the corner of his eye. Her haughty anger and indignant stature irritated him more than he wanted to admit. Guilt flooded him for his unforgivable action in nearly taking her in the dirt. A woman like her deserved courting and a romantic seduction scene—things he couldn't give her. Things he refused to ever give any woman again.

He shoved the self-condemnation away and concentrated on driving the buggy. If he concentrated hard enough, he might be able to ignore the stiff set of Jacey's back and the sweet smell of her scent.

There wasn't that much concentration in the world.

The ride was completed in uncomfortable silence. Stryker refused to apologize again, not when she had rejected his first attempt. The silence hung heavy between them, damning him for his actions, but refusing to douse the desire he still felt for her.

At last they reached the boardinghouse. This time he ensured he circled to her side before she could climb down on her own. However, when he lifted her down, he made certain their bodies didn't make any contact.

She kept her face averted from him, and he could feel her anger a tangible thing between them. She acted as if he weren't even there, much less walking close beside her. He reined in his own temper and escorted her to the door. Once there she hurried inside before he could say anything; then he heard the click of the front door lock.

The sound said plenty to him. Things were progressing from bad to worse. Now he was in for a reprimand from Rosalyn and Linda on his courting. And he could bet Jacey wasn't about to go through with the wedding anytime soon.

One fact was certain—his method of courting needed

improvement if he expected Jacey to go through with their bargain before his time ran out.

An hour later, Stryker sat in the saloon nursing his first drink and his foul mood. He leaned back in the chair, keeping his back to the saloon wall. Although he sat facing the door like he always did, he still felt uneasy, but he knew it wasn't from his usual innate caution at the possibility of a backshooter.

The cause was the scene with Jacey; it had left him unsettled. Reciting her encounter with the bull to his best friend didn't help any.

"You're making a big mistake," Brett Mason insisted for the second time in their conversation.

"Not likely."

"Doesn't Jacey's reaction to Bo tell you anything? Can't you see she's a city gal?"

"She's the perfect bride for my plan." Stryker took a sip of his drink to quiet the little voice that told him she was perfect in more ways than one.

"It won't work. She'll never stay on your ranch," his friend argued.

Her refusing to stay was exactly what Stryker had been counting on. Now a vague sense of defeat haunted him. He tried telling himself everything was working out as planned, but he wasn't assured things had changed since he had held Jacey in his arms and kissed her.

"Hey." Brett waved his hand back and forth in front of Stryker's face, getting his attention. "Why you didn't choose one the gals in town when you decided to get hitched instead of sending off for a mail order bride, I'll never understand. This gal has you tied up in knots."

"Not by a long shot she doesn't," he denied. "And one of the women in town wouldn't have worked."

"What do you mean worked?"

"Drop it." Stryker took a swallow from the glass.

"Like I said, she has you tied up in knots. You've got it bad." Brett rubbed his chin and studied his friend. "I haven't seen you this worked up over a woman since Madeline left you for old man Raines, and that was five years ago—"

Stryker fixed an ice-filled stare on his friend. In a deadly slow voice he stated, "Don't *ever* bring that up again."

Brett swallowed convulsively, then said, "Sorry. But you usually love 'em and leave 'em. No woman's got to you like this in—"

One look from Stryker sent the remainder of his words back in his throat. He coughed and took a swallow of the whiskey. Setting his glass back down, he leaned forward in concern.

"What do you know about this woman?"

"Enough. Stop interfering, Brett. It's all been worked out in detail. Down to the dollar."

Brett shook his head. "I don't like this—"

"Stop worrying about me like an old woman. Everything's been arranged. My heart is perfectly safe." He silently added that it was encased in steel, and no woman was getting through to touch it again.

A nagging doubt surfaced, and Stryker tossed it away along with the last swallow from his drink. He poured himself another, leaned back in his chair, and stared at the glass. He had nothing to be concerned about, he assured himself. He had worked too hard setting this bargain up for anything to go wrong. He wouldn't let it.

"What are you talking about?" Brett asked, puzzlement clouding his features. "The wedding—"

Stryker tightened his hand around the glass, then spoke, "Not real." He took a sip, letting the whiskey burn its way along his throat, hoping to burn out his doubts.

"What do you mean?"

Stryker leaned across the table and assured his friend in a low voice, "I mean I'm not really marrying her for keeps."

As he relaxed in his chair again, Brett stared at him in disbelief. He leaned closer and said in a terse voice, "What do you mean?"

Stryker set his glass away from him. He had lost his taste for the drink. One was enough. He nodded at his friend. "We made a bargain."

"You made a bargain with—"

Propping his elbows on the table, Stryker interrupted to explain, "Relax, it's only a temporary arrangement. Plan was I get hitched to the most unsuitable lady I can find— a citified gal. Then a month or two after the wedding, she up and goes back east with a nice bit of money in her hands. I'll be a married man, at least married enough to keep the town husbands from coming after me. And I won't have the bother of an unwanted wife hanging on my shirttails."

"You're serious, aren't you?" Brett stared across the table at his friend.

Stryker merely nodded, his back stiffening at the censure in his friend's voice. His own conscience prodded him, but he assured himself Jacey had agreed readily enough before he ever met her.

"Have you thought this through?" Brett asked.

Stryker merely sent him a direct look that said more than words could say. He had thought it through, all right. And now wasn't the time to have second thoughts.

"Yes, of course you have," Brett amended. He knew from past experience his friend never acted on impulse.

"It's settled," Stryker stated the fact.

When he didn't elaborate, Brett asked, "You mean she knows about this?"

"Yes."

"And she agreed?"

"Oh, yes."

"Well, I'll be hog-tied."

"That could be arranged if you utter one word of this conversation to anyone else."

Brett held up his hands. "You've got my word." A grin split his face, and he rubbed his hand back and forth over his jaw. "But blamed if I don't want to stick around to see this out. Have you thought about making it real?"

Stryker sent him a look that warned him to shut up.

His friend ignored it, instead lifting his glass in a toast. "To your temporary arrangement and your stamina. I've seen the lady, and if you can hold out against her, you're a better man than I am." He tossed back his drink with a chuckle.

Stryker pushed away from the table and stood. "I'm going to my office."

"I thought your deputy was on duty."

"I'm giving him the rest of the day off." Stryker strode out the door without even looking back. He needed to keep busy to keep his mind off Jacey and the persistent reminder of the feel of her in his arms.

Jacey reread the telegram and clenched her teeth together. Trust Jeanette to wire her at the worst possible moment. And with the most insane request she had ever heard.

She gripped the edge of the paper so hard it crinkled, then ripped in half. Giving in to her anger, she tore the remainder of the missive into tiny bits. The words remained crystal clear in her mind.

Aunt Cordelia abhors Franklin. Stop. Am beginning to entertain doubts. Stop. Do whatever you need to postpone vows. Stop. Hang on. Don't let him go before I wire you my decision. Stop. Jeanette.

Jacey stomped her foot in vexation. She would not keep hold of Stryker for her twin. Absolutely not. She had sworn he wouldn't touch her again. In fact, she never wanted to see him again.

What was she to do? How could she postpone the wedding when she had sworn it was off? She refused to try to attract his interest to hold him for her twin's decision. It was time she told him the truth. Let Jeanette straighten everything out with Stryker if she wanted to. If Jeanette wanted him, she could have him.

A surge of pain hit her at the thought of her sister in Stryker's arms. She pushed it away, telling herself she didn't care. She didn't. She merely enjoyed his kisses, nothing more. And she was beginning to enjoy them entirely too much. It was past time to put a stop to this insanity.

Jacey stormed out of her room and down the stairs. She had made her decision; she was going to see Stryker in the professional safety of his office. Even he wouldn't try to seduce her in a jail. Would he?

She closed her eyes against the thought. She doubted if her resolve was strong enough to resist him if he kissed her again.

She was going to tell Stryker the facts. She couldn't continue this masquerade another moment longer. She was tired of playing her twin and being engaged to her fiancé.

She wanted to go home.

* * *

Harvey Forester leaned against the support of a chair in the study and stared at his son in disbelief. He had come home only an hour ago to find Jacey and Jeanette missing, and his son making excuses. He ran a hand through his brown, thinning hair. His anger rose with each new excuse his son devised.

"Where are the twins?" He stamped his cane hard on the wood floor of the study.

Earl visibly paled, then stammered, "I . . . I . . . don't know."

"How could you let them leave?"

"I wasn't here when they sneaked away," he explained in defense. Then he added, "Like thieves."

The elder Forester cracked the floor with his cane. "Don't say it. Remember, they're my dead brother's children."

"But the policemen were here for Jacey—"

"I've already straightened out that misunderstanding. That fool Gregory Canefield. He'll never come near this house again."

"How was I to know—"

"Don't act the fool. This has all worked out too conveniently for you."

"How can you blame me? They've always been trouble."

The polished wood floor resounded with yet another stamp of the cane, silencing Earl.

"This time you're the one I'm blaming. Find them."

"I don't know where to start looking."

"If you don't find them and bring them safely home, then look for your livelihood elsewhere," Harvey threatened.

Earl visibly paled. "Father, you can't do that. I'm to inherit the company. I've worked too hard to—"

Mr. Forester turned his back on Earl. "The twins are my heirs, too. Refuse to find them, and you inherit nothing."

Earl took one last look at his father's stern posture and knew it would be useless to remain and argue. There was nothing to do but go after his cousins. The foolish girls were far more trouble than they were worth.

He was sure they had run off just to win his father's sympathy.

When he found Jacey and Jeanette, they would pay dearly for all the trouble they caused him.

Earl left through the back door. He knew Jeanette was infatuated with the worthless, fortune-hunting Franklin Prescott; all he had to do was track the man and he would surely find her as well.

The twins would rue the day they had crossed him this way.

Stryker looked up from his desk when the door of his office swung open. Thankfully the jail was empty; he was too distracted to notice if someone walked past him, much less attempted an escape. He was thinking of Jacey and half expected her to walk in the front door, but his visitor wasn't Jacey.

"Aw, hell," he muttered under his breath when he spotted Madeline Raines sauntering in, bringing with her the nearly choking fragrance of lavender.

"Go home," Stryker told her, not standing at her well-timed entrance.

"Darling, I know you're hurt—"

"Don't call me that."

"See, you are still hurting from my desertion." She patted a red curl in place, quite pleased with herself.

He shook his head and laughed at her. "Far from it. I've found someone else."

The look of shock on her face was worth every dollar of

the marriage contract. He leaned back in his chair and smiled.

"Don't be ridiculous." Madeline waved her hand, dismissing his statement. "You don't love that insipid creature. You're only doing this to get back at me."

"You're wrong, and my bride-to-be is far from insipid." A wide grin lifted his lips at his memory of Jacey's passionate response to his kisses.

Madeline paled and hurried forward. "You can't care about her."

Stryker merely grinned wider, leaving her to make her own assumptions.

"I won't let you marry her."

"There's nothing you can do to stop me, Mrs. Raines." He threw the taunt of her marriage for money at her.

She rounded the desk and threw herself onto his lap. Sniffing, she clasped her arms around his neck. "I'll do anything."

Stryker stood to his feet in disgust. "Don't make more of a fool of yourself than you already have." He reached up to disentangle her hands.

"Oh, I feel faint," she cried out and began to go limp in his arms.

Stryker forgot about releasing her hands. The gentleman in him demanded he keep her from falling to the floor. Carefully, he put his arms around her back to keep her upright.

Suddenly, she moved forward, grabbing his shirtfront and pulling him to her. "I knew you loved me."

Before he could deny it, she pressed her lips to his and ground her body against him, nearly causing him to lose his balance. He caught her arms in his hands, intending to shove her away.

At the same instant, Stryker heard the door crash against the wall with a resounding bang. He tore his mouth away from Madeline's kiss and looked up to see Jacey standing inside the doorway.

Her face revealed her shocked disgust. Her eyes looked as if they were filled with pain and fury.

"Don't let me interrupt you," Jacey forced out past her suddenly stiff lips.

She couldn't seem to take her eyes from the scene in front of her. She suddenly had the almost irrepressible urge to grab the woman by the hair and pull her away herself, then toss her out of the office on her derriere.

Jacey bit her lower lip in vexation, confused by the pangs of jealousy she now suffered. Stryker stared at her, surprise and guilt plainly showing on his face. She wished she could reach out and slap him, but she felt held in place.

Madeline curled one arm around his neck and looked over her shoulder at the door. "Do close the door on your way out, child." Her eyes glittered with triumph that clearly said, *I told you so.*

A shaft of pain cut through Jacey, and for an instant she couldn't even breathe. The pain lodged in her chest, and she was surprised anything could hurt so badly.

She raised her chin to force out the words, "I came to say good-bye. But I can see it wasn't necessary."

"Jacey."

Stryker pushed Madeline away, but she pressed herself against his chest.

"Let her go," Madeline insisted.

"Jacey," Stryker began.

"I'll be on the next train out of town," Jacey stated in a low, flat voice.

Bertram Raines pushed his way past her, and the fact that he had been standing beside her barely registered to Jacey.

"Bertram," Madeline cried out.

Jacey started to turn away to walk out the door, but the

banker caught her arm to stop her. "Oh, no you won't. This is all your fault for delaying the wedding."

"There isn't going to be any wedding," Jacey said with cold fury.

"Oh, yes there is," Raines insisted, his gaze locking with Stryker's across the room. "Isn't there, Marshal."

"No." Jacey yanked her arm from his hold.

"Tell her, Marshal." Raines said in a threatening voice. "Or I'll see the town demands your badge within the hour." He pulled out his pocket watch and flicked the case open with his thumb.

Jacey couldn't believe no one was even listening to her refusal. She stomped her foot, barely missing the banker's toes. "I'm not marrying you." She stared into Stryker's shuttered face.

Raines pointed to his watch. "You have one minute to give me your word"—he sneered at this and continued—"or I go start the foreclosure on your ranch. Without a job . . ." He let the remainder trail off.

Stryker tore his gaze away from Jacey's stricken face to meet the banker's hard eyes.

"Tomorrow at eleven?" Raines asked.

The question was a demand, and Stryker knew it. Nodding his agreement, he responded, "Fine."

Raines stepped forward and grabbed his wife by the hand. "It's time we left these two to plan their wedding, dear."

"But—" Madeline began.

Raines dragged her out the door behind him.

Madeline waved and said, "I'll see you later."

Three voices answered, "No you won't."

Jacey stared at Stryker and realized what she had just said. Well, she meant every word. Jealousy swept through her, and she was shocked with its intensity.

Unable to tear her gaze from his, Jacey continued to

stare at him. He had kissed her senseless this morning, then had the audacity to go to another woman this afternoon. She was furious, and hurt, and. . . .

The realization raced through her, sending her heartbeat speeding. Oh, no. No, she denied, but the truth wouldn't be pushed away.

She was falling in love with Stryker.

"Oh, no," she whispered.

"Oh, yes, Jacey." Stryker strode forward, catching her shoulders with his hands and pulling her into the room.

She shook her head, trying to deny her heart. She couldn't be falling in love. Yet that little voice whispered in the back of her mind, telling her that it was already too late.

Stryker held her with a gentle hold, but secure enough that she couldn't slip away if she had wanted to. Right now she wasn't sure if she could walk away.

He leaned closer, and she held her breath, waiting.

"We *will* be married tomorrow." His voice brooked no argument.

All Jacey could do was stare up at him.

"If you dare try to leave, I swear I'll hunt you down and bring you back to jail," he said in a low voice with an edge to it.

Pain hit Jacey at his threat, nearly taking her to her knees. She didn't have a choice. She would marry him tomorrow.

But she wished he had asked her.

Chapter Eight

Jacey stared at the woman in the mirror. She looked truly beautiful dressed in the white creation of rich material and lace. But didn't people say every bride was beautiful on her wedding day?

She also thought she looked pale, nervous, and nearly scared to death—which she was. Less than an hour remained until her wedding. She pinched her cheeks to chase away the stark paleness and bring some color to her face.

"Ouch," she muttered.

The pinch assured her this definitely wasn't a dream. Today was her wedding day. She should be happy. She should be excited.

She should run away as fast as she could.

And she would if she had a lick of sense or self-respect in her. Instead she stood, held in place by the memory of Stryker's kisses.

No, she couldn't run away. Truth be told, she didn't want to either.

She wished Jeanette could be here, then jerked herself up. Guilt flooded her. She was marrying her twin's fiancé.

"Jeanette, I'm sorry," she whispered, her voice breaking.

How was she to explain this marriage to her sister? Jacey had never trespassed on her twin's beaus—until now. Trespass, no, she had stolen him.

She closed her eyes against the guilt sweeping over her. A picture of Stryker sneaked into her mind, tall and strong. The memory of his touch followed, and her resolve weakened, then disappeared.

She opened her eyes and tore her gaze from the pale reflection in the mirror and looked down at the gown that flowed around her. It was a thing of beauty. She couldn't have wished for a more beautiful wedding gown than the one her two new friends had made for her. They must have worked around the clock to ensure it was ready in time.

The gown fit her perfectly, the bodice tapering to a full skirt that swirled around her ankles. A multitude of small buttons fastened with loops up the back of the gown. It had taken Rosalyn a full five minutes or more to fasten them all. Then after helping her dress, she and Linda had left her alone for a few minutes.

Jacey's stomach knotted. The time alone was supposed to be calming her for the wedding. It wasn't working.

She stared at her reflection again, wondering if the beauty in the mirror was truly her. If only this were a real wedding with love between the bride and groom. Instead it was the closest thing to a shotgun wedding she could imagine. A light tap at the door sent her nervous heart racing for her slipper-clad toes.

"Yes?" Her voice broke on the single word.

"Jacey, dear, are you ready? You look lovely." Rosalyn walked into the room.

"Beautiful," Linda added, coming to help place the veil atop Jacey's head.

The two women fussed over her, then stepped back and beamed, evidently proud of their sewing efforts. And perhaps proud of helping nudge the wedding along as well, Jacey suspected.

"Well, dear, it's time."

Butterflies took flight in her stomach, and she flinched. Could she go through with this?

"Dear, are you all right?" Rosalyn asked.

"You're not ill, are you?" Concern filled Linda's voice.

"No, I'm fine," Jacey assured the women.

Rosalyn caught Jacey's hand in hers and patted it reassuringly. "Everything is going to work out fine. Just you wait and see."

Linda nodded her head vigorously. "If ever I've seen a man in love, it's Stryker."

"Thank you, both. But you don't have to lie to me—"

"We're not."

"I know the way things are, and I'm going to go through with the wedding." Jacey fingered the corner of the veil. "You don't have to worry."

"We're not worried," both women put in at once.

Rosalyn hugged Jacey close and then pulled a box out of her skirt pocket. She opened it to reveal a string of beautiful pearls.

"Your gown needs one more thing." She held out the necklace. "I want you to have these, dear."

Jacey shook her head. "Oh, no, I couldn't."

Accepting a necklace was what had landed her in this predicament in the first place.

"I insist." Rosalyn stepped forward and clasped the string of pearls around Jacey's neck.

Jacey smiled at her friend. "I'll agree to borrow them—"

"Of course, dear," Rosalyn answered with a look that clearly said they would be discussing the subject more later.

Linda patted her hand. "Dear, everything is going to be fine."

Jacey only wished she could believe the assurance.

"Is Stryker . . ." Jacey's voice trailed off, unable to speak the remainder of her question, or the ones settled deep in her heart.

Would he escort her to the church?

Would he be waiting for her?

Would he ever be able to love her?

She forced a smile for the two women's benefit. Her new friends grinned in response.

"He's waiting at the church," Linda informed her.

"Humph, he's been waiting nearly all morning. Just pacing, according to Brett." Rosalyn handed Jacey a bouquet of beautiful wildflowers in a profusion of colors.

"They're beautiful." Jacey fingered the blooms.

"We thought you should have a special bouquet for today," Rosalyn told her.

"One you can only get in Texas in the spring," Linda added.

"Thank you." Jacey appreciated their kindness.

"There's more in the church," Linda told her, earning a poke from Rosalyn.

"That was supposed to be a surprise."

At Jacey's questioning look, Rosalyn explained, "We decorated the church with wildflowers for you. But *someone* ruined the surprise."

"What did I say wrong?"

"Thank you, both." Jacey reached out and caught both women's hands and squeezed. "That's the nicest thing anyone has ever done for me."

"Well, let's go see them, and that handsome bridegroom

of yours." Rosalyn tugged her to the door. "Bertram Raines is waiting to drive you to the church."

Jacey threw one last glance about the room. She wouldn't be returning here to stay with her new friends. A pang of nervousness hit her. What would it be like living at Stryker's ranch?

What would it be like living with Stryker?

Stryker paced back and forth in the area behind the small church. The last time he had been preparing for a wedding, the bride had run off with a richer prospect, leaving him feeling the fool.

He shut his eyes against the memory of Madeline's deception. In five years the humiliation and pain had lessened. It was in the past and had nothing to do with today. He wasn't marrying for love this time. And Jacey wasn't going to break his heart because he hadn't been fool enough to give it to her.

Turning back toward the church, he tugged at his cuffs. He would bet every one of the town husbands sat inside the church with their wives at their sides. Waiting.

Except Bertram Raines.

The banker stood in front of the boardinghouse with a horse and buggy to escort Jacey to the wedding. Was the man afraid she would sneak out a window and he would be deprived of seeing Stryker wed?

Stryker leaned his head back and stared up at the sunny sky. Wasn't the thought of Jacey finding a way out of town what was really bothering him? In truth he had to admit it.

"Will you quit fretting like an old woman." Brett clasped his friend on the shoulder and laughed.

"I'm not fretting," Stryker denied.

"Of course not. You've just worn a path through the grass pacing and worrying over your bride-to-be."

The clop of horse hooves signaled the arrival of a buggy and spurred Brett into action. He grabbed Stryker by the arm and turned him back toward the church.

"If I'm not mistaken, that's the arrival of your fiancée now in Raines' buggy. Let's get inside."

As they stepped through the side door into the church, it felt as if a fist closed around Stryker's throat. The realization of what he was about to do struck him. He was about to get himself leg-shackled to the most beautiful woman he had ever met.

He heard a door open and looked up to see Jacey standing at the back of the church, and all other thoughts left him. She was a vision of beauty in a gown that swirled and whispered around her when she walked up to join him at the front of the church.

She was his bride.

It's only temporary, a little voice whispered. He ignored it.

As she drew even with him, he took her small hand in his. All he could think of was that this was the woman he was pledging his heart to in front of the townspeople. She flashed him a hesitant smile, and he feared his heart was lost for good.

Jacey dared a brief glance up at Stryker, and almost wished she hadn't. He looked so tall and handsome standing beside her. His snowy white shirt offset his broad shoulders and strong arms. Her breath caught in her throat and lodged there. She swallowed down her sudden bout of nerves and gave herself permission to stare at him.

He greeted her with a smile that looked a little forced around the edges. She looked away and blinked back the sudden sting of unwelcome tears. With merely a look, she had been reminded this was a forced marriage. He didn't love her.

And she didn't love him. She absolutely refused to.

"Jacey," Stryker whispered.

She jerked her head up to face him.

Stryker nodded toward the minister, and she felt her cheeks redden with the blush of embarrassment. What had the man said to her?

"Excuse me?" she asked in a voice that came out scarcely above a whisper.

The minister repeated his words, and the remainder of the ceremony passed in a blur of disquieting emotions for Jacey.

Suddenly she felt the coldness of a band on her finger. She hoped it wasn't a symbol of what was to come. The coldness inched up her arm and came to rest in her chest. Stryker kept hold of her hand, wrapping his fingers around hers, and the ring warmed beneath his touch.

"You may kiss the bride," the minister announced.

Jacey looked up at Stryker in hesitation. Would he kiss her? Would he. . . ?

Stryker bent over and brushed his lips against hers. All coolness fled her body, chased away by the reassuring warmth of his lips. Jacey returned the light kiss, raising up on her tiptoes.

It was as if a dam burst in him at her action. Stryker responded with the pent-up longing and desire that had been driving him crazy. He deepened the kiss, slanting his mouth over hers and taking her fully in a kiss destined to meld them together.

He pulled her to him, not even caring that he had lifted her off her feet. He held her close, his mouth devouring hers. Over and over again.

Jacey slid her arms up around his shoulders to his neck and held on. Her bouquet slipped from her hand to fall at her feet, and she didn't give a whit. His kiss swept her away from everything and everyone else in the world.

The sound of applause penetrated the cloud of desire surrounding them. Stryker groaned against her lips and eased her down the length of him. Slowly, inch by painful inch, he slid her down until her feet touched the floor.

Brett stepped forward, hand extended to congratulate his friend, but Stryker ignored him. Instead he swept Jacey up into his arms and carried her down the aisle and out the door of the church.

Jacey buried her face in his chest and gave herself up to the enjoyment of being carried close in Stryker's arms. He made her feel cherished, treasured, and loved. She knew it would end soon enough.

Once outside, her pleasure came to an abrupt halt. Stryker stood her on her feet and took a step away as if he had realized what he had done. Immediately the two were surrounded by well-wishers. The men clasped Stryker on the back and shook his hand. The women congratulated Jacey with distant politeness that left her wondering. Madeline Raines remained a distance away, a hate-filled gaze fastened on Jacey.

However, Rosalyn and Linda made up for the lack of sincerity she had felt from most of the townswomen. Not even Madeline's animosity could spoil the beauty of the sunny day and the kernel of happiness in Jacey's heart.

"Well, folks," Bertram Raines shouted above the din of the crowd. "We got ourselves a celebration to go to." He gestured to the town hall.

Rosalyn caught Jacey's hand. "I hope you don't mind, but Linda and I took the liberty of preparing a little celebration, as Bertram called it."

Their generosity touched her, and Jacey blinked back the sudden moisture of tears. "Thank you again." She squeezed their hands.

Stryker slid an arm around Jacey's shoulders and led her to the town hall and the well wishes of the townspeople.

For Jacey the next hour passed in a blur. The ring on her finger felt unfamiliar and insisted on reminding her she was married now. For better or worse. She gulped at the thought.

Brett pulled Stryker from her side and raised his glass to him in a private toast between the two of them.

"To you and your new *bride*," Brett said loud enough for everyone to hear.

As cheers followed, he leaned closer and added, "Even if it is temporary."

Stryker winced at the reminder.

With a smile, Brett drained his glass, then said in a low voice for his friend's ears only, "I wager fifty dollars that you won't last out the night."

Stryker clenched his hand into a fist. "I made a bargain," he gritted out, "and I intend to keep it."

"Even if it kills you?" Brett chuckled.

"Yes."

Stryker looked across to where Jacey stood, and he let his gaze follow her every movement. Brett was right. Being with his new bride and not being able to touch her was going to be slow death.

Jacey felt a warmth start at her spine and work its way through her body. Slowly she turned to find Stryker staring at her. There was no mistaking the heat in his darkened eyes, even from the distance separating them.

He turned back to his friend, and Jacey returned her attention to her two friends standing beside her. A question nagged at her until she couldn't hold it in any longer.

"What's a shivaree?" Jacey asked Linda in a low voice.

"What?"

"I heard someone whispering about it earlier," Jacey explained. "What is it?"

Her friend blanched and looked around the room. "Pray you don't find out."

"But, what—"

"Don't you worry. Rosalyn and I will have a little talk with the men. They'll leave you two alone tonight." With this cryptic remark, she swept off.

Jacey meant to tell Linda that she had heard the women discussing it, but at the thought of spending the night alone with Stryker, she forgot all about her friend. She trembled, but it was inside where no one else could see it. Her stomach tumbled over and over. Realization hit her, stealing her breath away in its wake.

Tonight was her wedding night.

At long last the festivities ended, and Stryker dutifully swept his new bride up in his arms and carried her out to the borrowed horse and buggy. He struggled to keep a smile fixed on his face in spite of the thought rolling over and over in his mind.

Tonight was his wedding night. And he couldn't touch his bride! The night and the ones to follow were going to be pure torment.

Since Brett and Bertram Raines insisted on escorting the newlyweds to the ranch, there was little chance for conversation. Stryker kept his arm around Jacey during the ride, and she wondered if it was for the other men's benefit. Nervous butterflies kept her stomach as unsettled as her thoughts.

Once at the ranch, their escorts left quickly, but Brett turned back a moment. He tipped his hat to Jacey and winked at them both.

"I gave you two a little gift. Made everyone who works the ranch promise to keep clear of the house tonight." He kicked his horse and galloped off.

Stryker swallowed down his comment. He might just shoot Brett for his "gift." Jacey looked at him, her eyes wide, and he wanted to reassure her. Right then he needed some reassurance of his own that he could keep his hands off her.

Trying to smile, he lifted her out of the buggy and quickly set her on her feet. The last thing he needed at that moment was to risk their bodies touching.

"I'll show you the house," he told her, attempting to fill the silence between them.

"That would be nice." Jacey winced at her comment. Why couldn't she be natural?

Because the house tour is destined to end in the bedroom, a little voice insisted on informing her. She gulped at the reminder.

Indeed, the brief tour of the ranch house ended when Stryker opened a door leading to a large bedroom. Jacey stared, then stepped across the threshold into the room.

"There's a second bedroom across the hall," he told her.

"Umm."

What else was she supposed to say? she wondered. She couldn't very well question him now about the sleeping arrangements.

"Jacey?"

His low voice stroked her, sending the butterflies tumbling into sudden flight in her stomach. She had eaten little at the celebration. She couldn't for the life of her turn and face him right then. It was completely unlike her to be this nervous.

She took a hesitant step farther into the room and nearly tripped on the hem of her wedding gown. She straightened up as a sudden realization struck her. There were no servants in the house tonight. She squeezed her eyes closed and drew in a breath.

"Ah, I . . ." her voice trailed off.

"Jacey, what is it?"

Irritated at her meekness, she raised her chin and pointed to the gown. "It took your two friends to button this gown. I'm afraid I'll need some help unfastening it."

Without waiting for a response, she turned her back to him. *Act naturally,* she told herself. In spite of the order, she held her breath as she waited for his assistance.

Jacey didn't realize she was holding herself so stiffly until the brush of his fingers on her shoulder made her jump. She tried to make herself relax; however, the feel of Stryker's fingers at her neck was hardly conducive to relaxation.

He raked her hair aside and fiddled with the first button. At last he worked it through the loop. He moved on to the second button. Then the third.

Jacey closed her eyes against the pleasant feel of his fingers brushing against her bare skin. If she had thought the fastening of the buttons had been endless before the wedding, it was nothing to the slow passing of time now. She sucked in a gulp of air and forced herself to stop keeping count of the buttons as he released them from their loops.

She had expected the air to be cool on her back since her skin seemed so heated. But the air was surprisingly warm. Then she realized it was Stryker's breath on her neck warming her skin. Unable to help herself, she moaned.

Stryker fumbled with the next button. The low sound from Jacey was playing havoc with his self-control—and so were the small buttons.

He forced himself to concentrate on pushing the button through the loop. Once it was finally freed, he worked on the next one. And the next.

And the next.

The row of buttons seemed endless. He drew in a bracing breath and smelled the enticing scent of roses. Jacey's scent. His gut tightened, and he clenched his fingers. He leaned closer to focus on unhooking the next button.

He could see the creamy skin of her back between the open folds of the gown. He swallowed down the sudden rush of desire. It welled up in him again, unheeding his attempt to push it aside. Instead, he pushed the unfastened section of gown aside. Unable to resist any longer, he brushed a light kiss across the silken skin of her back.

Jacey sighed and pressed closer. He continued kissing her back, lower and lower until he reached the barrier of material. Unloosing the next button, he drew his mouth lower.

He flicked his tongue back and forth above the next button, then thumbed it free. Inch by inch, he freed the buttons, trailing his mouth along in their wake. Jacey whimpered and moved beneath his hands.

At last he reached her waist and paused to span its narrow width with both his hands. Her bare skin was warm beneath his thumbs. He ran a row of kisses the length of her back, not stopping until he brushed the curve at the base of her spine.

Just a few more buttons to go. The gown had been designed with seduction in mind. He wasn't sure how much more he could take of this exquisite torture. He wanted her with a burgeoning desire that could barely be held in check.

Tonight, he would make slow love to her. He would. . . .

Realization of what he was about to do shot through him. He was about to make love to his bride. That act would make her his wife in every sense of the word.

And bind him to her.

Stryker forced himself to regain his control. Bit by bit he fought the battle between desire and self-preservation. He won, but he wasn't sure that he hadn't lost.

Straightening, he took a step away from Jacey. He couldn't think with her so close to him, within the reach of his hands. He took another step back. It was the hardest thing he had ever done in his life. He damned himself for doing it. He didn't have a choice. He had made his vow not to make her his, and he would keep it. For his own good.

"I think you can finish this," he informed her.

His voice cooled her more than the rush of cold air across her moist skin. The sound of the door shutting behind him chilled her. He had been about to make love to her. What had happened to change his mind? One thing was clear.

He didn't want her.

He couldn't have made it plainer if he had shouted it at her.

She wrapped her arms about herself, holding the wedding gown up. Right then she thought she hated the beautiful dress.

Chapter Nine

Jacey paced back and forth in front of the door. Her dressing gown floated out behind her. She couldn't believe Stryker had left to tend to his cows.

His cows.

And on their wedding night.

She had watched him taking care of the animals from her window. She still couldn't believe it.

Anger stiffened her spine, but the feeling of abandonment crushed her resolve. Didn't he want her?

She bit her lip, then admonished herself. She wasn't about to become some insipid little miss waiting for her man to decide if he wanted her or not. She would go find him and settle this between them. Once and for all!

Whirling around to the door, she reached out her hand, but a sound outside stopped her.

"Jacey," someone called out in a near whisper.

A shiver flickered along her neck, but she brushed it off as bridal jitters. After all, she was unfamiliar with the ranch.

Without thinking, she swung the door wide open. She looked out, but no one was there.

"Jacey," the call came again.

"What?" Her voice filled with irritation when the speaker didn't show.

Curious, she stepped outside and looked around. She heard a rustle, then the sound of several women giggling. It reassured her, and she took a step forward.

"Hello?" she called out.

Someone grabbed her from behind, and before she realized what was happening, she had been trussed up like a calf. Hands lifted her and placed her in the back of a buckboard.

When she opened her mouth to scream, a gag was shoved in. Terror gripped her, and she tried to kick out with her bound ankles. She heard someone yelp in pain and felt a brief moment of satisfaction before she was pushed down in the wagon. Then the terror returned to eat at her.

"Relax, it's just a shivaree," a woman's voice assured her.

Jacey turned her head and recognized several of the townswomen from the wedding. Two women sat up front, driving the buckboard. As the driver turned her head to send a cold smile her way, Jacey realized the leader of the women was none other than Madeline Raines. She wished she could scratch out the woman's eyes then and there. If her hands weren't bound, she might attempt it.

"Sit back and enjoy the ride." Madeline sneered. "You'll see your *husband* soon enough. Stryker can have you if he can find you."

A round of laughter followed the remark.

One woman leaned forward and patted her arm gently. Jacey thought she recognized her as the wife of the mercantile store owner.

The woman patted her arm again. "It's traditional to

hide the bride from the groom and make him find her," she explained. "Stryker's a good tracker. He'll find you right quick. So, sit back and enjoy your shivaree." She giggled and covered her mouth.

At the laughter, Jacey relaxed slightly. These women didn't intend to harm her. It seemed they were having some fun at her expense.

She recalled her question about the shivaree. It appeared she now had her answer. This was a shivaree. She didn't think she liked it one little bit. And she intended to inform these women of the fact the minute they set her free.

The bouncy, jostling ride seemed to take forever, and Jacey's temper inched upward with each mile they traveled. Enough was enough. She fully intended to say it as soon as they stopped and removed her gag.

Minutes later, the buckboard slowed to a stop. Jacey sighed in relief. At last she could—

Suddenly the women jumped up and pulled her down out of the buckboard. Instead of untying her or removing her gag, they half carried her forward.

As a shape loomed up out of the darkness, Jacey let out a muted scream. At the sight of the headstone, she realized where they had taken her.

A graveyard.

Fear crept through her anger, cutting a wide swath into her courage. The women surrounded her, then eased her down until she was sitting with her back against cold stone. She shivered at the knowledge that it was a headstone.

Laughing, the women turned and ran for the wagon. One stayed behind, tying her firmly to the solid marker. Jacey could hear her breathing at her side. She turned her head to meet the malevolent stare of Madeline Raines.

"They think I'm untying you. But I'm not going to."

Madeline traced a finger along Jacey's jaw. "Enjoy your wedding night. And remember, Stryker's mine!"

Jacey mumbled her argument around the gag, but the words came out indistinguishable. It was just as well. She had uttered some very unladylike words at Madeline's departing back.

As the wagon pulled away, true fear swept over Jacey. She gulped in as deep a breath as she could manage, refusing to give in to the fear nipping at her mind. Instead, she thought of Stryker and set out to free herself from her bindings.

Ten minutes later, the only thing she had accomplished was to make her wrists sore and raise her temper several degrees. At least the anger covered the fear, keeping it at bay. This was not how she had envisioned her wedding night.

Twisting and turning her head, she at last managed to dislodge the gag from her mouth.

"Help!" she cried out, then followed it with a very healthy scream.

The sound made her feel better, but brought no results. She hoped Stryker was as good a tracker as the woman claimed. Jacey wanted to see him right now more than she had ever wanted to see anyone in her life. She had a few things to tell him!

None of them were very nice.

He could take his mistress and go to the devil for all she cared! Tears pricked her eyes, but she held them back. No one would reduce her to a sniffling miss.

"Stryker," she angrily yelled into the darkness surrounding her.

Stryker stormed out of the empty bedroom. Jacey was gone!

He reached back and slammed the door. She had left him. Fled in the darkness. He gritted his teeth in his fury. She had broken their bargain.

A thought nagged at him. Something about the room hadn't been right. He turned back, pushed open the door, and walked into the room. Glancing around, he studied the contents.

Jacey's wedding gown hung in the closet. Varying colored gowns hung beside it, taking up a goodly portion of the space. Her valise sat on the floor inside the closet.

He frowned, disturbed by what he saw. What woman left all her clothing behind?

The lawman in him took over. He flicked a glance to the dressing table, searching for clues. Her brush lay tilted on its side. A strand of pearls trailed across the table. When he noted the velvet reticule sitting on the table, he knew something was very wrong. His gut knotted in apprehension.

Stryker rushed outside and began to search the area. He spotted the fresh wagon tracks with a sense of impending doom. The mark of one chipped side wheel told him the vehicle belonged to Jake and Clara.

Rosalyn and Linda had assured him they had spoken with the men about the planned shivaree, and the men had agreed to desist. Apparently they had underestimated the womenfolk of Braddock.

As he saddled his horse, he had a sinking feeling he knew exactly who was behind his bride's disappearance. Madeline Raines.

He tasted fear in the back of his throat. Madeline could be vindictive when crossed. He knew that for a fact; he had let his guard down, and Jacey was paying for his mistake. He knew this was more than an innocent prank.

Where was the worst place Madeline could think up to

hide Jacey? The answer came to him, and he kneed his horse into a gallop. He had to get to Jacey!

Stryker heard her voice at the outskirts of the old grave-yard. He swallowed his relief at finding her. She sounded furious. And scared.

Dismounting, he called out her name and raced to the center of the graveyard. He found her tied against a head-stone. Anger burst in him. Someone would pay for this. He would see to it personally.

"Jacey, it's all right. I'm here." He knelt beside her.

When he saw the faint traces of tears on her cheeks, his heart turned over for her. "I'm sorry. I'm so sorry."

His hands were unsteady as he freed Jacey from the ropes tying her to the headstone. She sat perfectly still, staring at a spot over his shoulder.

"I'm sorry. I had no idea Madeline would be so vindictive." He removed the gag and helped her to her feet.

The instant she was free, Jacey whirled on him. "Keep your mistress away from me, or I may kill her."

"She's not my mistress!"

"Save it for when I'm in the mood to hear lies."

She turned and stomped away from him.

The minute Stryker and Jacey reached the ranch house, she dismounted without his help. Before he could stop her, she stomped to the house, slammed the door, and locked him out.

Locked him out of his own house.

Stryker shook his head in disbelief. He had to be the only man in history to save his bride, then be rewarded by her locking him outside on their wedding night.

He led his horse to the barn. It looked like he would be spending his wedding night in the barn. Alone.

A fine way to begin a temporary marriage, he thought as he lit a lantern and grabbed up a blanket. He had been worried about Jacey's delicate constitution on their silent and tense ride home. He could have saved himself the effort. His *bride* was just fine, not to mention in a fine temper.

Rearing back, he kicked at the pile of hay in an empty stall. Muttering about women in general and his new bride in particular, he stomped down the hay into a bed.

"Hey, men. Here he is," someone shouted from the open doorway of the barn.

Stryker spun on his heel, drawing his gun out of habit. "Whoa, buddy."

He recognized Brett's voice immediately. Slowly he reholstered his gun, letting his friend wonder for a moment if he was going to put it away or not.

"Glad to see marriage hasn't improved your disposition any," Brett said. He hauled up a bale of hay and propped one foot on it.

"What's this?" Stryker was in no mood for a friendly chat, tonight of all nights.

"Heard the ladies got to shivaree your bride. Now it's our turn."

"Brett, don't even think about it."

His friend grinned widely. "It wasn't my idea. Seems all promises by the men to Rosalyn and Linda are off now." Turning, he called out over his shoulder, "Fellas, I found him. We're in the barn."

"Should I thank you now or later?"

"You can thank me for not asking what you're doing out here instead of being in the house with your new bride," Brett said in a low undertone, then fell silent.

The barn door was swung wide open, and in trooped half a dozen of the town husbands. Stryker bit back his groan. He didn't like the looks of this one bit.

"Congratulations." Jake walked in and scooted another bale of hay to join them. "Sorry 'bout what my wife was a part of tonight. Clara didn't mean no harm." He had the grace to look chagrined. "And she won't be giving your bride any more trouble from now on either."

"Don't you have business to tend to at the mercantile?" Stryker asked pointedly.

Jake merely laughed at the question and sat down on the bale of hay.

Chet sauntered in with the bowlegged walk he was known for, come from years of breaking horses for the livery stable. "Annie sends her apologies. How about a game of poker, old boy?"

"Poker?" Stryker asked. While the men were busy pulling bales of hay off the stack to set up the game, he tossed the blanket into an empty stall out of sight before anyone could ask unwelcome questions.

No need for the town husbands to know he had been locked out of his own house on his wedding night. He would never hear the end of it. He would go along with their game of poker and let them think it was their idea to keep him and Jacey apart for a couple of hours. He wasn't likely to get much sleep anyway. Not tonight.

Four more men entered, giving their congratulations and apologizing for their wives before they sat aside from the poker game. Stryker met each man with growing amazement. Had all of the men's wives been in on the shivaree of Jacey?

"Evening, gentlemen." Bertram Raines strolled into the barn, dusted off a bale of hay with his handkerchief, and sat down.

Trust old Bertram to be the last one in and attempt an important entrance.

"How's the bridegroom doing?" he asked, folding his handkerchief.

Stryker held back his response with a great deal of effort.

Instead, he forced a smile, and asked, "Leaving your wife at home tonight, Bertram?"

The banker narrowed his eyes, then nodded. "Madeline offers her apologies for her part in the 'festivities.'"

"Festivities?" Stryker strode over and towered above the shorter man sitting on the hay. "She left my *wife* tied to a headstone in the graveyard."

"Clara said Madeline set her free," Jake put in, trying to cool the rapidly overheating situation.

"Not likely," Stryker gritted out. "She was still tied and gagged when I got to her."

Brett caught Stryker's arm, holding him back from punching the banker.

Bertram wiped a hand over his forehead and couldn't meet Stryker's hard gaze. "I'm sorry. She will be apologizing to your *wife* tomorrow."

"See that she does." Stryker turned away, kicked a bale into position, and sat down. "Who's dealing?"

One game of poker turned into two, then three. By the time the next hand was dealt, Stryker realized the men intended to see the sunrise with him.

Aw, hell, he swore to himself.

Across from him, Jake hid a yawn behind his cards. Stryker took heart at the action. The soft snores of two other men came from an empty stall. It looked like he might manage to send the men off before Jacey roused and came out in the morning. She might well still be in a high temper. In fact, he was certain she would be.

Sunrise came, and still he couldn't budge the men short of shooting them. Disgruntled, he studied his cards. His one consolation was that he had been winning most of the hands, and most of the men's money. It gave him a brief sense of satisfaction until he noticed that every man was staring at the door. Most of them had their mouths gaped open.

"Good morning, gentlemen." Jacey greeted the men with a smile of welcome.

Stryker stiffened, tensed for whatever she was going to say next.

Her smile never left her face, even when she glanced briefly at him. The only sign of her remaining anger was the slightest chill in her eyes as her gaze swept up and down him.

He couldn't take his eyes off her. This morning she wore a gown the color of her eyes. The ever-present bustle drew his gaze to her backside. Irritation rushed him as he noticed that the other men's gazes traveled to the same place.

What did she think she was doing?

Stryker stood to his feet out of irritation. The men all followed his action, but theirs was out of politeness.

"Morning, ma'am," Jake greeted her.

"Mrs. Stryker," Bertram said, tipping his bowler hat.

"How are you, ma'am?" Chet asked.

Jacey blushed under their combined greetings. "I'm sure by now you gentlemen would like a nice cup of coffee. If you all would follow me to the house, I think I can throw together a little something for you."

With this, she turned about and led the way to the house, her hips swaying enticingly. What was she up to now? Between her dazzling smiles for the other men and her overly friendly attitude, Stryker knew she had something planned. He gritted his teeth until his jaw ached.

The involuntary reaction of her "husband" didn't miss her attention. Jacey pounced on it with relish. She intended to pay him back in spades for what she had been put through.

When she had woken alone, then realized Stryker had never even attempted to join her during the long night, she had been hurt. Anger had soon taken its place. She had dressed and slipped out to find the cluster of men playing cards in the barn.

Cards!

Stryker had spent the night playing cards with the men and enjoying himself, while she had tossed and turned most of the night. It had not improved her temper one whit.

In the midst of her anger, an idea had reared. How would Stryker feel about the men fawning over her the way women did over him?

She imagined the men would welcome a pot of coffee. And if they would like some coffee, think of how they would feel about being offered a hot breakfast. She would have them falling at her feet, just see if she didn't.

So she had sneaked back to the kitchen and set to work frying up slices of ham, eggs, and making Rosalyn and Linda's specialty of bear sign. The western doughnuts were supposed to be a favorite here, named for the way they looked like what a bear left in the woods. She wrinkled her nose at the memory.

The men dutifully followed her into the house like a batch of obedient puppies. She smiled in enjoyment and anticipation of their coming surprise.

"Gentlemen, please take your seats." She gestured to the dining room table.

She kept her smile in place, refusing to laugh at their startled expressions as they took in the scene before them. The table was set with the exact number of necessary place settings. Serving platters sat waiting, heaped high with food. The aroma filled the room.

She heard one man groan aloud.

"Ma'am, you didn't need to go to this trouble," Jake insisted.

Jacey recalled him from the mercantile store. She sent

him a dazzling smile and watched his face redden at her attentions.

"She can cook?" Brett asked Stryker.

"Doesn't it look like it?" Chet responded in her defense.

Jacey merely laughed off their brief spat. Everything was working out beautifully. The men were practically drooling over the display of steaming food. And she still had one more item to tempt them.

"Why, thank you, Mrs. Stryker." Bertram Raines seated himself and reached for the platter of ham.

The remainder of the men joined him. Jacey left the room with a smile. By the time she returned carrying a plate of bear sign, she had the men in the palm of her hand.

One man jumped up to take the plate from her, insisting she shouldn't be carrying anything for them. Another man rushed to serve her a cup of coffee. A third man filled a plate against her ladylike protests. Even Stryker's best friend Brett hurried to the kitchen to fetch her a glass of water.

Jacey sneaked a glance from lowered lashes to where Stryker sat at the table. His attention was focused on his plate, but she could see the dark frown on his face. She smiled. He didn't appear in the least bit pleased with his friends.

Serves him right, she thought with secret glee.

Stryker was in for a bit of turnabout. Let him see how he liked the townsmen falling all over her, instead of the women falling over him!

Brett returned a while later with the glass of water, and Jacey thanked him prettily. For a moment he returned her smile; then as if remembering his friend, he glanced at Stryker and winked.

From the corner of her eye, Jacey watched Stryker for his reaction. He stiffened, straight and tall in the chair.

His jaw clenched, he looked from one man to another as they served her. She made sure to thank each and every one.

Her surprise breakfast was a certain hit. She had managed to win over every last one of the men. Even Bertram Raines had stopped studying her with cold scrutiny and rushed to get sugar for her coffee.

Eventually, one by one the men thanked her and departed, except for Bertram Raines, who stayed behind to be the last one to leave.

At the door, he caught her hand in his and pressed a kiss to her knuckles. "My thanks, Mrs. Stryker."

She forced a smile. "You're most welcome."

He reddened and looked away. "My wife will be coming today to offer her apologies. I hope you will accept."

Jacey's eyes sparkled for a moment, before she schooled her features. "I'll be waiting for her." She ended her remark with a disarming smile.

She would be waiting for Madeline Raines all right. Ready and waiting.

Intent on making plans for the woman's arrival, Jacey scarcely noticed Stryker head out the door. He muttered something about "work," and she held in her grin.

It definitely looked like he wasn't at all pleased by her wifely breakfast—much less the attention she had received from the other men.

Serves him right, she thought again.

An hour later, Jacey heard a knock at the back entrance. Peeking out a window, she spotted Madeline Raines standing at the door. Haughty and proud with her nose in the air, the other woman tucked a red curl beneath her fancy feathered bonnet. She wore a bright rose gown with a low-cut bodice. *Too daringly cut for any proper daytime visit,* Jacey thought to herself.

Was Madeline hoping to find Stryker at home and finagle some time alone with him? If so, the scheming woman would be sadly disappointed.

Jacey smiled to herself. Too bad he wouldn't be seeing her today. She intended to ensure her husband's mistress left suddenly from a very memorable visit.

Jacey took a moment to savor her intended greeting. The woman's brightly colored gown was perfect for her plans. The low-cut bodice and feathered bonnet were a bonus for what she had planned for the woman. She tossed her head, smoothed back a stray tendril of hair, and made the woman wait another minute. Smiling to herself, she strolled over to the door and opened it to her visitor.

"Well, good morning," Jacey said, fake sincerity filling her voice.

Madeline brushed a speck of dust from her skirt with marked disdain. Looking back up, she smiled like a cat intending to pounce, then covered her mouth with her fingertips. "Oh, dear me. I do hope you don't mind me using the back door. I didn't stop to think. Stryker and I never had much reason for formalities."

The words hung between them for the space of a heartbeat. Jacey knew the other woman was attempting to provoke her, so she wouldn't have to apologize. Jacey wasn't about to let her succeed. Yet.

Jacey deliberately waved off the comment with a flick of her wrist. "That's quite all right, Mrs. Raines. I'm sure you're used to back doors."

Madeline opened her mouth, then snapped it closed. Jacey merely smiled sweetly.

"This visit wasn't my idea. Bertram insisted I pay you a call." Madeline waved a handkerchief back and forth in front of her face.

"I was expecting you."

"How?"

"Bertram told me." Jacey smiled genuinely this time.

Madeline's eyes narrowed to slits. "He what? When did you see my husband?"

"Why, when he had breakfast here this morning. Was there something you wished to say to me?"

"It's rather warm standing out here."

Jacey cocked her head and waited.

Madeline stomped her foot in anger. "Ohh. I apologize. There, I said it."

"Yes, you did."

"It is warm standing here. If you had any manners, you'd invite me inside for a cool drink."

"Oh, yes, now that you mentioned it. I do have something that will cool you off."

Jacey let her smile widen as she took a small step backward. Reaching down, she grabbed up the half-filled bucket of cold water from beside the door and upended it over Madeline's head.

The other woman screeched.

Jacey watched the cold water turn the bonnet into a sodden lump and Madeline's fancy, upswept hairstyle into a mass of wet tangles. Water ran down Madeline's face and into the low-cut bodice.

"Cool enough?" Jacey asked, her voice coated with honeyed sweetness.

"Ohh!" Madeline shoved a wet string of hair out of her eyes and patted her prized bonnet.

The bonnet's feathers drooped to one side, steadily dripping water down over the shoulders of her dress. The brightly colored gown was now splotched and hung heavily on the sputtering woman's shoulders.

Jacey leaned forward and said in a firm voice, "Stryker's mine now."

Chapter Ten

Stryker exited the barn to see a very wet Madeline Raines climbing into her buggy. It took her two attempts to clamber aboard since she had to stop to push dripping strands of hair away from her face. Her bright gown was a sodden mass of drooping fabric.

He stared in amazement, then folded his arms to observe the spectacle. At last she sent the horse and buggy careening away from the ranch house. Stryker turned to spot Jacey standing outside the door. The pleased grin on her face told him more than words could say about how Madeline came to be so wet.

When Jacey spotted him watching her, she crossed her arms and lifted her chin in defiance. Feeling like he did when he was about to face a gunfight, he strode across the distance separating him from his *wife*.

"Jacey—"

"Oh, you just missed Mrs. Raines." She waved at the buggy in the distance.

"Jacey, what—"

"Tsk. She seemed in an awfully big hurry to get back to town." She smiled at him in feigned innocence.

"What did you do?" he gritted out past clenched teeth.

He realized he seemed to be constantly clenching his jaw or gritting his teeth since Jacey had come into his life. She sobered and turned a look of amazement on him. He didn't like it one bit.

"Me?" she asked, her eyes wide with innocence.

"Yes, you," he demanded, his voice raising in response to her game.

"I only gave her what she asked for."

He shut his eyes a moment and opened them. "Which was?"

Jacey's lips twitched before she schooled her features again. "Why, to cool off."

Stryker's eyes met hers, and he saw the twinkling mischievousness there. An answering smile tugged at his lips. Jacey had every right to get even with Madeline as far as he saw it, but he was sure the other woman wouldn't see it that way.

"She didn't look very 'cool' to me," he pointed out, his lips twitching at one corner.

"Oh, my. Then, I must not have succeeded." Jacey looked disappointed.

"Oh, I think you succeeded quite well," he corrected. He glanced pointedly at the empty water bucket sitting on the ground.

"We'll see," she said cryptically.

Stryker didn't think he wanted to know the true meaning behind her curious remark. Something told him he would be a lot better off not knowing.

As he remained silent, Jacey fidgeted from one foot to the other. Finally, she raised her chin and faced him squarely in challenge. He had been expecting to see that gesture from her before now.

"I suppose you're going to want me to apologize?" she asked.

He couldn't believe what he had heard her ask, nor could he mistake the defiance in her voice. His lips twitched again. He had to bait her. "And would you?"

Jacey tossed her head, never breaking eye contact with him. She planted her hands on her hips and leaned forward. "Not even after a certain place freezes over."

She whirled on her heel and flounced into the ranch house, her bustle bouncing with her walk. Stryker stood for several seconds staring after her; then he leaned back his head and laughed.

There would probably be trouble to pay for her actions from Bertram Raines, but right then he couldn't blame her in the least. In his opinion, Madeline had gotten what was coming to her.

But Jacey wasn't finished yet.

By the end of the day after Jacey finished straightening up from the shivaree, her mood had worsened. She had found the flour hidden away in a drawer and the sugar on top of the coffee. It appeared that Brett Mason had been busy in the kitchen when she wasn't looking this morning. See if she ever fed him again. As far as she was concerned, the entire town could take its shivaree traditions and disappear with them!

Dinner with only her and Stryker was a quiet and nervous affair. He ate her carefully prepared meal, but neglected to compliment her cooking, and even worse, he seemed distracted.

Distracted! She glared at him, and her anger began to simmer.

Jacey decided then and there that he could spend the

night alone. She didn't want to think about what might be distracting him, but questions insisted on plaguing her.

Was he regretting their hasty marriage?

Was he angry over her earlier revenge on Madeline?

Was he thinking of his mistress?

Sorely vexed with the disturbing questions, she stood abruptly, nearly knocking her chair over in her haste. "I'm going to bed," she announced with all the dignity she could muster.

Stryker's head snapped up at her words. Jacey held her breath as his gaze probed hers. She couldn't look away from him. When he surged to his feet, her stomach dipped, then dropped in response.

Was he—

"I'll show you to your room." He crossed to her, and his firm voice brooked no arguments.

Her room? He had phrased his comment oddly. Did he intend that they sleep in separate rooms? Surely not.

Jacey swallowed down her doubts and started for the stairs. His footsteps sounded loud behind her. As they reached the doorway to the main bedroom, he stopped.

"Jacey, I—"

She turned and tipped her head back to look up at him, not realizing until that moment how close they stood. She refused to back away, even though a little voice warned her to do so. Instead, she threw caution to the wind and rested her hand on his chest. After all, they were married.

"Jacey," Stryker hesitated and cleared his throat.

"Yes?" She waited and knew her heart showed in her eyes.

He took a step forward, then stopped himself. Stiffening with resolve, he stepped away from her, until her hand fell from his chest.

If he had slapped her, Jacey couldn't have been more hurt. She forced herself to lift her chin with pride and step back through the doorway. Reaching out, she caught the open door and slammed it shut as hard as she could right in his face.

She couldn't recall when she had been so hurt, or so angry. Each emotion warred within her for control. Finally she gave in to the anger. What she wanted to do was throw something. For lack of anything better close at hand, she grabbed up the pillow and threw it against the wall as hard as she could. The muffled *thump* brought her no satisfaction, but the small cloud of feathers floating upward brought a smile.

Crossing over, she scooped up the pillow, then noticed a cut in the end of the pillow. Odd, she thought. Stryker needed to learn to take better care of his bed linens. He needed to learn a lot of things as far as she was concerned!

Right then she wanted to throw herself onto the bed and pound the pillow until all the stuffing came out. She would imagine it was Stryker's chest. Letting out a muffled curse, she stomped across the width of the room to the bed.

Stryker jerked back at the oath from the other side of the door. He stared at the door, stunned by her fury. The flash of pain that had crossed her face had nearly tempted him to change his mind and throw out his resolve. Then, before he could act, she had slammed his bedroom door in his face.

He turned away and crossed the hall to the other bedroom. At least he wouldn't be spending the night in the barn.

He told himself he should thank her for stopping him from taking her into his arms. He should be thanking her for keeping his resolve not to consummate the temporary marriage.

But he wasn't.

Stepping into the smaller bedroom, he threw a disgruntled glance around. Only by using a great deal of control did he resist slamming the bedroom door behind him.

He strode across the room, unbuttoning his shirt as he walked. When he reached the side of the bed, he threw back the sheet. Suddenly a loud crash sounded from across the hall.

At Jacey's scream, he turned and ran for the door. Throwing it open, he rushed across the hall, nearly breaking down Jacey's door in his haste to reach her. He stumbled into the room, frantically searching for her.

When he found her it was all he could do not to laugh. Across the room, the mattress sagged, nearly folding in half with two of the wooden support slats missing. In the middle of the mattress lay his bride, her legs sticking up in the air and her arms waving.

He couldn't see her face; it was covered with a flurry of feathers as they floated downward. She lay amidst a tangle of sheets and feathers, thoroughly stuck and held in place by the folded mattress.

As relief rushed through him that she wasn't in any danger, it took all his self-control to hold in his laughter. She looked so funny, and unladylike, and appealing. Not to mention furious. He could barely distinguish the muttered words coming from her mouth.

At last Jacey spit out a mouthful of feathers with a very unladylike snort. "Stryker! Get me out of here!"

She enunciated each word of her demand with complete clarity and undisguised anger. He bit his cheek to keep back the threatening laughter and strode across the room.

He reached down and caught her hands to pull her up, but she was too thoroughly wedged into the sliding mattress. As he braced one foot forward to heave her free, he slipped on the corner of her fine lacy nightgown, losing his balance. He released her and flailed his arms to regain his balance.

A second later, Stryker landed atop Jacey. He grunted, and she muttered something he didn't quite catch. He figured he was better off not knowing what she had said, but it had sounded remarkably like it ended in the word *jackass*.

A chuckle slipped free in spite of his efforts. He levered himself away from her and caught a glimpse of her face. Fury glittered in her eyes, and for a brief moment he was glad she was too tightly wedged into the bedding to throw a punch in his direction.

"Of all the mean, sneaky, low-down tricks—"

Stryker shook his head. "I didn't touch the bed."

"Get off me," she demanded.

He didn't hesitate to obey her gritted order. Pushing himself to his feet, he reached down and slid one arm under her back. He used his other arm to shove himself away from the crumpled mattress. They both came free with a sudden *whoosh* that landed them on the floor with Jacey now sprawled across him.

She shook her head, blew out a feather from the pillow, and pushed herself to her feet. As Stryker felt his lips twitch, she glared down at him. He decided right then wasn't the time to give in to the laughter that threatened to burst free, even though she looked delightfully funny with goose feathers sprinkling her hair, and one clinging to the corner of her mouth.

"If you dare laugh at me, I swear I . . . I'll kick you," she threatened.

Stryker swallowed and nearly choked with the effort of holding back his chuckle. This was a devil of a time for his sense of humor to surface. He couldn't think of a much more vulnerable position than lying at a furious woman's feet. His chest hurt with the control he was exerting not to laugh. Looking at the ceiling, anywhere but at Jacey, he shoved himself to his feet.

Unfortunately, he couldn't resist the urge to glance at her. He watched as one feather slipped down a curl, drifted across her forehead, and landed on her nose. That did it. He burst out laughing.

Jacey reached up, plucked the feather from her nose, and stuck it to his chin. Planting her hands on her hips, she tilted her head to stare into his twinkling eyes."

"Since you think it's so funny, why don't you—"

Stryker bent toward her and scooped her up into his arms. "Let me put you to bed, Jacey. Before you hurt yourself." He bit off the last word as a chuckle slipped out.

His chest shook beneath her body. Jacey crossed her arms, refusing to touch him, and glared up at him. His eyes shone with suppressed mirth. The feather remained clinging to his chin, nearly undoing her resolve to stay angry.

As his nose twitched with a threatening sneeze, the feather slid down his chin and along his jawline. It fluttered, then clung again. She released a pent-up breath, and the feather fluttered back up to land on his nose. She couldn't hold out any longer. Covering her mouth, she began to giggle.

"Oh, you think it's funny when I'm covered with feathers, do you?" he asked in a voice of pretended irritation.

Jacey answered him right back. "Absolutely." Then she caught up a handful of feathers from the front of her nightgown and blew them in his face.

Stryker blinked, then sneezed. Once, twice. Then a third time.

"Put me down," Jacey ordered, giggling and covering her face with her hands.

Sniffing and rubbing his chin against her shoulder, he refused. "Not until you can't hurt either one of us."

With this, he turned and strode out the door and across the hall. He kicked open the other bedroom door fully with his foot and shouldered his way into the room. Crossing to the bed, he playfully dropped Jacey onto the mattress. As he began to follow her down, a cow bell jangled loudly. Over and over again.

The sound came from under the bed. With each move Jacey made, the bell rang again. Her good humor vanished much quicker than it had appeared.

She had had enough.

Shoving herself upright, she cringed at the telltale ringing of the cow bell. *Clang, clang, clang.*

It broadcast her every move. Putting her hands over her ears, she turned her anger on Stryker. The bell clattered a final time. She raised herself up to her knees.

"Get out," she yelled.

"But—"

Jacey dropped her hands from her ears and plated them on her hips. "Enough. I've been kidnapped, have cooked for an army of men, had my *husband* stalk out of the bedroom."

At his startled glance, she continued without giving him an opportunity to speak. "Had a bed fall apart on me. And now I hear cow bells."

"Jacey—"

She held up her hand, then pointed to the door. "Not one more word. Out!"

Stryker opened his mouth, but decided it was useless to attempt to reason with her. The town had definitely gone overboard with their shivaree. Maybe he would try talking to her later.

Much later.

Grabbing up his hat, he slapped it on his head and, turning on his heel, strode out the door. This time he was the one to slam it closed.

Jacey fumed and stared at the door. She wanted to scream in frustration. Instead, she crawled off the bed to the floor and looked under the mattress for the offending object. She spotted the cow bell immediately. Reaching out, she yanked it free and threw it across the room. The bell bounced off the wall and fell to the floor.

The act made her feel better. Crossing to the window, she watched Stryker walk to the barn. When he didn't ride out, she released a sigh of relief. He was sleeping in the barn.

She whirled away and crossed to the bed. The linens were rumpled. The bed looked far too lonely for a newly married, virgin wife.

She was beginning to think they were destined never to make love.

The next morning, Jacey awoke lonely, but in a better mood. As she dressed carefully, she thought out what she wanted to say to Stryker. She intended to have a long talk with him today. And the sooner the better.

Stryker came into the kitchen as she was finishing preparing breakfast. When he announced he needed to go to town, she pounced on the opportunity to accompany him.

"It will only take me a few minutes to get ready." She smiled at him, offering an unspoken apology.

"I was going in to work, not do shopping."

He didn't tell her that he needed desperately to put some distance between them. The sight of her in his kitchen, fixing his breakfast, had nearly been his undoing. All he had wanted to do was pull her into his arms and carry her off to the bedroom.

Only their previous bargain and his vow to keep free of marital entanglements prevented him from doing what he wanted. Instead, he turned and started for the door.

"Stryker, don't you dare leave me behind."

He spun around at her tone of voice, but the mutinous look on her face kept him from speaking.

"I'll be ready in a minute. And I am going with you," she announced. "So sit down and eat your breakfast. I'll be right back."

As she waltzed out of the room, back held stiff, he sank into a chair. Just whom had he married? Jacey definitely wasn't a meek, sweet miss. No, he told himself, she was his *wife*.

He decided he had better take Jacey along with him so he could keep an eye on her. He didn't trust the certain glimmer he had caught in her gaze before she walked away.

She was as good as her word and minutes later walked back into the kitchen in a blue gown that matched her eyes. Stryker closed his own eyes against the temptation. If he didn't watch himself, he would be a goner.

It took nearly all his self-control to lift Jacey into the buggy, when her bustle brushed his stomach.

He sucked in several deep breaths on his way around to the other side of the borrowed vehicle. He supposed he would need to be buying one of his own now that he was married.

The course of his thoughts brought him up short. He didn't like the direction his mind was taking in the least. Hadn't he gone down that road once before, nearly marrying Madeline? He would not become an obedient slave to any woman ever again.

Not even Jacey.

At the thought of Madeline, he felt nothing this time. Not giving himself a chance to ponder this, he grabbed at the opportunity presented to put some distance between him and Jacey. As he flicked the reins and headed the buggy to town, he watched her out of the corner of his eye.

"I wanted to say Madeline had nothing to do with the bed," Stryker assured her and waited for her reaction.

Jacey merely glared at him and turned her head away. He had succeeded in distancing them. He knew she couldn't remain quiet for long, not with her temper sizzling the way he had come to recognize well.

He was right. A minute later, he heard her mutter, "Trust you to defend her."

"I'm not defending her."

Jacey met his gaze squarely and held it.

Stryker could see her mind already working on a suitable plan of revenge. He knew he had better put a stop to it now, before she had a chance to take action. The last thing he needed was an all-out war between the two women.

"Brett fixed the first bed," he told her to diffuse the situation.

She raised her eyebrows. He could tell she didn't believe him.

"If you think back, he was gone overly long when he fetched you the glass of water. About long enough to remove a couple of strategic slats from the bed."

He could see comprehension dawn on her. She narrowed her eyes, and a certain glimmer shone in their blue depths. It did not bode well for his friend, Stryker was sure of it. Well, Brett would have to fend for himself.

"I see you remember," he nudged her along.

"Ah, yes. Perhaps I should, ah, thank him," she said, her tone leaving no doubt of her true intention.

Stryker grinned at her and winked, tempted to let Jacey get her own revenge. A recollection of the way Brett had rushed to do her bidding at breakfast changed his mind. No, he would take care of his friend himself. He didn't want Jacey spending too much time in Brett's company. The man could be a charmer when he wanted.

"No, I don't think you should be the one to 'thank' him. I'll see to Brett myself," he instructed.

At Jacey's sputtered protest, he fixed her with a firm stare. "Stay out of this one."

She crossed her arms over her chest and sighed in resignation.

Then she turned to face him. "And the cow bell? Was that compliments of Brett, too?"

Stryker shook his head. "That's more the mark of Chet and his livery stable."

"I—"

He held up his hand. "Why don't you leave the men to me?"

Jacey looked him over for a moment, then glared at him.

He met her stare. "I think you've had enough revenge for a little while, don't you?"

At the memory of Madeline Raines dripping wet, Jacey smiled. She would let Stryker have his own fun. Chet, the owner of the livery, had looked a little large and burley for her to tackle.

"Whatever you say," she said in a syrupy voice.

That particular tone from Jacey gave Stryker a great deal to worry about. The only good thing was it took his mind off the feel of her delectable body against his. At least for a minute or two it did.

Once in town, he dropped her off at the mercantile store, and she agreed to meet him at the marshal's office later. He hoped for his sanity it would be much later.

Jacey wandered about the mercantile, making a few small purchases, before boredom set in. She faced the truth— she missed Stryker. Perhaps she would drop in on him. She never had gotten around to having her talk with him. Now seemed the perfect opportunity. At the jail, she would have a captive audience, so to speak.

Gathering up her courage, she walked down the board-walk and into the marshal's office. Stryker looked surprised to see her. Since he was speaking with another man wearing a badge, she wandered around the room. It was much different from the offices back in Baltimore.

That recollection brought a flutter to her chest. She was wanted for theft in Baltimore. This was as close to a jail cell as she ever wanted to get. She whirled around just as another man walked into the office. She recognized him from the breakfast she had served, but couldn't recall his name.

"Ma'am," he greeted her. "You look mighty pretty today." He stopped and grabbed his hat from his head. "I wanted to thank you again for the meal."

"You're welcome." Jacey smiled at his nervousness.

Stryker looked up, scowling at the man. "What is it, Matt? Did a telegram come in?"

"Yup."

As Stryker reached out his hand, Matt added, "But it's for Miss Jacey." He handed her the missive.

At Stryker's deep frown, Matt amended, "I mean, Mrs. Stryker."

"Thank you," Jacey murmured, her mouth suddenly dry and her palms sweating.

As Matt left, she clenched the telegram so tightly in her hand the paper pinched her palm. It had to be from Jeanette.

She resisted the urge to rip open the missive right then. Heaven only knew what her twin might have said in the note. Jeanette had never been known for her discretion. Jacey wasn't so sure she wanted anyone else to see the telegram. Especially Stryker.

"Excuse me." She stepped toward the door. "I think I need a breath of air."

Stryker stood deep in conversation with his deputy again,

and she wasn't certain he even knew she left. For once she was glad of his distraction.

Stepping outside onto the wooden boardwalk, she took a few hurried steps away, then paused and ripped open the telegram. She began to scan her sister's message. One bit of information jumped out at her, catching her off guard and nearly causing her to fall off the boardwalk.

Jeanette was coming to Braddock.

Chapter Eleven

Jacey clenched the telegram so tightly, her knuckles turned white. Jeanette was coming.

Her stomach took a nosedive for the wooden boardwalk beneath her feet. She closed her eyes a moment and took in a deep, calming breath. Oh, dear heavens.

"Good morning." The feminine voice from behind her startled her out of her thoughts.

Jacey jumped and quickly folded the telegram before anyone could notice it, then shoved the missive down her bodice and out of prying eyes. She would finish reading it later. Feeling guilty, she whirled around and met the apologetic smile of Clara.

"Good morning." Jacey tried to sound normal and not let the panic show through.

"I wanted to say I'm sorry about the shivaree," the other woman said. She looked away, then back. "Honest, I didn't know Madeline had left you tied."

Her mind refusing to close out the telegram tucked away in her bodice, the best Jacey could manage was a stiff smile.

"I just wanted you to know that," Clara continued at Jacey's silence. "And I don't blame you for not forgiving me."

The hurt look that crossed Clara's face caught Jacey's full attention. She brought herself up. The woman had apologized to her, and here she was letting her think she was still angry and ignoring her.

"I forgive you," Jacey assured Clara and clasped her hand.

"Thank you. Listen, come over to the store anytime you're in town and we'll have coffee." Clara patted her hand and walked down the boardwalk toward the store.

Jacey watched her walk off. The sharp edges of the telegram poked her tender skin beneath the bodice of her gown, bringing her attention back to the missive from Jeanette.

She could well imagine it being her twin sister's accusing finger poking at her instead. Jeanette would be furious when she arrived to learn the wedding had already taken place without her as the blushing bride.

The truth of the situation struck her, robbing her of both breath and speech.

She was married to another woman's man.

A trembling began deep in Jacey's stomach. Shame flooded through her. She had promised her twin she would watch over Stryker, and that job did not include marrying him. Not only had she stolen her sister's intended and his affections, she had married him for herself. At least that was most assuredly the way Jeanette would see it.

Jacey would never admit they had spent their wedding night apart. Her pride wouldn't let her.

She retrieved the telegram, then slowly unfolded it. It was lengthy, and definitely from her twin. Only Jeanette acted without ever considering cost.

INTRODUCING BALLAD,
A BRAND NEW LINE OF HISTORICAL ROMANCES.

As a lover of historical romance, you'll adore Ballad Romances. Written by today's most popular romance authors, every book in the Ballad line is not only an individual story, but part of a two to six book series as well. You can look forward to four new titles a month – each taking place at a different time and place in history.

But don't take our word for how wonderful these stories are! Accept our introductory shipment of 4 Ballad Romance novels – a $22.00 value – ABSOLUTELY FREE – and see for yourself!

Once you've experienced your first four Ballad Romances, we're sure you'll want to continue receiving these wonderful historical romance novels each month – without ever having to leave your home – using our convenient and inexpensive home subscription service. Here's what you get for joining:

- 4 BRAND NEW Ballad Romances delivered to your door each month

- 25% off the cover price (a total of $5.50) with your home subscription

- a FREE monthly newsletter, *Zebra/Pinnacle Romance News,* filled with author interviews, book previews, special offers, and more!

- No risks or obligations…you're free to cancel whenever you wish… no questions asked.

To start your membership, simply complete and return the card provided. You'll receive your Introductory Shipment of 4 FREE Ballad Romances. Then, each month, as long as your account is in good standing, you will receive the 4 newest Ballad Romances. Each shipment will be yours to examine for 10 days. If you decide to keep the books, you'll pay the preferred home subscriber's price of $16.50 – a savings of 25% off the cover price! (Plus $1.50 shipping and handling.) If you want us to stop sending books, just say the word… it's that simple.

If the certificate is missing below, write to:

Ballad Romances, c/o Zebra Home Subscription Service, Inc.,
P.O. Box 5214, Clifton, New Jersey 07015-5214

OR call TOLL FREE 1-888-345-BOOK (2665)

Visit our website at www.kensingtonbooks.com

FREE BOOK CERTIFICATE

Yes! Please send me 4 Ballad Romances ABSOLUTELY FREE! After my introductory shipment, I will receive 4 new Ballad Romances each month to preview FREE for 10 days (as long as my account is in good standing). If I decide to keep the books, I will pay the money-saving preferred publisher's price of $16.50 plus $1.50 shipping and handling. That's 25% off the cover price. I may return the shipment within 10 days and owe nothing, and I may cancel my subscription at any time. The 4 FREE books will be mine to keep in any case.

DN050A

Name _____

Address _____

City _____ State _____ Zip _____

Telephone ( ) _____

Signature _____

(If under 18, parent or guardian must sign.)

For your convenience you may charge your shipments automatically to a Visa or MasterCard so you'll never have to worry about late payments and missing shipments. If you return any shipment we'll credit your account.

☐ Yes, charge my credit card for my "Ballad Romance" shipments until I tell you otherwise.
☐ Visa ☐ MasterCard

Account Number _____

Expiration Date _____

Signature _____

Orders subject to acceptance by Zebra Home Subscription Service. Terms and Prices subject to change. Offer valid only in the U.S.

Get 4 Ballad
Historical Romance Novel
FREE!

BALLAD ROMANCES
Zebra Home Subscription Service, Inc.
P.O. Box 5214
Clifton NJ 07015-5214

She read the message, both eager and dreading to see what news it had to impart. As she read, Jacey knew her mouth had dropped open since she could feel the air on her tongue. With an effort she clamped her mouth closed, then reread the words more slowly, hoping she had read them incorrectly the first time.

She hadn't. The words resounded in her head.

Aunt Cordelia despises Franklin and locked her jewelry in the safe. Stop. Am having doubts myself about our future. Stop. Hang onto my intended for me. Stop. Am coming to Braddock to wed. Stop.

For the first time in her life, Jacey felt truly faint. She found it difficult to breathe, and the boardwalk tilted beneath her feet. Her stomach lurched, then sank along with her heart. Her sister had changed her mind. She should have known to expect it.

Jeanette had decided to marry Stryker.

But she couldn't because he was already married to Jacey.

She groaned aloud. What right did her sister have to do this to her? Jeanette fluttered from man to man without a single concern. She moved on to the next with no pain, while Jacey felt as if her heart was being ripped out at the thought of her sister wanting Stryker for herself.

"No, no, no," she muttered, tearing the telegram into pieces.

She tossed the scraps of paper to the ground without thinking what she was doing.

"Oh, dear me, I think you dropped something," a snide voice informed her.

Jacey spun around to meet the narrowed gaze of Madeline Raines. She bent down before Jacey could stop her and snatched up a piece of the message.

Jacey immediately grabbed for it but Madeline, being taller, held it out of her reach. The other woman smiled, her eyes glittering.

"Umm, what have we here?" Madeline taunted, continuing to hold the piece of torn paper up high.

"Give that to me," Jacey demanded, tempted to kick the hateful woman until she dropped the edge of paper. She inwardly cringed at what might be betrayed in the retrieved scrap of telegram.

Madeline looked at her; then squinting at the paper in her outstretched hand, she read the remaining scattered words aloud. "Doubts myself . . . my intended . . . Braddock to wed." She raised her eyebrows at Jacey. "Another wedding?"

As Madeline bent down to pick up another piece of the telegram from the boardwalk, Jacey gave her a nudge with her hip. The other woman tumbled off the raised platform and landed in the dusty street.

"I hope you didn't hurt yourself," Jacey said sweetly, with false concern. Reaching out a hand to the sputtering woman, she snatched up the remaining scraps of paper with her other hand. Then she ripped the lone piece from Madeline's hand as well.

"Why, you . . . you . . . thief!" Madeline shrieked, jumping to her feet in a huff.

"No," Jacey corrected her. "I merely keep what is mine." She smiled and nodded in return as she saw the other woman get the meaning of her remark. "And now I think it's time I joined my *husband*."

"He won't be your *husband* for long when he hears what I have to tell him."

Jacey forced herself not to react to the woman's threat. Instead, she smiled sweetly and asked, "And what is that?"

"About your telegram."

"That's hardly news to him. He was standing there when I received it."

Madeline's eyes narrowed, and she asked, "But does he know you're planning to marry someone else?"

Jacey laughed aloud at the absurdity of Madeline's conclusion from the scattered words of the ripped telegram. She walked away, not even giving her the satisfaction of a response.

Madeline's next words nearly made her steps falter. "I'll get to the bottom of this, see if I don't."

Jacey concentrated on walking as nonchalantly as possible, as if she hadn't a concern in the world. In truth, the woman's threat scared the daylights out of her.

Her only hope was if Jeanette kept her promise to slip into town quietly and get word to her first.

Stryker drew the buggy to a stop behind the ranch house. The ride from town had been a quiet one; Jacey seemed worried over something. Several times he had caught her chewing her lip, but each time he questioned her, she assured him everything was fine.

Fine?

Fine was the last word he would use to describe the strained situation between them. She had barely spoken a word all the way home. They couldn't go on like this.

He couldn't go on this way. Something had to be done, and soon.

He glanced over at Jacey, but she had her face averted from him. He could see her nibbling on her lower lip, a habit she acquired only when she was distraught. She caught up her skirt to step down from the buggy.

Before she could move to climb down, he hurried around to her side. He didn't stop to wonder at his devoted action; it just seemed right.

Slipping his arms around her waist, he lifted her out of the buggy. She stared at him and let the folds of her skirt fall from her hands. She looked delectable, he thought to himself, resisting the temptation to kiss her pinkened lips. If he didn't set her down, he would give in.

Unable to break the eye contact, he forced himself to ease her down. But a part of him insisted he performed the action slowly. Too slowly.

She felt so good in his arms. Her waist fit his hands perfectly. He slid his thumbs upward, massaging her rib cage lightly. As she sighed, her breath blew against his cheek. He tried to swallow, but couldn't. The knot tying his stomach up spread to his throat.

Enjoying the feel of her body against his, he eased her down a little more until her lips were even with his. Something tugged on his shirt, and he looked down. An edge of the frilly lace at her bodice had caught on the third button of his shirt. He lifted her slightly, hoping to release his button. Instead, the lace entangled around it tighter, pulling them together.

Jacey lifted her chin, and their noses bumped. Her indrawn breath feathered against his chin. It was more temptation than any man should be given to bear.

Stryker decided he had had enough himself. Everything conspired to throw him and Jacey together, and they invariably ended up in each other's arms. He was tired of fighting the unavoidable.

He knew with certainty making love to Jacey was an inevitability. He might as well stop denying it. And himself. Tonight he would have a talk with her about canceling the one part of their "bargain."

Later.

He surrendered to temptation and took Jacey's lips in a kiss destined to draw them even closer together than the tangled lace had. He held his breath until she slid her hands around his neck, surrendering herself to the fire engulfing them with the touching of their lips.

As she sighed against his mouth, he probed her lips with his tongue, then eased between her lips to the velvety softness within. She tasted so sweet. It was paradise, and hang the consequences.

Sliding her down the length of him, he leaned lower, never breaking the contact of their mouths. He drew one hand upward, exploring her body with his palm. Her breast fit his hand perfectly, and he continued his upward path until he reached the top of her bodice. Pulling the lace loose, he tugged her gown downward, exposing the top of one creamy breast.

At Jacey's moan, he trailed his mouth over her lips to her chin and down the slender column of her neck. Her skin was like the finest silk to his tongue. He continued lower, loving her with his mouth until he could dip his tongue between her breasts. He wasn't sure who sighed this time, Jacey or him. It didn't matter. Nothing else mattered.

Jacey tangled her fingers through his hair, tugging his head upward, and this time she was the one who initiated the kiss. She covered his mouth with hers, her tongue joining with his in a dance of passion. The kiss deepened, their bodies closing the small distance separating them. They melded together.

"Stryker, we got trouble," someone called from across the yard.

Jacey felt Stryker stiffen at the foreman's statement. She was losing him; she could tell it.

"Hey, Stryker," Hank yelled. "That fool bull Bo has got himself messed up in—"

Hank stopped abruptly, obviously realizing what he was interrupting. "Ah . . . ah . . . I'm sorry, boss . . ." He let the remainder of his words trail off.

Stryker pulled away from Jacey, torn between his duty to his ranch and his desire for her. He stared down into her upturned face for endless moments before he eased her arms from around his neck.

"Let's go take care of it, Hank." He gritted the words out past clenched teeth and abruptly turned away from her to disguise his burgeoning desire.

As she stood there watching, he walked off across the yard. Jacey felt as if she had been slapped. She had been so caught up in Stryker's lovemaking that she had lost track of their surroundings. She had forgotten that the hired help had returned to the ranch house today. Nothing had existed for her except the two of them and their wondrous lovemaking.

Lovemaking, hah!

A faint breeze blew across her, making her aware of the dampness of her skin both above and below the neckline of her bodice. Her face heated in embarrassment. She couldn't believe what she had been doing. Outside and in plain sight.

She raised her chin, trying to ignore the shame that threatened to sweep over her. What had happened between her and Stryker had been nothing more than simple lust. Outside in the open and in broad daylight, at that.

Hadn't his abrupt withdrawal shown her the truth?

Well, she had a thing or two to show him!

And he wasn't going to like it one bit.

If things kept on this way, she just might give him to Jeanette. It would serve him right.

The next morning, Jacey wished she could trade places with her twin sister. Let Jeanette take care of the wifely chores—at least the chores Jacey had been assigned so far.

The most pleasant act of being a wife had been denied her. Again. Thanks to the stupid bull. Stryker hadn't come to bed last night, so she had slept alone. Again.

She stomped across the yard to the chicken house, or whatever it was called. It didn't matter a whit to her—she hated the creatures. Yanking the door open, she ducked her head and hurried inside.

She hated the chickens most of all. The feeling appeared mutual.

She was in no mood to gather the eggs. It was as if the chickens knew what she came for and were waiting for her to make one wrong move, which she invariably did. This time she tried staring the hen down first. She and the beady-eyed chicken looked fixedly at each other. Neither one blinked. Jacey couldn't believe she had been reduced to attempting to stare down a chicken!

How much lower could she sink?

The bird in question turned its head slightly, and Jacey jumped at the opportunity. She shoved her hand under the chicken's feathers and triumphantly pulled out her prize of one egg.

Before she could place the egg into the basket sitting on the ground, the chicken whirled around, flapping its wings, and pecked Jacey soundly on the hand.

"Yeow!"

Jacey jumped back, knocking over the basket of eggs. Her foot stepped on something slippery, and she lost her balance. Waving her arms wildly, Jacey swore at the chicken and landed on her behind in the slippery stuff on the floor.

Eyes flashing in anger and humiliation, she stood to her feet. Looking over her shoulder at her skirt and the mess clinging to it, she swore at the chicken and Stryker both in the same breath. Her gown was covered with broken egg yolks and what looked like something from the wrong end of a chicken.

"I don't care if I never see another egg again. I quit!" she shouted, loud enough to set the population of the hen house to squawking.

When several chickens swooped down at her, she grabbed up her skirt and ran out the door. She didn't stop until she was halfway across the yard. Whirling around, she plopped her hands on her hips and faced the chicken house.

"You stupid creatures can sit on those eggs until they cook for all I care."

Stryker rounded the corner in time to hear her blaming the entire chicken world. He hoped all her anger was directed at the unfortunate birds, but he figured most of her temper was headed his way.

"Have a little mishap?" he asked, his lips twitching.

Her anger simmered, then reached the boiling point. Jacey wiped off a handful of the mixture on the back of her skirt and threw it straight at him. It landed squarely on the front of his shirt.

"What do you think?" she shouted.

Shoving her way past him, she walked with all the dignity she could muster to the back door of the ranch house. She made certain to slam the door behind her, not giving a whit what she tracked into the kitchen. Then she whirled around and locked the door for good measure.

As the cook, Mrs. Carson, turned to her, Jacey said, "The only way I'll touch another chicken again is fried, with biscuits and gravy!"

The older woman looked her up and down, then forced her lips into a firm line. "Yes, ma'am," she answered in a voice strained with holding in laughter. "Would you like a nice bath?"

Jacey was so furious all she could do was nod sharply.

The cook coughed and covered her mouth with her hand. Her body shook with her effort to control her mirth.

"Oh, go ahead and let it out," Jacey said, "before you choke yourself."

The woman obliged her.

Jacey heard the doorknob rattle and tightened her grip on her skirt, prepared to run.

"Aw, hell," Stryker swore and pounded on the door to his own house.

The cook burst out laughing again and started for the door. Jacey ran for the relative safety of the bedroom and its sturdy lock. She wasn't about to face Stryker right then. A memory of his face when she had thrown the mess at him nearly sent her into a fit of giggles.

"Served him right," she snickered, stopping inside the bedroom doorway.

When he didn't immediately run up the stairs after her, she relaxed enough to strip out of the filthy gown. She wrinkled her nose and gave the garment a kick. Toeing off her slippers, she left them beside the gown.

Clothed in her petticoat and chemise, she crossed to the washstand and poured water into the bowl. She took her time washing her hands, wanting to cleanse away every trace of the disgusting chickens.

She walked to the window and dared to sneak a peek outside, looking for Stryker. Across the distance, she spotted a figure at the open doorway of the barn and sighed in relief.

Taking a leisurely look around the area outside, she admired the ranch. As Stryker had told her, it was a nice spread. She smiled at the word *nice*. Then she realized in surprise that she was beginning to like the place.

Heaven forbid.

Another smile tugged at her lips. If Jeanette could see

her now. Quickly she sobered. If her twin did see her now, she would likely shove her out the window.

The arrival of the bath water interrupted her troubled thoughts. Once the tub was filled, Jacey added a sprinkling of rosewater. The scent wafted up, tempting her with the luxury of a scented bath. She resisted the temptation long enough to step a distance away to rid herself of the remainder of her soiled clothing.

The door eased open, and Jacey spared it only a glance. She was certain it was Mrs. Carson coming to either check on her, or laugh at her. She reached down and untied her petticoat, then let it fall into a disheveled pool at her feet. When she tugged at her chemise, warm male hands got there ahead of her, spanning her waist.

"Let me help," Stryker said, his voice deceptively low and close against her ear.

She jumped away as if scalded. "I . . . I . . . was going to take a bath."

He stared at her, and she saw his gaze darken with the heat of desire. It was unmistakable.

"I think we both need one," he suggested, his voice a soft purr that stroked her bare skin.

He reached down and unfastened his belt buckle with one hand. His gaze trapped her, holding her in place, while he unbuttoned the top button of his shirt, then the second and the third buttons.

"Ah . . ." Jacey moved away a step, but couldn't for the life of her take her eyes off Stryker revealing his muscular chest button by button. She tried to swallow, but couldn't. "Ah . . . you're welcome to the water when I'm finished." She struggled to inject a bit of haughty indignity into her voice, but knew she failed since she had trouble even getting the words out.

Stryker merely smiled and shook his head.

He pushed his shirt off and let it fall to the floor. Next

he removed his boots and socks. Jacey knew with absolute certainty he intended to strip off his clothing right then in front of her. She opened her mouth to protest, but a soft sigh came out instead.

Stryker pinned her with his intense gaze and slowly unfastened his pants. He dragged them down his hips and kicked them aside. She stared, mesmerized by his actions. She had never seen a naked man before in her entire life. And he was magnificent.

"You . . ." Words failed her.

"You have too many clothes on," he told her in a voice that was pure temptation.

Stepping closer until they were almost touching, he slid his hands down her chemise, then inched it upward, ever so slowly until he pulled it over her head and dropped the garment from his fingertip.

Jacey swallowed. Once. Twice. The third time, a lump lodged in her throat as Stryker cupped her breasts in his hands. Slowly, he caressed her body, as if acquainting himself with her by touch alone. It was the most sensual thing Jacey could have ever imagined. Her breath quickened until her breasts rose and fell with urgency.

Stryker pulled her to him, then scooped her up and carried her the short distance to the large, claw-footed tub. She found she loved being lifted into his arms. Once at the bathtub he eased her down the full length of him until her feet were dipping into the warm water. She savored the heat from both sources, Stryker's body against hers and the heated bath water. She decided her husband was the hotter source. Embarrassed at her flagrant thoughts, she looked down at the water.

"Um . . . you . . . it smells of rosewater," she said in a voice that had gone nearly breathless. "I added scent . . ." Her voice trailed off.

His slow smile answered her, telling her he didn't give

a care. He slid her lower, until her feet rested on the bottom of the bathtub.

As his dark, velvety eyes devoured her, all ability to reason fled her. She couldn't think when he looked at her that way. He stroked the curve of her back with his hand, and she no longer wanted to think. She only wanted to feel.

He stepped into the tub, joining her, and the water lapped up against their legs. It was warm, but not as warm as the heat in her husband's gaze. It surrounded her, enveloped her, consumed her.

"Jacey?" Stryker asked the question with only one word. It was her final chance to tell him no.

Denial was the last thing in her heart. She knew she couldn't deny him, not when she wanted this as much as he. She gave him her answer, pulling his head down to hers and pressing her mouth against his. Their lips touched gently at first, then with increasing demand, until she thought he would consume her completely.

Stryker slid his hands up to her shoulders, then eased her down into the water, until she was sitting in the bathtub. He leaned closer and closer, kneeling into the water, then kissing her with a passion that demanded full surrender.

Jacey leaned back against the enameled tub, the water rising and falling around her in sensuous waves. It lapped at the bottom of her breasts, and he bent his head and flicked his tongue over one nipple, then teased the other one. Releasing a soft whimper of delight, she grabbed on to his shoulder with her hands. She thought she might faint dead away if he kept this up much longer. In her inexperience she had to ask; her curiosity could not be denied.

"How long does this . . . this . . . go on?" She found she was unexpectedly breathless.

The room seemed to go silent around them. Then his

shoulders shook, and he looked up to smile at her. She thought it was the most beautiful smile she had ever seen.

"Much longer, my love." The laughter left his eyes, and they darkened again with desire. "Much longer."

"Oh, good," Jacey murmured before he kissed her thoroughly and most completely.

Her curiosity disappeared, overtaken by heat and a desire she had never experienced before. She gave herself over to the kiss, nibbling his lips in return when he nibbled hers. Stryker groaned against her mouth.

He slid one hand behind her neck, drawing her fully into the melding of their mouths. His other hand slid lower, down over and around her breasts, then across her stomach. And lower.

She gasped as he touched her intimately. Ripples of pleasure followed in the wake of his loving fingers. He teased, tempted, and took her higher and higher—until she dug her hands into the corded muscles of his shoulders. A low cry of fulfillment slipped past her lips, and he took it with his own, capturing it, urging her to deeper delights.

At last she slipped her mouth from his and rested her forehead against his chin. Sucking in several breaths, she smiled to herself.

"So that was lovemaking," she murmured, her breath feathering his skin.

Stryker slid his hands along her thighs and back over her stomach, then up to her waist.

"No, my love, we've only begun," he said, pressing his lips to her forehead.

"Oh. I might faint."

"Oh," he answered, suddenly standing to his feet and sending the water in the tub up and over her breasts. He smiled a slow smile that sent her heartbeat speeding. "Then, maybe we should get you out of the water. Umm?"

The warm water seemed to caress her this time as it ebbed and flowed over her along with his inviting words. Stryker reached down and took her hands in his, then drew her gently and tenderly to her feet.

Grabbing up a towel from the stack of two beside the tub, he wrapped one around her. Slowly, with infinite care, he toweled her dry, sliding the towel down her arms, then back up to her breasts. Once there, he started a sensual journey down her body with the cloth. He bent down and followed the towel's path with his tongue.

Jacey cried out in pleasure and tangled her fingers into the thick hair at his nape. He savored the journey to her center, then eased his mouth upward until he captured her breast, where he stayed.

She reached out and took the towel from his hand. Stepping out of the tub and following his lead, she began to dry his body, muscle by muscle. She paused at the juncture of his thighs, then slipped her hand free of the towel to run her fingers over his length.

Stryker moaned aloud and pressed against her body, trapping her hand. Jacey gasped, and he took the sound in a kiss that made her legs go weak. She clung to his shoulders with one hand, leaning into his embrace.

His eyes darkening to velvet blackness that nearly absorbed her, he scooped her up against his chest and carried her to the bed. He laid her down gently, tenderly, then followed her body with his, bracing his hands on either side of her slightly damp and glistening shoulders.

Jacey leaned up, wanting to be closer, and she initiated the melding of tongues that stole her breath before it ended. He eased down closer. And closer.

His chest brushed her breasts. Once. Twice. She sighed against his mouth, and he answered her invitation. He slid one knee between her thighs, urging them apart. Jacey complied, parting for him, and returning his fervor breath for breath.

He pressed into her softness until he made her his. Jacey caught his broad shoulders and held on. Together they soared higher and higher until she thought surely they reached the heavens.

Stars twinkled behind her eyelids, and she followed him to paradise.

Chapter Twelve

The morning sun shone through the window, draping itself across the entwined bodies. Jacey stretched her arms over her head, smiling in contentment and pure joy.

"Morning." Stryker nuzzled the greeting between Jacey's breasts.

She giggled at the tickling feel of his morning whiskers against her skin, and answered, "Morning yourself."

"I'd make that a *good* morning, but I need sustenance to keep up with a wanton woman like you," he teased in a low voice that once again stroked her like a feather across bare skin.

She tilted her head and smiled at him. "Liar."

He opened his mouth, then closed it and grinned. "Shall I make this a *good* morning?"

Giggling, Jacey caught up the sheet and jumped out of bed. Before he could do more than stare at her naked backside, she whirled to face him.

"Now that you mention sustenance, I am starving. I must have worked up an appetite last night," Jacey teased.

He grinned, enjoying this playful side of her and his tantalizing memory of their night together. Following her out of bed, he stood before her in all his glory. She couldn't resist gazing at him. A smile tipped her lips.

"I'd race you downstairs, but Mrs. Carson would likely faint dead away," he said, grabbing up his pants.

"Oh, and have you done that before?"

He grinned widely, pausing until she stomped her foot. "Now that you mention it . . ."

"Stryker." She stomped her foot again.

"No, I haven't."

With this, he walked over to the wardrobe and pulled out a shirt. After buttoning it, he grabbed up his boots and ducked out the door. "See you downstairs, wife."

Jacey's smile turned into a full grin of delight. She loved that word, *wife*, especially the way he said it.

Hurrying to dress, she soon joined him downstairs. Mrs. Carson didn't faint at the sight of them. Instead, she looked from one to the other, then beamed at them with a wide smile.

Halfway through breakfast, Stryker stretched out his leg and ran his foot up Jacey's calf. She jumped in her chair, letting out a muffled yelp of surprise.

"Are you all right, ma'am?" Mrs. Carson asked, a worried frown creasing her face.

Stryker ran his foot back down Jacey's leg and caught up his napkin to cover a strangled cough.

"Jacey has a headache." He lowered the napkin and locked his gaze with hers. "I'm going to put her back to bed," he said in a slightly strained voice, the corner of his lips lifting in a sensual smile.

Mrs. Carson wiped her hands on her apron and struggled to pull her lips into a straight line. "You do that. Fact is, I think it's the best idea you've had in a long time," she announced, then broke into pleased laughter.

Grinning, Stryker led Jacey out of the room. He bent down to whisper, "Race you to the bedroom—"

Before he completed his sentence, Jacey dashed off ahead of him. Startled, it took him a moment to pursue her, but he did and with relish. She beat him to the door by a hand; hers reached the doorknob first.

Smiling a smile of pure temptation, she tilted her head back and asked, "What's the winner get?"

"Me."

She looked him up and down slowly in a way guaranteed to heat a man's blood. Cocking her head, she nodded. "I guess you'll do."

"You guess?"

"I know you'll do just fine."

Stryker shoved the door open, then took a step forward. Smiling, Jacey backed up a step through the doorway. He walked her backward, step by tantalizing step, all the way to the bed.

"Let me show you 'fine,' wife."

"Yes, please do."

Easing her down onto her back on the bed, he proceeded to do just that.

The sun was higher in the sky when Jacey and Stryker descended the stairs again. Both wore smiles of contentment.

Stryker caught her hands in his. "I need to ride into town." He bent down and kissed her. "I—"

"Take me with you."

He grinned, then asked, "Do you think we'll make it all the way to town?"

Jacey cocked her head, then looked him up and down. "I think you're safe for a while."

Laughing, he pulled her out the door after him. In no time the buggy was readied, and he lifted her onto the seat. He followed the movement with a long, leisurely kiss, then strode around to the other side and climbed in.

This time the ride seemed to take much less time than ever before. Jacey didn't bother trying to hold herself in a ladylike posture. Instead, she scooted over and snuggled into Stryker. He draped one arm around her shoulders.

"So you don't fall out," he said, grinning widely at the reminder of their previous ride.

"And if I fell out, would you rescue me?"

"From what?" he laughed, looking around at the trees.

She batted her eyes at him. "Why, from the big, bad wolf."

"Maybe I am the big, bad wolf."

"Maybe, indeed."

She laughed, the tinkling sound warming him deep inside. She rested her hand on his thigh, and he smiled in enjoyment.

Jacey peeked up at him and felt the warmth seep into her from his muscular thigh. She wondered how she could have ever doubted this marriage between them. She watched him, taking pleasure in his sure moves and control.

Last night and this morning had been wondrous. And she had fallen more deeply under his spell. Spell? No, he hadn't woven a spell and entrapped her. She had fallen in love with him willingly. The realization of her thoughts struck her with a jolt much harder than the rutted road.

She was in love with Stryker.

She let the truth sink in, filling her inch by inch. Smiling, she savored the feeling. Yes, she was in love with Logan Stryker.

Thoroughly . . .

Completely . . .

Eternally in love with him.

"What are you smiling about?" he leaned his head down and asked.

Jacey swallowed down her announcement. She wasn't ready to say it out loud yet. She needed time to savor the realization before she could speak it to anyone. Even him.

"Why, I guess I'm happy." The half truth nearly stuck in her throat, choking her with the omission.

Far too soon they reached town.

"I'll try not to be too long," he assured her. "It's time my deputy started pulling his share." He didn't tell her that the diminished duties of the deputy had been his idea.

He lifted her out of the wagon, set her on her feet, and gave her a thorough kiss. Jacey stepped back, dazed for a moment. At the knowing twinkle in his eyes, she batted his shoulder playfully.

"Don't get yourself fired." She cocked her head and grinned up at him.

"Bertram Raines wouldn't fire me now." He winked back at her. "He's far too impressed with my wife's cooking."

Jacey laughed in pure enjoyment of the day. "Perhaps I'll take Clara up on her offer of coffee and a chat. Then I want to visit with Rosalyn and Linda."

He widened his eyes in mock fear that brought a giggle from her. Then he turned and headed for the marshal's office. He couldn't resist one look back at Jacey as she walked toward the mercantile store. Her bustle swayed in the tantalizing way he had come to recognize as pure Jacey. His grin widened, and he leaped up onto the boardwalk, eager to finish what needed to be done and head back to the ranch with his wife.

At the doorway of the mercantile store, Jacey was nearly

knocked off her feet when someone leaving the store in a hurry bumped into her. Madeline Raines stepped back and sent her a patronizing smile.

"Oh, I hope you're not hurt, my dear Jade. Or was your name Jacey? I never can recall it."

Jacey forced herself to smile back as if unperturbed by the intentional insult, and answered, "That's all right, Mrs. Raines. I understand at your age things can be difficult to remember."

The other woman's indignant shriek brought Jacey a real smile this time. She continued, "Since you can't remember, you can call me *Mrs. Stryker.*"

"Never."

"Forever," Jacey said with finality.

Madeline's harsh laughter cut a swath through Jacey's confidence. Something about the other woman's consummate assurance disturbed her, more than she liked to admit even to herself.

She didn't like the look on the other woman's face one bit. She reminded her of a hungry cat who had just devoured a poor little bird, feathers and all, and was now quite pleased with itself.

"You really don't know, do you? He never told you the truth."

A chill skittered its way along Jacey's spine, beginning at her neck. She told herself the woman was only trying to make trouble.

Madeline put a hand to her bodice and laughed. "This is truly choice."

A moment later she stopped laughing and leaned closer. "Why don't you ask Stryker about . . ." She paused and widened her eyes. "Oh, but he if hasn't told you yet, then I suppose it will be his little secret. For a while."

"What are you talking about?" Jacey couldn't stop the question from slipping out.

"I think it behooves Stryker entirely too much not to tell you."

At the other woman's self-assured smile, Jacey's temper rose. She had had enough from the spiteful, conniving woman. Raising her chin in determination, she faced her squarely. "I'm tired of your little game, Mrs. Raines. Either tell me or move out of my way."

"Oh, the little kitten has claws, does she?"

Jacey resisted the urge to tell her they were enough to scratch her eyes out.

"Well, I think I'll go on home and savor this moment." Madeline laughed with a low chuckle. "I'm sure Stryker is laughing as well. Good-bye."

With an airy wave, Madeline stepped down off the boardwalk and walked across the street. Her laughter drifted across the distance, sending a chill deep into Jacey's heart.

She tried to tell herself the woman was only being spiteful. There wasn't any secret between Madeline and Stryker. Of course there wasn't.

Jacey knew she could tell herself that all day, but she didn't believe it. Distrust sprouted and began to grow. The seed of doubt had been planted and couldn't be dislodged with mere self-assurances. Not until she knew the truth.

Nibbling her lower lip in vexation, Jacey spotted Brett Mason down the boardwalk. He tipped his hat to her and entered a building. An idea caught her. Brett was Stryker's closest friend. Surely he would know what Madeline Raines had been talking about, and if there was any truth to her insinuations. She started after him.

Jacey resisted the urge to catch up her skirt in her hands and run after Brett. If she did, she would likely break an ankle on the uneven wood comprising the boardwalk. Not to mention the scandal she would create by running through town with her stockings and petticoats showing for all to see. She forced herself to take a deep, calming breath and walk down the wooden boardwalk like she had been taught back home. It nearly killed her to do so.

Keeping her eyes trained on the building front where she had seen Brett disappear, it seemed to take forever to reach the establishment. As she drew even with the beginning edge of the building, she read the sign on the plate glass window.

Her mouth gaped open, and she stopped dead still.

The sign proclaimed the place to be *The Wild Bull Saloon.* She closed her mouth on her startled exclamation. Then she stared at the window. The sun reflecting off the glass prevented her from getting a clear picture of the inside of the establishment.

Oh, heavens.

Dare she go inside? Even she knew what kind of women frequented a saloon. Or rather the kind of women she would be likely to find working inside.

She stomped her foot in vexation. She needed to talk to Brett. Now, not later. Was she going to let a little thing like the name of the place stop her?

No, she refused to let anything deter her. Not even a saloon.

Determined, she stepped forward to the door, then stopped in her tracks. The doorway looked like nothing she had ever seen before. It was open, save for a pair of about three-foot tall doors mounted in the middle of the full doorway. She reached out and pressed against one side. It swung freely back and forth. Gathering up her courage, she pushed the strange swinging doors wide open and stepped into the room.

The saloon was dark inside, compared to the bright sunlight outside. She blinked several times until her eyes adjusted to the dimmer interior. She took note of the tables and chairs placed around the room. A long, tall wooden bar with shiny brass railings dominated one part of the room. Behind it hung a large mirror.

As she surveyed the room, an uncomfortable feeling started at her neck and inched downward to her slipper-clad toes. She realized every person in the place was staring at her. Openly staring in the most impolite fashion. She gulped down her sudden nervousness.

She knew without a doubt that she had made a mistake in entering the establishment. She should have asked someone to have Brett come outside to her. She *should* have waited outside, but it was far too late for that now. There was nothing for it but to proceed.

Fixing a smile to her face, she stood her ground without flinching at the stares directed her way and glanced around the room, looking for a familiar face. At the back, sitting at a table with four other men, she spotted her quarry, Brett Mason.

A sigh of relief slipped past her lips, breaking her smile. She took a step forward.

"Ma'am, you shouldn't be in here." A voice from behind the long bar stopped her.

She knew the man was correct, but she wasn't about to leave until she had spoken to Brett.

"I'll only be a minute or two," she assured the barrel-chested bartender.

"Ma'am, ah . . ." The bartender seemed at a loss for words.

Jacey waved a hand to reassure him. "This will only take a few minutes." She took another step forward.

The bartender rushed around from behind the bar. "Ma'am, I wish you'd go, ah," he faltered, then continued, "Ma'am, would you please leave before there's trouble?"

"I'm not going to cause any trouble," she said with a burst of indignation.

He shook his head and crossed his arms over his chest.

"Ma'am, you were trouble the minute you walked through that there door."

Jacey leveled a firm glare at him. "Well, I'm already inside, and I intend to talk to—"

"Let her stay!" a man hollered out.

The bartender groaned and shook his head. Then he rolled his eyes. "See," he told her.

Raising her chin in determination that told anyone she would not be easily deterred, she clenched her hand around the strings of her reticule and walked across the room to the table at the back.

Later, she decided the only thing that prevented her from being accosted was that the men, both drunk and sober, were too startled to move until she had reached her destination.

"Brett, I—"

The tall, blond man dropped his cards, and his jaw followed suit. He worked his mouth twice before a sound came out. "Jacey! I mean Mrs. Stryker, ah, I, ah."

She nodded in greeting. "Hello, Brett. I need to talk to you for a few minutes."

One of the men jumped up to offer her his chair. She accepted it with a polite nod and sat down, straightening her skirt around her.

Beside her, Brett's eyes widened, and he opened and shut his mouth again. "You shouldn't be here."

"Let the gal stay!" a man yelled out from several tables away.

Jacey politely ignored the remark. It didn't matter; she intended to remain until she had finished her business with Brett and had her answers.

"Stryker—" he began.

"That's what I'm here to talk to you about," she told him, leaning forward.

"Jacey," Brett pleaded, "you need to get out of here. And quick."

She narrowed her eyes, any attempt at politeness fleeing. "Not until you give me some answers."

"Oh, no," the bartender muttered from behind her. "Please, ma'am, don't start no fight."

She turned in her chair to send him a disparaging glance, then turned back to her quest. "Brett, I just ran into Madeline Raines." She didn't tell him the woman had nearly run her down.

"Oh, no," Brett groaned. Without thinking about it, he rubbed the back of his neck the way he had seen Stryker do when he was bothered.

"Oh, yes." Jacey caught his hand. "Tell me what happened between her and Stryker. What is she to him?"

"Nothing now."

Jacey pounced on his slight slip. "Now?"

"I mean, there's nothing between them."

"But there was," she said with surety in her voice.

Brett took a quick swallow from his nearly full glass of whiskey on the table.

"Tell me," Jacey ordered.

"Ma'am," the bartender interrupted, nervously looking around the room. "You need to get on out of here."

"Not until he tells me what I want to know," she tossed over her shoulder without turning around.

"Brett, tell her," the bartender said. "Tell her what she wants and get her out of here."

Brett sighed and stared at the table. "Jacey, are you sure? This all doesn't matter anymore—"

"It does to me."

He sighed again, this time deeply, then gave in. "They were engaged to be married."

At her gasp, he stopped.

"Go on."

"Jacey, it was about five years ago."

"What happened?"

"She jilted him for somebody richer."

"Bertram Raines," Jacey said.

"Stryker was pretty torn up about it. Swore never to marry again. But, you can see that's all changed. Why, look at you two—"

"Will you get the *lady* out of here so we can play poker?" one man at the table prompted to the bartender.

Jacey turned her glare on the new speaker. "This will only take a few minutes. Then you can go back to your little game of cards."

The man's eyes narrowed on her. "Lady, if you were a man, I'd—"

"George, leave her be," Brett ordered.

"You telling me what to do?"

"Yes."

The man named George pushed away from the table and surged to his feet. Before Jacey do more than widen her eyes in shock, he reached across the table and grabbed Brett by the shirtfront. His chair tumbled back to the floor with a crash.

She jumped to her feet and slapped at the man. "Stop it!"

Brett pulled away from the man's hold, ripping his own shirt and sending the table rocking over on its side. Cards, glasses and a bottle of whiskey fell to the floor along with the table in a resounding crash. Jacey ducked, then jumped out of the way as Brett swung at the other man. His fist connected solidly with the man's jaw, but the man didn't go down.

The fight was on.

Another man at the table swung at George and missed. George sent the man to the floor with one punch. A third man joined in, pulling Brett around to face him. Two more men entered the fray.

Jacey yelped, then scooped up the bottle from the floor and brandished it. "Stop it!"

No one listened to her. The man swung at Brett, and Jacey brought the bottle down on the man's exposed shoulders. He crumpled to his knees, then surged back to his feet and turned on her with a roar of anger.

Jacey jumped back, but the stranger came at her. The bartender grabbed Jacey around the waist, swinging her around and out of the way. He lifted her onto a table and pointed his finger at her. "Stay put."

Muttering, "I knew you'd cause trouble," the bartender shoved his way into the melee.

Jacey flinched at the sound of glass breaking and glanced over her shoulder to see the fancy mirror over the bar shatter. She bit her lower lip.

A second later, the saloon doors crashed open, hitting the walls with the force. A gunshot ripped the air, loud even above the sound of the fighting.

Jacey dove off the table and scurried underneath it. Peeking out, she looked over to the doorway and the man who had fired the gunshot.

Stryker stood there.

Jacey closed her eyes. Oh, heavens.

Around her, the fighting stopped as suddenly as it had started.

"Clear it out," Stryker shouted in a deadly voice.

Silence filled the saloon.

"Who started it?" Stryker demanded. His badge shone in the dim overhead lighting, giving credibility to his question and demanding a quick answer.

Two men responded at once with, "She did!"

Stryker looked from the men to where they pointed at

a table. Striding across to the table, he stopped then bent down and peered underneath.

Jacey smiled up at him.

Stryker closed his eyes, and she could have sworn she heard him groan.

"I can explain," she began.

"Not now." He reached down and pulled her out from under the table.

Jacey brushed off her skirt and faced him. He looked angry. Very angry. "But, I didn't—"

"Not now—"

"But, Stryker—"

"Jacey, shut up."

She opened her mouth, then snapped it closed again at the look he sent her. He caught her by the hand and tugged her along with him.

"Where are we—"

"I'm taking you to the jail. Where you'll be safe."

"Stryker!"

"Not now, Jacey."

Wisely she decided to remain quiet, but only until they reached the jail. There was no way her husband was locking her up. No way at all.

Stryker led her across the street and down the boardwalk in silence. She could tell he was furious. She nibbled her lower lip and thought over how to explain what happened without relating what she had learned about his past with Madeline.

Once inside the office, Stryker slammed the door shut. The glass pane rattled in the door, and Jacey winced, waiting for it to shatter like the mirror over the saloon bar. Her lips twitched at the humor of comparing the marshal's office to the Wild Bull Saloon. One look at Stryker's face made her change her mind; perhaps the two buildings had more in common than she had surmised. It looked like a fight was brewing here as well.

Suddenly the door opened and slammed again. Stryker flicked a glance at the doorway, then relaxed slightly. Brett strode over to where they stood like two combatants. He laid a hand on Stryker's arm.

"Brett, stay out of this," Stryker ordered, his gaze never leaving Jacey's.

"It wasn't her fault."

"See," Jacey put in. "I told you so."

"Jacey," Stryker warned with a single word.

She ignored the admonition and stomped her foot.

Stryker looked pointedly at her feet, then back up at her face.

Brett quickly stepped between them. "Honest, it wasn't her fault. I threw the first punch."

"You what?" Stryker shouted.

"I started it."

"Over what?"

Brett made the mistake of glancing toward Jacey for an instant. Stryker intercepted the telltale action.

"I knew she was at the bottom of this." Stryker shook his head, then rubbed the knot of tension building at the back of his neck.

"Now, Stryker—" Brett took a step closer to him.

"Don't interfere, Brett." Stryker's voice lowered to carry a distinct threatening note.

While Stryker and Brett were deep in argument, Jacey inched away from them. She didn't intend to be close in case the men came to blows. She stopped when she backed up against the corner of the desk, dislodging a stack of papers. They fell to the floor in a disorderly heap.

Quickly Jacey bent down to pick up the papers. Hand outstretched, she froze dead still. She couldn't breathe as her throat closed in shock.

Her own face stared back at her from one of the fliers on the floor. Above her picture the word *Wanted* was emblazoned. She stared at the wanted poster, and the room tilted around her. No! She couldn't faint now. She wouldn't let herself.

Forcing herself to move, she reached out and snatched up the wanted poster. Folding it, she stuffed the paper into her reticule.

She must never let Stryker see the wanted poster.

Everything depended on keeping it from him.

Chapter Thirteen

The next morning, Jacey stomped out of the stables and all the way back to the house. Her mood was darker than the inside of the barn. Last night she had slept alone. In his anger over the saloon brawl, Stryker had spent the night in the other bedroom. Alone.

This morning his temper obviously hadn't improved one whit. She kicked at a clump of dirt, wishing it was his shin. She fumed each time she thought about what Stryker had told her before he swung up onto his horse to ride out to town.

He had *ordered* her to stay at the ranch.

Ordered!

She had never been so insulted in her entire life. No one ordered her around, and hadn't done so in too many years to recall.

He blamed the entire trouble at the saloon squarely on her. One would have surmised she had entered the place solely to cause trouble. Obviously, he hadn't listened to

Brett's argument any better than he had to hers. She wasn't the one who started the fight.

Well, brawl to be truthful. But she hadn't thrown a punch at anyone. Would he listen to her explanations? Oh, no. He got his temper up and fixed the blame firmly on her. She admitted to herself she likely shouldn't have gone into the establishment, but he should forgive her. Not issue her orders.

Turning on her heel, she stared at the cloud of dust marking Stryker's departure, then stuck her tongue out at his back. He would soon see that he couldn't order her about as if she were someone she employed for pay.

Even worse, he had calmly ridden off as if he expected her to meekly obey his directive to not dare leave the ranch. She hadn't meekly obeyed an order since she was a child—if even then. And she wasn't about to start now.

She would show him.

He could take the list of chores he had given her and. . . . Her temper continued to climb. Well, he could take his chores . . . and stick them where the sun didn't shine.

She was going for a walk.

She hadn't taken more than a dozen steps when her conscience started to bother her. In truth, she admitted being angry at Stryker since she had learned of his past love for the hateful Madeline Raines. *But apparently he doesn't find her hateful,* a little voice whispered the taunt.

If there was nothing between them as Brett claimed, then why had Stryker hidden the truth from her?

Isn't that like the pot calling the kettle black, the little voice of her conscience nudged again. The wanted poster lay inside her reticule, hidden away upstairs in a bureau drawer. A shudder coursed through her. He could never know about that. As a lawman, he would never understand.

Never.

She walked on, hoping to exorcise her irritation. Minutes

later, she stopped to kick at another clod of dirt, sending it flying through the air. It landed with a *plop* next to a mesquite bush. Suddenly the bush rustled, sending her scurrying in the opposite direction. She stopped, several feet safely away, and looked over at the scraggly bush. It rustled again, and she backed up a hurried step.

Something small and dark in color poked out from the side of the bush, and Jacey let out a small yelp. She jumped back farther away.

She thought she heard a hiss.

Jacey resisted the strong urge to turn and race for safety. Glancing about the open area, she didn't see any semblance of safety within sight. She had left the ranch house far behind while walking off her anger.

Peering at the bush, she held herself still, hoping *whatever* was hidden inside would go back to what it was doing. Or slither or crawl away from her.

The only creature she could recall that made any kind of a hissing sound was a snake. A shiver wiggled its way up her back. She hated snakes! Worse than chickens!

Jacey willed the creature to go back to sleep, or hibernation, or whatever they called it when the sun was beating down hot. Her wishful thinking appeared to work when after minutes of holding herself motionless, the bush stayed quiet.

Carefully, she took a step back, then another tiny step, widening the distance between herself and the unknown danger that could at any moment strike out at her. She eyed the mesquite with distrust, then slowly turned away and began to tiptoe in the opposite direction, concentrating on putting one foot in front of the other without making a single sound. One . . . two . . . three, she counted. When she reached ten, she would risk breaking into a run.

Another rustle behind her warned of impending danger,

and she whirled around. An instant later, a low blur of movement raced for her.

Jacey screamed and grabbed up her skirts to run. Before she could take a step, a ball of fur pounced on her feet. She froze, looked down, and broke into laughter. Her "attacker" was a fluffy kitten.

A giggle slipped free as the kitten spun around and scampered away at the sound. The little animal halted at the edge of the bush and looked back at her hesitantly. When Jacey didn't move, the kitten sat down and blinked big blue eyes at her.

Bending low, she held out her hand to the animal. It hunched up at her movement. She giggled at the ferocious action from the kitten. Well, actually it was an oversized kitten.

"Little one, you're too small to be that fierce," Jacey told the animal with a soft laugh.

The kitten looked half-grown. Studying the animal, she took in the dappled spots of rust, brown and black on its cream-colored, furry coat. She had never seen a kitten such as this one before. Certainly there wasn't anything like it back home in Baltimore.

Inching forward, she stretched out her hand and whispered her encouragement. "Here, kitty, kitty."

When the animal merely stared at her, Jacey laid her hand in the dirt, then wiggled her fingers back and forth. Sure enough, the kitten watched and waited a moment, then bounded out at her, pouncing on her hand.

It meowed, the sound almost like a high-pitched whine, and Jacey's heart turned over in sympathy at the lonesome sound.

"I know just how you feel, little one. I bet you've been abandoned, too."

She gently petted the soft fur, and the kitten snuggled

her hand, sucking on a fingertip. That did it. She was taking the poor thing home and feeding it.

"Come on, sweetie," she soothed. "Let's get you something to eat. Bet you're hungry."

As if to answer her, the kitten suckled her finger harder, then licked her fingers with a tiny, rough tongue. A minute later, it bit her finger.

"Ouch," Jacey yelped and nearly dropped the kitten. "You are hungry."

Gently scooping the kitten into her arms, Jacey stood slowly. She didn't want to frighten the poor thing into scratching her or leaping out of her arms and running away. It needed nourishment. The kitten snuggled into her arms, shivering slightly. "Poor little stinker, are you frightened? That's what I'll call you. Tinker."

A name settled on, she turned and headed back to the house. Since she wasn't certain of Mrs. Carson's opinion on animals in the house, especially a stray kitten, she decided to sneak her new pet in and straight upstairs.

She murmured assurances to the kitten on their way back to the ranch house. In response, the small animal kept attempting to nurse on Jacey's fingers. By the time she reached their destination, she wasn't certain of the kitten's age. While it kept trying to nurse, for such a hungry creature, it was surprisingly heavy.

As the house came into sight, she practically tiptoed across the open distance to the door, carefully looking around. Heavens, she felt like a criminal.

A sudden recollection of the wanted poster with her name and likeness on it, hidden away in her reticule, prodded her. It was true—now she was a thief. Hadn't she stolen the wanted poster?

But she had a good reason. Yes, she was saving her hide.

A little voice in the back of her mind prompted a thought of Jeanette, and Jacey gulped down the accompanying rush of guilt. By rights, Stryker belonged to her twin, until she had stolen him from her.

She sucked in a deep breath between clenched teeth and pushed the thought aside. However, the nagging guilt remained. Slowly, she rubbed her chin against the soft fur of her new pet, seeking comfort for her aching conscience.

"I guess you might say we're hiding out right now, huh, Tinker?" she whispered.

Easing the kitten into the crook of one arm, she carefully opened the door and stepped inside. In the next room she spotted Mrs. Carson turned away from her. She sighed in relief, then caught up her skirts and held the kitten close against her.

On tiptoes, Jacey crossed the room to the stairs. She half expected the cook to call out to her before she reached the safety of the bedroom. Biting her lower lip, she crept up the stairs as fast as she could manage, hoping the kitten didn't make a giveaway noise.

She didn't breathe easy until she shut the bedroom door behind her. Sagging against the wooden door, she eased the kitten down to the floor. Immediately Tinker scampered off and under the bed.

Dusting off her hands, Jacey left the kitten in its hiding place and slipped out into the hall, careful to shut the door behind her. As casually as possible, she walked down the stairs and sauntered into the kitchen.

Mrs. Carson greeted her pleasantly, but with a hint of surprise.

"I'm thirsty. Is there any milk?" Jacey asked with as much innocence as she could muster.

"Milk, ma'am?"

"Um huh." Jacey entwined her fingers together in a rush of nervousness.

"Sure. Let me get you a glass."

As the woman left to get the milk, Jacey scooped up a bowl on the counter and hid it in the folds of her skirt.

"Here you go." Mrs. Carson sent her a strange look.

"Thank you. I think I'll take it upstairs." Jacey smiled her thanks and turned away.

She recalled seeing a full-sized cat dash out of the barn the other day. It fostered an idea. She took two steps, then nibbled her lower lip. "Ah . . . does Stryker ever complain about the cats in the barn?"

"Heavens, yes. Always saying how they're in the way." Mrs. Carson tucked a stray wisp of hair into the neat bun at the back of her neck.

"Oh. I was just wondering." Perhaps it would be better for all concerned if she kept the kitten hidden away for at least a few days.

Without another word, Jacey returned to the bedroom. After several tries she managed to coax the kitten out from under the bed. She sat on the floor with the little creature and set to feeding it. It took several attempts to get the little animal to begin drinking the milk. Both Jacey's fingers and the kitten's front paws were covered in creamy froth. At last, once it caught the gist of the bowl, the kitten licked it clean.

Jacey stroked the soft fur, then sniffed and wrinkled her nose in distaste.

"We both smell like milk, Tinker. Except you smell worse. You most assuredly need a bath," she announced.

The kitten sat on the floor, blinking bright blue eyes at her in answer.

Jacey gently scooped up the fury bundle and crossed the room to the washstand. She dreaded this undertaking. Cats notoriously hated water in her experiences back home. At least the one Jeanette had claimed as hers years ago had hated even being near water.

"It's all right, Tinker," she assured the kitten.

Shifting the animal into the crook of one arm again, she poured the tepid water from the pitcher into the large, deep bowl. As gently as possible, she eased the kitten into the water, paws first, and waited for the explosion of meows.

Nothing.

The creature appeared to actually like the water. Relieved, but surprised, Jacey quickly cleaned the kitten and dried it before it changed its mind.

What an unusual creature, she thought; maybe it was some rare Texas breed of cat. Either way, she had best keep her new pet hidden until she found a way to convince Stryker to allow her to keep it.

But first, she had to convince him of her innocence in the brawl, before she dared ask for any favors.

As Stryker left the jail, he glanced down the street to the Wild Bull Saloon with a grimace. Yesterday's brawl had taken its toll on the establishment and him.

Today the saloon was closed for repairs, and he was paying for them. It had been a heck of a brawl with his wife as the instigator. He recalled his shock when he had spotted Jacey hiding under the table right in the middle of a brawl. A shudder ran across his shoulders, and he attempted to shrug it off.

His concern for her had quickly been replaced with anger. Today he had ordered her to stay home and out of trouble. The woman could cause more trouble with a look than a bank robber with a six-shooter.

He should have arrested her. Several men from the saloon had stopped by to insist he do his job. He had refused and paid for the repairs instead. Maybe he should take the cost of the saloon repairs out of the money due to Jacey when she returned back east.

His chest constricted, and it felt as if a fist tightened around his heart, squeezing tighter and tighter. The thought of Jacey leaving shook him to his boots. He didn't want her to leave him to return to Baltimore or anywhere else. He never wanted her to leave him.

The realization stopped him in his tracks. He wanted the marriage to be real, not temporary.

He clenched his jaw until his teeth ached. It was time to end this farce of a marriage he was in. Past time to have a talk with Jacey. He would settle it between them tonight. One way or another.

Tonight would change his marriage and his life.

He wondered a moment if Jacey would agree to cancel their previous bargain. Or was she truly as mercenary as he had believed her to be from her letters? Would she hold him to their agreement? Did she care for him in the slightest, or was she merely biding her time and fulfilling her part of their cursed bargain?

Jacey seemed to like the lovemaking between them, but could it mean more to her? Could she come to care for him?

Stryker walked down the wooden boardwalk, deep in troubled thoughts, his boot heels clicking in the afternoon quiet. He scanned the street quickly out of sheer habit before he crossed to the other side and the mercantile store.

"Hey, Stryker. Wait up!"

He spun around at the cry, his hand going to the gun in his holster. At the sight of Brett dashing across the street to join him, he sighed and rested his hand on his hip.

His friend leaped up onto the boardwalk beside him. He nodded to Stryker's gun hand with a half smile. "Thinking about shooting me?"

"Should I be?"

Brett shrugged. "Just wondering if you're still angry about yesterday."

"You're right, I am."

"Still mad at Jacey?"

The question hit him hard, like a blow to the gut. He realized he wasn't angry with her. He had foolishly been using the brawl as an excuse to keep his distance from her. Not any longer—it was time to settle some things.

The glare Stryker sent didn't leave his friend in doubt of the state of his mood.

"Surely you can't still blame her—"

"Leave her out of this. And anything in the future," Stryker ordered in a cool, level voice.

Brett dared to smile at his reaction. "Is that a touch of jealousy I'm seeing, old friend?"

"No."

"Wanna bet?"

Stryker sent him a level stare.

"If I recall correctly, we had another bet." Brett cocked his head, looked his friend up and down, then held out his hand. "Looks like you lost that one. Pay up, friend."

"What for?"

"Are you denying you're a truly *married* man now?"

Stryker gritted his teeth and reached in his pocket. Brett's laughter goaded him. He couldn't believe he had forgotten about the foolish bet he had made that he could keep his hands off Jacey. But in truth, it was a bet he didn't mind losing.

An unexpected sound from down the street startled him. It had sounded like a single gunshot. No further noise followed, but the silence felt uneasy.

Stryker didn't like it one bit.

Instinct told him something was wrong. Drawing his gun, he flattened himself against the front of the building housing the mercantile store and studied the town.

Brett stepped up beside him. "What—"

"Get back," Stryker hissed, pushing his friend against the wall of the building.

He scanned the street, his gaze coming to rest on the bank catty-cornered from where he stood. Everything looked normal, but he knew something was brewing.

The first sign of trouble came with a bullet thudding into the storefront beside him. Stryker dove for the cover of the nearby horse trough. Brett followed right on his heels.

Stryker leaned around the left side of the trough enough to get a clear view of the door to the bank. Two men ran out onto the boardwalk lining the front of the bank, guns in hand. One man held a bank bag in his other hand.

"There's two of them that I can see," he told his friend quietly. "But I don't spot any horses."

Suddenly the two bank robbers began shooting, firing their guns into the air. Stryker knew it was a signal to their man hiding with the horses.

He wasn't about to let them ride out of town. Not with the proceeds from their bank robbery. As he raised up, he caught a movement from the corner of his eye. Whirling around on his knee, he leveled his gun, then immediately lowered it. Rosalyn stood framed in the doorway of the mercantile. She made the perfect target for the thieves.

"Get down," Stryker yelled, lunging for her at the same moment. The sharp crack of gunfire answered his warning shout.

He surged forward, standing and shoving Rosalyn down to the wooden boardwalk. The action left him exposed for the brief moment.

Stryker didn't see the man they had posted as guard standing around the corner of the building until he stepped out to save Rosalyn. The man fired, and the bullet caught Stryker in the shoulder. The impact of the bullet sent him staggering backward.

He raised his gun and fired, hitting the third robber in the chest. The man dropped to the ground, dead still.

Stryker struggled to stay upright; he knew he had to get to the cover of the horse trough. He was too exposed on the boardwalk. Everything about him moved as if in slow motion. He heard Brett yell something, but couldn't make out the slurred words.

Brett stood, and Stryker forced himself to raise his gun and pull the trigger as one of the robbers pointed his gun straight at Brett. He saw the robber go down and heard the retort of his friend's gun echo in his mind.

Stryker took a step forward, stumbled on the boardwalk, then crumpled to the ground. He struggled to push himself to his feet, but only got as far as his knees before he fell back to the hard dirt. Groaning, he tried again. Had to get to cover. His mind whirled with orders.

Had to take care of Brett, see if he was hit . . .

See if anyone in the bank was hurt . . .

Had to take care of the town. . . .

He pushed himself up by sheer force of will. One glance showed his friend a few feet away, walking toward him. Opening his mouth, he tried to shout out a warning to Brett.

Stryker wavered unsteadily on his feet. The ground tilted, straightened, then tilted again beneath him. Time blurred for him, and he attempted to shake his head to clear it.

An image of Jacey hiding under the table of the saloon flashed through his mind. She was in danger. He forced himself to take a step forward.

Had to get to her. . . .

He stumbled, tried again, then sank to the ground. As his vision began to darken, he had only one thought. Jacey.

His last word was a cry of desperation. "Jacey," he called out.

Then blackness closed around him, taking him farther and farther away. Until all that remained was darkness and pain.

Then only darkness, taking him away from her.

Chapter Fourteen

Jacey walked to the bedroom window again and looked outside at the late afternoon. She couldn't seem to sit still. A vague sense of unease nagged at her, prompting her to pace. Tinker padded along beside her, jumping back and pouncing, reacting to her mistress's nervous movements.

Absently, Jacey bent down and stroked the kitten on the head, then straightened and nibbled on her lower lip. She rubbed her hands up and down her arms, with the sudden onset of a chill.

She attempted to shake off the feeling, but it persisted in spite of the sun shining brightly outside. Shivering, she wrapped her arms close about herself. The only other time she had this sensation was when her twin Jeanette was in danger, but somehow she knew this wasn't about her sister.

"Stryker," Jacey whispered in the stillness.

Her throat constricted, and she covered her mouth with one hand.

Something has happened to Stryker!

She knew the fact with absolute certainty. There was a bond joining them now, one she could feel in danger.

Catching up her skirts, she whirled about and ran out of the bedroom, pausing only long enough to shut the door behind her. She didn't stop again until she reached the downstairs window looking out into the yard.

Over the next hour, Jacey kept her vigil at the window, afraid to leave, almost as if standing there was her only link with Stryker. She knew it sounded foolish, but she couldn't walk away.

At the sound of wagon wheels rumbling into the yard, Jacey whirled and ran for the door. Without pausing to look out to see who might be coming, she raced outside. She knew this wasn't a polite social call.

When she spotted the buckboard wagon rumbling into the yard with the group of men riding alongside, her heart nearly stopped beating. She searched frantically, but couldn't see Stryker. He wasn't with the men . . .

Unless he was in the back of the buckboard. Panic caught her in its terrifying hold, and she suddenly felt icy cold all over.

"Stryker?" she called out, running for the back of the wagon.

Brett intercepted her before she reached the buckboard, grabbing her shoulders and dragging her to a halt. "Jacey, wait. Listen—"

"No!"

Frantic, she pushed at Brett, attempting to break his hold. He held her firmly, and she couldn't jerk free. When she stepped back and raised a foot to kick him, he evaded her with a swift dodge to the side.

"Jacey, stop it."

"Let me go."

"Listen—"

"I've got to get to him."

"Jacey, there was a holdup at the bank." He paused.

"No," she moaned. She had known something was wrong. Her breath caught in her throat, and she sagged in Brett's determined hold.

He eased his grip and faced her again.

"He's ... he's ... not—" She couldn't say the hope-condemning words.

"No, no, Stryker's alive," Brett assured her. "He's been shot, but—"

"Then, get out of my way!" Jacey yanked her arms free of his hold.

Dodging his outstretched hands, she whirled away and ran for the back of the wagon. Two men stepped in front of her to bar her way. She recognized one of the men from the morning she had served them breakfast.

"Get out of my way," she repeated, her voice carrying a note of determination.

"Ah, ma'am, you shouldn't see ..."

"Oh, for heaven's sake, I'm not going to faint at the sight of a little blood," she informed them.

There was more than a little blood.

At the sight of Stryker lying on his back, swathed in bandages and his clothes stained with blood, she gasped. The ground tilted beneath her feet, but she refused to give in to the light-headedness. Raising her chin in sheer tenacity, she leaned closer until she could touch his hand.

"Stryker?" she whispered. "It's Jacey. I'm here."

"Ma'am, he can't hear you."

"Of course he can." The faint movement beneath her hand assured her he knew she was at his side.

Turning back to the men, she began to issue orders. "Get him inside. The bedroom on the right will be the most comfortable." She hastily added the word *please* as an afterthought.

The men jumped into action, obviously surprised at her sudden control and command of the situation.

"What did the doctor say? How is he?" She flooded the men with questions. "Who can tell me what happened?"

Brett stepped forward. "I can tell you what you need to know."

She narrowed her eyes on him. "No, you'll tell me everything."

Brett opened and closed his mouth in indecision. There were some things a gentleman didn't discuss with a lady. Especially not with his friend's wife. He knew Stryker would be furious if he learned Brett had caused Jacey distress or induced a fainting spell.

"Brett. Tell me now, or I'll find someone else who will." She crossed her arms over her chest. "Don't you think Stryker would want me to hear this from you?"

He nodded. But he would also be the one his friend blamed for causing her upset.

From the corner of her eye, she watched the men lift Stryker from the back of the buckboard. "Gentle," she called out to them.

"Yes, ma'am."

Jacey supervised the settling in of Stryker. Then she returned her attention to Brett.

"Now, talk," she ordered, peeking over her shoulder at Stryker as he lay in the bed. "But first I want to be at his side."

Jacey walked back to her husband and took up a position at his bedside. She felt his forehead and brushed a strand of dark hair from his temple.

"He was a hero today—"

"Of course he was. But I don't care about that. How is he?" She touched his forehead again tenderly.

"Doc Bradley got the bullet out. Said he'd lost a lot of

blood. But as long as a fever didn't set in . . ." He left the rest unsaid.

Jacey swallowed down the lump of fear that rose up into her throat at the implication of his words. Brett reached out and squeezed her shoulder.

"I'll take good care of him." Her voice wavered for an instant. "What happened?"

Brett stepped closer and slipped an arm around her shoulders. She sent him a wan smile of thanks.

"The bank was robbed this afternoon. Stryker was the first one to get there as the robbers were leaving." He paused to scrutinize how well she was taking the news. All he saw was interest and impatience.

"Go on," she prompted, attempting to exert a small measure of patience for Stryker's sake.

"And then Rosalyn stepped out of the mercantile."

Jacey covered her mouth with one hand. "No. Is she all right?"

"A little bruised and plenty mad at Bertram Raines and his bank, but thanks to Stryker, she wasn't hit."

Jacey stared down at the man in the bed and smoothed her hand across his forehead. She had always known he was brave, but today he had risked his life for a friend. And for the town. They had better appreciate it.

"While he was out in the open, he was shot. There were three of them. He got two men, but one . . ." The words trailed off, and he rubbed a hand over his face. "None of us saw the one concealed beside the building." He stiffened. "Jacey, I'm sorry."

"Don't blame yourself." She offered what comfort she could to Stryker's friend.

"If he—" Brett cut the remainder off suddenly, glancing down at Jacey.

She stiffened and bit her lower lip. She didn't have to ask what he had been about to say; she could feel the anxious words as if they hung in the room, waiting to be voiced. The uncertainty tore at her.

She forced herself to ask, "Brett, how is he? The truth." She looked up into his face, determined to watch for any signs of a lie.

"It'll be rough for a while. But he's a tough man."

He didn't have to tell her that. Stryker was also strong, and brave, and tender . . .

And the man she loved with all her heart.

But the words Brett hadn't spoken worried her. Stryker *would* make it through this. He had to. She wouldn't let him die. She blinked away the sting of tears. She would not cry. Not in front of Stryker. Not now.

He needed her strong for him. For both of them.

"Are you going to be all right?" Brett asked her, giving her shoulder a comforting squeeze.

"I'm not as fragile as you think," she informed him. "I can take care of him. I did some work at the hospital back home."

Actually it had been more than a little work. She had helped one of the doctors for months until Uncle Harvey found out about it. She always suspected Cousin Earl had tattled on her out of spite.

"You don't have to do it alone. Mrs. Carson and Hank know how to handle gunshot wounds."

Brett's remark told her this wasn't the first time Stryker had been shot. She stiffened in shock; the thought of him being shot before had never crossed her mind. Until now.

"I forgot all about them." Jacey took a step toward the door. "I'd better tell them—"

"They already know."

"Oh."

"Why don't you go lie down and rest—"

At her sudden look of defiance, he amended his remark. "Ah, why don't you sit in here awhile and rest?" he offered.

"Thanks." She sent him a forgiving smile. "I'll check his bandages."

"Ah—" He swallowed down his objection after one glimpse at the set look on her face. "I'll go see about Hank and Mrs. Carson."

Jacey nodded and went to stand beside Stryker. He commanded her full attention, and she barely heard the soft click of the door as Brett left.

She stared down at her patient. He looked so helpless lying on the bed. His skin had paled beneath his tan, and she couldn't resist stroking her hand lightly down his cheek. Then she leaned forward and pressed a feather-light kiss against his cool, still lips.

She vowed not to let anything happen to him and set to work checking the bandages wrapped around his broad chest. Crossing the room, she poured water from the pitcher into the bowl and carried it back to the bed. Carefully she began to clean around the bandages, wiping away the dried blood.

Stryker lay motionless, except for one low moan as she cleaned his side. Flinching at the sound, she bit her lip and dropped the cloth into the bowl of blood-stained water.

Straightening up, she pulled up a chair and began her vigil beside him. No one was going to make her leave his side until he was awake and better.

Much better.

The next evening the fever set in. The uncommon paleness fled his face to be replaced by a heated flush. She carefully wiped his face with a cool cloth.

Heat radiated out from his body, almost as if reaching out for her. She brushed a lock of dark hair back from his forehead and winced at the hot, dry skin beneath her fingers. If only he would sweat, then he would break the fever that held him in its dangerous grasp.

Jacey sponged off his chest with the cool water, careful not to get the bandages wet. Thankfully Hank had removed Stryker's clothes yesterday, although Jacey had worried the entire time about him tearing open the wound and starting it bleeding again. Later, Mrs. Carson had offered to relieve Jacey, but she refused to let anyone care for Stryker except her.

Now she worried if she had been selfish in her insistence to care for him. Had she made a mistake? Could someone else have cared for him better, have prevented the fever? The doubts and questions nagged at her, threatening her composure and her lagging confidence.

She sucked in a deep breath and stiffened her back. The knowledge she had acquired in Baltimore stood her in good stead. She knew what she was doing, and she was doing the best that could be done for him. She chased the doubts away. Stryker needed her focused on him, not on her personal worries and lack of self-confidence, she chided herself.

Fretful, she paced to the window and back. Over the past two hours, she had wiped him with cool cloths, laid one over his forehead, and even tried covering him with two woolen blankets from the bureau. His body remained fevered in spite of her efforts.

At the sound of a crash from across the hall, Jacey jumped to her feet. It was past time to check on her kitten again. Since yesterday, she had alternated between the two rooms, daring brief moments away from Stryker to feed and care for the kitten. She dared not leave the kitten alone in the other bedroom indefinitely.

Jacey changed her mind about keeping her pet hidden

away. She didn't want to be separated from Stryker for even a moment until his fever safely broke. She dashed across the hallway and gathered up Tinker, then quietly slipped back into the other bedroom.

Putting together a makeshift bed in the corner, she settled the kitten in, glancing over to Stryker every few moments until she was finished with the task. The inquisitive kitten sniffed the area, then gradually picked a spot on the blanket and made herself a nest.

Jacey spared her pet a quick stroke, then hurried back over to check on Stryker. She laid her hand on his forehead and frowned. His skin persisted to be hot to the touch. If anything, he was warmer than a few minutes ago.

She attempted to give him a drink, raising his head slightly up off the pillow and holding the cup to his mouth. The water trickled past his lips and across his cheek.

Muttering her frustration, she wiped his face again and eased his head back down onto the pillow. Something had to change and soon.

"Sweat. Stryker, come on, sweat," she said out loud to him, but it didn't do any good.

She talked to him, ordered him, pleaded with him. Nothing helped. His fever remained as firmly as before. Only her fear changed, growing with each passing hour of the seemingly endless day.

She continued to wipe him with the water until he began to thrash beneath the covers. He moaned, the sound tearing at Jacey's heart. She wished fervently for him to get well as she prayed.

Finally, he seemed to relax and sleep for a little while. She kept up her vigil at his bedside, half-afraid to leave him. Mrs. Carson brought up a plate for her, and she picked at the food, giving some of the meat bits and the milk to Tinker.

As the time wore on, Jacey's worry turned to fear. Stryker's breathing slowed, then turned shallow. She watched the rise and fall of his chest. Each breath seemed an effort for him as if his thrashing had exhausted his strength.

"Come on, Stryker, fight," she urged him, holding his hand tightly in hers. She tried to will her own strength into his body.

She couldn't let him die. She wouldn't.

Jacey blinked away the rush of tears that filled her eyes, threatening to spill over. She loved him too much, and if he wouldn't fight the fever, she would fight it for him.

Once again, she began wiping his heated skin with the cloth. Over and over, she tried to cool his burning skin. At last, exhausted, she sank back into the chair and rested her head against the top.

For only a moment, she told herself.

Sometime later, she jerked awake at a muffled outcry.

"Mmm," Stryker mumbled.

She sat forward, scooting her chair closer to the bed, and felt his forehead with her hand. The fever still held him.

He mumbled something again.

She leaned closer, attempting to catch what he was trying to say.

"Stryker?" she prompted.

"Madeline?"

Jacey's breath froze at the name uttered from his parched lips. No, he couldn't be asking for his former fiancée.

She rested her hand on his possessively. "Stryker?" she spoke past the lump in her throat. "It's Jacey. I'm here with you. I—"

"Madeline!"

Jacey sucked in her breath, then forcefully calmed herself.

"Stryker," she tried again. "It's Jacey—"

He threw out an arm as if reaching for something. Or someone.

"Come back. Madeline, darling, come back."

Jacey jerked back, feeling as if she had been slapped. She didn't think he could have said anything that could have hurt her more than hearing him call for his former intended, begging her to come back to him.

She tried to tell herself it was the fever making him think of the other woman. Fever such as his made people do and think strange things. She knew it from her work with the doctor in Baltimore. She kept telling herself this, and almost succeeded in convincing herself. Almost, but not quite.

The seed of doubt settled in the back of her mind, waiting for the slightest thing to foster it into full growth. She sank back into the chair, surrendering to the exhaustion claiming her body.

Hours later, Stryker jerked awake with a start, his right hand reaching for his gun. His gun belt was gone and his gun along with it.

He attempted to sit up, but something or someone held him down. He pushed at the barrier, finally succeeding in shoving it out of his way. As he sat up, pain shot through his chest, robbing him of the power of breathing.

The memories came back to him in scattered bits. Gunfire . . . the bank robbers . . . Rosalyn stepping out of the doorway. . . .

Was she wounded?

No, he recalled taking her to the ground and safely away from the gunfire. He closed his eyes and once again felt the searing jolt of the bullet hitting him.

He had been the one shot. He remembered the burning pain, the bullet tearing into him, and the horrible weakness that had overcome him when he needed to act. Opening his eyes, he leaned up onto one elbow, but the pain nearly crushed his chest.

Fighting for breath, he slid back down into the softness beneath him. Within a moment, he could breathe again. This time he only lifted his head to look around.

In his mind's eye, he saw Rosalyn lying on the boardwalk, her hands over her head. Near the horse trough, he could see Brett raising upright. No, he flung out his hand, but couldn't reach his friend.

"Brett!" he shouted out the warning.

Then Jacey's face came into his blurred vision. He blinked, and she wavered before him. He raised a hand to shove her down to safety, but couldn't summon the strength to move her away.

"No," he cried out. "Get away," he ordered in a hoarse, strangled voice. "Get away."

Shoving with all his strength, he pushed her back away from him. He heard her cry out an instant before the darkness claimed him again.

Jacey stepped back to Stryker's bedside. As she reached out to pull the sheet up to his chest, a single tear rolled down her cheek. She sank into the chair beside the bed, fighting the tears that burned behind her eyes.

His words resounded and resounded in her head.

"Get away," he had shouted at her.

She tried to tell herself it was his wound, but his words had rung so true and so desperate she had to believe them. He didn't want her anymore.

A light tap at the door jerked her up. Raising her chin and scrubbing at the trace of the single tear, she crossed to the door and swung it open.

Mrs. Carson stood in the hall. "How is he? Has the fever broke?"

Jacey shook her head, unable to speak past the lump closing off her throat.

The woman's eyes clouded with sympathy. "Dear, why don't you go sleep awhile? I'll watch him."

"No, I can't." Jacey barely got the words out. She couldn't leave him now, not with the fever trying to claim him. He needed her to help him fight. No matter what he had told her.

"You need to get some sleep," Mrs. Carson insisted.

Without realizing it, Jacey raised her chin in desperation. "Not until the fever's broke."

The other woman smiled at her in understanding. "All right. I've brought some fresh, cold water."

"Thank you."

Jacey took the pitcher of water and glanced back to the bed. Stryker lay still and unmoving, but a tiny nose peeked out from under the bed. It was confession time.

"Ah, I found a kitten and brought it to the house," she admitted in a low voice.

"That's nice, dear," Mrs. Carson said absently. "It will help take your mind off worrying so much."

"Thank you," Jacey said.

"I was wondering about that milk. That explains it." She shook her head and smiled. "You need me, or if there's a change, you just holler for me." Giving Jacey a comforting pat on the shoulder, Mrs. Carson returned downstairs.

Jacey crossed to the bed. Bending over Stryker, she noticed beads of sweat on his forhead. Relief nearly caused her to crumple, and she sat on the edge of the bed suddenly weak in the knees.

The bed shook beneath her, and she whirled to stare at Stryker. He shivered, the action causing the mattress to move again. Jacey's heart sank. Now that the fever had broken, chills racked his body.

She pulled the covers up to his chin, but he shoved them away. His body convulsed in a violent shiver. He couldn't go on this way. He could rip out the doctor's stitches.

Quickly, Jacey kicked off her shoes and crawled under the sheets with him. Pulling the covers over him, she clamped an arm around his waist to keep him from dislodging the blankets again. She snuggled close against him, willing her body heat to warm him. Stryker stiffened a moment; then his body relaxed, and she heard his breathing even out. At last he slept peacefully.

She rested her head on the edge of the pillow and let a sigh slip out. He was going to be all right. She was sure of it now. The warmth of his body next to hers, combined with the relief and simple exhaustion, lulled her to sleep at his side. She slept soundly through the night with her head close to his, sharing the feather pillow.

The next morning, sunlight streamed through the window, bringing Jacey slowly awake. She felt warm and cozy in the bed. She snuggled against the warmth behind her back, not awake enough yet to think.

"Morning," Stryker mumbled in a hoarse voice near her ear.

Jacey turned over so fast she nearly fell out of the bed. Her eyes met Stryker's clear gaze.

"You're awake," she cried out with happiness.

"I think," he murmured, then shook his head as if to clear it.

"Lie still," Jacey ordered, resting a hand on his arm. "You'll pull your stitches."

"What stitches?"

She studied him closely for any sign of fever. There wasn't any. His gaze was level and clear on her.

"The ones in your chest. You were shot stopping a bank robbery," she told him in a soft voice.

He closed his eyes and groaned in remembrance. "Yeah, I remember now."

"Lie still. I'll get you some water." She eased back the covers. "And something to eat." A smile of happiness lit her face.

"Umm." He cleared his throat; then against her instructions he leaned up on one elbow.

"Lie down," she ordered.

Suddenly the covers at the foot of the bed moved, and a small head poked out. A blur of cream, brown and rust tumbled forward, then suddenly stopped.

Stryker jerked back against the pillow. "What the hell is that?"

Jacey winced at his strangled shout. She glanced down to see Tinker backing up against the covers. Blue eyes glittering, she began spitting at Stryker.

"That's my kitten, Tinker—"

"Tinker?" His voice gathered strength, and a slight edge of concern.

"Yes. I found her a few days ago. She'd been abandoned, and I've been taking care of her."

"Jacey—"

"She isn't a bother. Honest, you'll hardly know she's around."

"Jacey—" he tried again, inching his feet away from the animal bit by bit.

"Let me keep her?" she asked in a pleading voice. She reached toward the kitten, but Stryker grabbed her arm, stopping her.

"Jacey, don't touch it. That's a damn wild cat!"

Chapter Fifteen

"No, you're wrong," Jacey argued. "It's a kitten. I found it—"

Stryker kept hold of her arm with his uninjured one. "Listen to me. I know what that thing is."

"But—"

"That's no tame house cat. That's an ocelot."

"A what?"

"An ocelot. A *wild* cat."

Jacey turned her head and studied her pet. Granted, Tinker didn't look exactly like the kittens she had seen back home in Baltimore, but surely it wasn't "wild." Could it be true? Could the fluffy kitten be a wild cat?

No, she refused to believe it. Stryker hadn't fully recovered yet. He wasn't seeing her pet clearly. He would react differently later when he felt better.

"Don't worry." She eased her arm from his hold. "You lie back and rest. I'll take Tinker out of here, and you can meet her again when you've rested and are feeling like yourself."

Stryker groaned and closed his eyes. "That's no kitten. Will you listen to me." He forced his eyes open, but his voice sounded weary. "Get rid of that thing," he ordered as his eyes drifted closed again.

"I will," she assured him.

As he fell into sleep, she hurriedly scooped Tinker up into her arms, rubbing her behind the ears to soothe her. The kitten snuggled into her. Tiptoeing out of the room, she placed the kitten into the other bedroom before going downstairs to tell Mrs. Carson the news of Stryker's recovery.

She was certain he would see things clearer after he had slept and eaten something. Meanwhile, it might be wise to keep her pet and herself out of sight for a little while. And she had gotten rid of Tinker as he had ordered. She merely had done it in her own way by putting the kitten out of his sight.

By the next afternoon, with no sign or mention of the cat, Stryker convinced himself that he had hallucinated the entire episode with the ocelot. It didn't make any sense that Jacey had brought a wild cat into the house, much less into his bed. The memory was jumbled together with a vague dream about Madeline jilting him, Brett being shot, and something about Jacey leaving him.

He shook his head to clear it. In another day or so, the pieces would straighten themselves out. According to Jacey he had had a bad fever, nearly scaring her to death.

A memory of her body snuggled up against his, her arm wrapped around his waist, tantalized him. He could almost feel her hands stroking him with the cloth, the recollection was so vivid. He drifted off to sleep with a smile on his face.

Over the next two days, Stryker slept and obediently ate the rich broth prepared by Mrs. Carson to speed his healing. Well, maybe obedient wasn't an accurate word, Jacey thought, as she attempted to coax him into finishing the latest bowl she had been feeding him.

He pushed it away. "No more broth."

"But you need nourishment."

"Then, get me a real meal," he insisted.

"You're not ready for that yet," she told him firmly.

"I'm ready for a lot more than you think." He flashed her a grin.

The gleam in his eyes caught her off guard. Had he forgotten what he had said to her days ago? She looked away and clenched her teeth against the rush of pain that accompanied the memory of his harsh order for her to "get away." He had even repeated the words to her. Twice he had told her to "get away." But she couldn't leave while he was so ill.

Disobeying his order, she had stayed, refusing to leave the ranch until he was well. She stiffened her resolve against both the memory and the pain and forced herself to look back at him.

Stryker smiled at her softly, his lips tipping up at the corners. That smile made her heart nearly flip over in her chest. He still had that devastating gleam in his eyes. He couldn't mean what she thought he meant. He couldn't be wanting to make love to her. Could he?

Was it possible the fever had made him say those hateful words? Had he not meant them? Perhaps he did not even remember uttering them.

Gathering up her courage around her, she opened her mouth and asked, "Do you want me to leave?"

She held her breath waiting for his answer. It seemed

her entire future hung in the balance of his response. If he said yes, she would pack her things and go. He was well enough now, and she couldn't bear the pain of staying when he no longer wanted her around.

Stryker frowned at her, and she waited. Questioning. Daring to draw faint hope at his long pause.

"Leave? Why?" he asked.

She sucked in a tiny bit of air, then pressed on. "Leave here."

His frown deepened. "Not unless it's to bring me something to eat other than this watered-down meal."

Jacey smiled, her heart lifting with her lips. He didn't remember. It had been the fever talking, not him. She closed her eyes a moment in silent thanksgiving, then impulsively leaned forward and kissed him quickly on the lips.

"I'll be right back." She whirled around, bowl in hand, and dashed for the door.

"Jacey?"

Smiling, she took the stairs at a near run. He was hungry. That was a wonderful sign of his full recovery.

"Jacey!" His shout echoed down the stairs. "Come back here."

She looked back over her shoulder and laughed gaily. Yes, he was recovering.

Perhaps after he ate, it was time to introduce him to Tinker again.

Jacey stalled on taking the kitten to Stryker's room. Hank, the ranch foreman, had confirmed that Tinker was an ocelot, but remarkably tame and very young. The latter made her even more determined to keep the kitten.

After cuddling Tinker a moment, she set her on the floor and squared her shoulders. It was near supper time.

She would wait until afterward to introduce Stryker and her pet. She waited through his meal, sitting with him beside the bed. She even waited while he rested. She told herself he needed to build up his strength.

Later that evening she finally admitted she was using any excuse to delay the encounter. She had to stop. It was time Stryker and Tinker met again.

She crossed her fingers beneath the kitten's soft tummy and tapped lightly on the bedroom door. She had it all planned out. First, she would wake Stryker gently, maybe with a kiss; then she would introduce him to her new pet.

"Stryker?" she called out softly, easing the door open a crack.

"Jacey." He was sitting up in the bed, his back propped against a pillow.

She worried her lower lip a moment, then pushed the door open and stepped inside. "Stryker, there's someone I'd like you to—"

"What the—" he roared at her.

Tinker startled, arching her back in Jacey's arms.

"Stryker, you're scaring her."

"Scaring *her!*" He rubbed the back of his neck with his hand. "I thought I'd dreamt that thing."

"Her name is—"

"I don't care what its name is. I thought I ordered you to get rid of that thing," he shouted.

"You were delirious from the fever then."

"No, I wasn't. And what am I now?"

She grimaced. "You're angry."

"You're right," he muttered.

He stared at the ocelot kitten in Jacey's arms. The thing stared back at him with large blue eyes. It snuggled back down in her arms and blinked at him.

"That thing can't be more than a few weeks old," he observed.

"All the more reason to keep her."

"Jacey," he warned.

"Don't you see, she'd never survive if I abandoned her out there." She gestured with one hand to the window.

"It's a wild animal—"

"No, she isn't. Look. She's as tame as a kitten."

To emphasize her point, she set the kitten on the bed. It bounded over to where Stryker's feet lay beneath the covers and pounced on them.

"Yeow," he yelped, scooting his feet away.

"She didn't bite you," Jacey admonished.

"It attacked."

Jacey laughed outright. "She's playing, like any tame cat." She shrugged one shoulder. "She just likes feet."

"Yeah, for a meal."

He eyed the ocelot warily as she waddled over to his feet again, then snuggled down against them.

"Hank says she'll only eat mice and birds."

"Hank knows about it?"

She gave him a frustrated look. "Yes, and so does Mrs. Carson."

When he opened his mouth, she quickly added, "And Tinker has won them both over."

She didn't bother to tell him that feat had taken a lot of time, and apologies, and effort on her part, especially after Tinker dashed out and startled Mrs. Carson into dropping a plate of biscuits.

"Jacey, you have to get rid of it."

"Stryker, I can't get rid of her. I can't. Please don't ask me to."

"I'm not asking you, I'm telling you."

She raised her chin and faced him. He nearly groaned aloud. He knew by that defiant gesture she wasn't going to simply obey him meekly. Not his Jacey.

His Jacey?

The thought hit him hard. When had he started to think of her in that way?

He stared up at her in surprise. Her eyes met his, and he saw a spark of stubborn defiance. It brought him back to the matter at hand.

"Jacey—"

"No!" She stomped one foot in emphasis.

This time he did groan aloud.

Quickly, she reached across the bed and plucked up the ocelot. Snuggling it close to her chest, she backed away from him. Her withdrawal startled him and bothered him more than he wanted to admit.

"Stryker, I've never had a pet of my own before." She swallowed and added the word, "Please."

She turned her head away, but not before he saw the sheen of tears in her eyes.

"Stryker, please . . ." Her voice wavered, then broke.

As he watched her, one tear slid down her cheek to her chin, then dropped onto the bodice of her soft pink gown.

If she had broken into sobs, he could have withstood that act. He had given in to Madeline's sobbing fits too many times in the past to be affected by those kinds of tears. He had learned his lesson well and sworn never to let a woman's crying affect him again.

He swallowed and groaned under his breath. He had no defense against Jacey's silent, pain-filled tears. Not the few silent drops that slipped free. He could see she was trying to hold them back so hard that her shoulders stiffened until he thought they would snap into pieces.

"Jacey," he said softly.

She didn't answer, only wiped a hand over her cheek and kept her face averted from him.

"All right," he muttered. "You can keep it. Only keep it away from—"

He never finished his instruction. She quickly set the

kitten on the floor and practically threw herself into his arms.

"Thank you."

She kissed him soundly on the lips, and when she started to pull away and stand, he reached out and held her to him. Pressing his hand against her back, he eased her back down atop him.

"Your wound," she murmured against his mouth.

"Is fine," he whispered, before taking her lips in a kiss that settled all argument.

Jacey melted into his tender embrace, hungry for his touch. Mindful of his wound, she eased her weight to the side, and he rolled to his side, never lessening his hold on her. It was as if he was afraid she would disappear.

There was an urgency to their caresses. Stryker kissed her, savoring her taste as never before. It felt as if this were the first time they had made love, or was it just more precious after coming so close to losing each other forever in death.

He held her close in his embrace, taking her mouth in kiss after breath-stealing kiss. Jacey returned his passion, her own rising to a new pitch never reached before. She had come so close to losing him, first to death, then to his fevered order for her to leave. She ran her hands down his body, cupping him. It was as if she couldn't touch him enough. She needed to feel his skin against hers to chase away the fears of losing him.

Stryker sighed deeply in pure enjoyment of her touch, then began to unfasten her gown. Slowly, he eased each button free, leaning back only to slide the gown from her shoulders to expose her breasts. He hooked the straps of her chemise with his thumbs and pulled it down.

As he fused their mouths together again, Jacey raised her hips and shoved her clothing down. Kicking it aside, she snuggled into him. He cupped her breast with one hand, then ran his palm down over her rib cage to her waist and lower. He traced the outline of her hip and ran his hand around to the small of her back. He pulled her tighter against him, sliding his palm over her backside and holding her to him.

Jacey felt his swollen desire and sighed her surrender into his kiss. He took her surrender and gave up his own control as she ran her palm along his side to slide her hand between them and hold him.

Stryker groaned against her lips, easing her mouth open to plunder the velvet softness. Jacey gave back to him, touch for touch until pleasure gripped her, carrying her higher and higher in its grasp.

As she began to come down, he slid his knee between her legs and rolled her to her back. With infinite tenderness, he slid into her, savoring the feel of her wrapped around him. She arched her back to meet him, nearly driving him over the edge.

They made love gently, tenderly, as never before. This time bound them together with threads of steel that held them tightly, even as they soared for the heavens together.

Stryker was smiling the next day when Brett stopped in for a visit. He motioned his friend to a chair beside the bed.

"You're looking good," Brett observed.

"I've had good nursing."

His friend laughed, then put a hand to his head and groaned. "Maybe we should keep it quiet for you."

Stryker chuckled at the suggestion. "Maybe it's your hangover that needs low voices."

Brett nodded, then groaned again.

"Looks like you outdid yourself."

"Even worse. I barely remember last night. Madeline

waltzed into the saloon and bought me a bottle. Seems Bertram is out of town for a day or two and she was lonely."

Brett glanced at Stryker for his reaction. There was none. "You have any problems with that?"

Stryker smiled and shook his head. "You're welcome to her, but watch yourself. Another night like last night and—"

"I've sworn off whiskey."

"Sure you have," Stryker taunted. "May I remind you of that vow in a month?"

"All right. I'm swearing off at least for a while."

Stryker chuckled again.

"Hank told me Jacey has a new pet."

"Brett, she's keeping a wild cat in the house as her pet." Stryker leaned back against the headboard to watch his friend's reaction.

Brett crossed his foot over his knee and leaned back in the chair. Laughter filled the room. It took him a full minute to stop before he could speak.

"You are kidding, aren't you?" A touch of doubt tinged Brett's voice as he stared at the man in bed. "She doesn't have a—"

Stryker groaned. "I only wish I were. And yes, she has adopted an ocelot."

"A what?" Brett's foot hit the floor with a *thump*.

Stryker couldn't help but grin at the other man's reaction. Brett looked about the same way Stryker suspected he had looked when he first saw the kitten. On his bed no less.

"An ocelot," Stryker enunciated clearly.

"I heard you the first time; I just didn't believe you said it," Brett snapped.

"You should have been in my place when the thing pounced out from the covers on the foot of the bed."

Brett stared in shock, then burst into fresh laughter. "That I would have loved to see."

"Don't say I didn't warn you. The thing bounds out at the oddest moments."

"It's in the house?"

Stryker hesitated, not willing to admit he had given in to Jacey's pleas. The fact still goaded him. He feared he was becoming as controlled as he had once been with Madeline years ago. He had sworn he would never again hop to do a woman's bidding, and here he was doing just that thing.

A little voice whispered softly in his mind, *But this time it's different.*

He shook his head to dispel the disturbing thoughts. Brett stared at him in confusion.

"Which is it? Yes or no? Is that thing in the house?" He looked around uneasily, lifting his feet off the floor.

Stryker chuckled. "You're safe. She's keeping it out of my sight. For now."

The other man gingerly set his feet back down onto the wooden floor. Then he looked to the door as if to make certain it was tightly closed.

A grin tugged at Stryker's lips, and he held it in check with an effort. He couldn't resist goading his friend a little bit. "Beware in the rest of the house," he warned.

"What do you mean?"

"According to Mrs. Carson, the kitten rules the household. Prowls wherever it chooses." Stryker sneaked a glance at his friend.

Apprehension strained Brett's face, and once again he flicked a glance to the door, then shifted uneasily in his chair.

"Hear tell it's taken to hunting, too."

"Hunting?" the other man's voice rose a notch.

"Yup. Hunting. In my own house." Stryker lowered his voice so his friend had to lean closer to hear what he had to say. He wasn't going to reveal the kitten's prey was the straw broom. Not just yet.

Brett shifted in the chair again, and Stryker knew he had him right where he wanted him. He paused, long enough to make his friend uneasy.

"Yup. It attacked Mrs. Carson's—"

"What?" Brett shouted, jumping to his feet.

"Broom. Almost knocked it right out of her hands." As he watched comprehension dawn on his friend's face, he let his laughter free.

"That was uncalled for."

Stryker's laughter eased to a chuckle. "Oh, I enjoyed it immensely."

Brett dropped back into the chair, crossing his arms. "So it was all a joke. I knew there wasn't any wild cat in the house. I never believed it for a moment."

"Well, you'd better believe that part. It's true. Jacey has even named her new pet. Tinker. Can you believe that? A wild cat with an innocent name like that."

"Well, I'm glad to see you're feeling good enough to joke around. Even if it was at my cost."

Stryker's lips twitched, but he resisted laughing again. He would let his friend see for himself the truth about that blasted cat. According to Mrs. Carson, the kitten greeted each new visitor in the same manner. Tinker hid behind or under something, her blue eyes gleaming in anticipation. Once the visitor stood still for any length of time, the ocelot dashed out of hiding and pounced on the person's feet. He grinned at the memory of Jake's meeting with the new pet. He had heard the yells all the way up here.

"What are you smiling at?" Brett asked, suddenly suspicious.

"Nothing. I'm just feeling better."

Stryker couldn't wait to hear about the upcoming

encounter between his friend and the ocelot. He grinned at Brett. Yup, he was definitely looking forward to it. It would be amusing as anything, and pay him back for the shivaree prank with the bed.

Brett stood, eyeing him warily. "I'd better be getting on back to town."

"Thanks for stopping in," Stryker answered. "I appreciated the entertainment."

"Entertainment?"

Hiding his smile, Stryker said, "Your visit."

"Yeah." Brett turned, with a confused look on his face. Stryker heard him mutter something that sounded like, "Must be the fever."

Then Brett walked across the room and into the hall.

"Leave the door open, will you?" Stryker called out.

"Sure thing. See you later."

Smiling, Stryker crossed his arms and waited. He was certain he would be seeing his friend again real soon. He didn't have long to wait for his shivaree's revenge.

Sure enough, within minutes he heard Brett's yell, followed by a few choice swear words. Then the sound of footsteps pounded up the stairs. Stryker cocked his head and greeted Brett with a smile.

"Problems?"

Brett crossed the threshold and slammed the door shut, then winced at the loud noise. "Hang your hide. That *thing* attacked me!"

Stryker laughed at his friend's indignant look. "According to Jacey, her kitten Tinker merely likes feet to play with." He raised an eyebrow.

"You're actually letting her keep it?"

Chagrined at the question, Stryker shrugged. "Seems so."

"What did she do to get you to agree to it?"

A wry grin tugged at his lips, and he looked away when he answered, "She cried."

"And you fell for that trick? She manipulated you, old friend. And you fell for it."

Brett glanced down to examine his boot for damage and missed the suddenly harsh look that crossed Stryker's face.

"It seems I'm not the only who fell for a trick," Brett observed in a derisive tone. Turning quickly, he strode out of the room, leaving Stryker staring after him.

The joke on his friend left a bad taste in his mouth. And a worse feeling in his gut.

Trick . . . Manipulated you . . . You fell for it. . . .

Brett's words hit their mark, making him feel a fool. Did Jacey control him so much that even Brett could see it? With only a few tears, she had reduced him to do her bidding, precisely as she had wanted. And likely as not had planned.

Disgust rose up in him at the loss of his self-control. He had always prided himself on that, on being able to set the limits himself. Now a woman had taken that power from him. And he didn't like it one bit.

He was becoming ensnared by Jacey, as surely as a rabbit in a hunter's trap. The knowledge shook him to his core. He didn't want to feel this for her, or on account of her. Hadn't he learned his lesson with Madeline? She had nearly destroyed him with her manipulations and deceptions. He had sworn, vowed on his badge, he would never allow it to happen again.

It was happening now.

He refused to accept it as the truth. He could change the fact. And he would.

Bit by painful bit, he began to withdraw emotionally from the hold he felt Jacey had over him. He would never allow her to deceive and manipulate him to her biding.

Never again, he vowed.

The ache in his shoulder intensified, but somewhere deep inside another ache began, stronger and immune to any effort to relieve the pain.

Chapter Sixteen

The longer Stryker stayed in the bed, the more disgusted with himself he got. He had been lying abed too long and letting Jacey order him about. While he admitted he had enjoyed the time apart from the rest of the word with his new wife, it had come to an end. He had been a fool.

She was no different from Madeline with her tricks and schemes. She was no different from any other woman. Although he told himself the fact, a part of him stubbornly refused to accept it.

Anger and disgust built up in him. He hated nothing worse than being played for a fool, and Jacey had played him brilliantly. He had been so wrapped up in her, he hadn't seen the truth until Brett pointed it out.

It was past time he got back to work—work he had neglected in order to spend more time with Jacey. It was time he started the process of putting Jacey out of his life.

When she entered the room some time later, Stryker avoided meeting her eyes. He couldn't risk one look at her destroying his resolve. She had that much power over him.

He harshly reminded himself their marriage was a sham, a "bargain" she had readily agreed upon for sufficient money from him. His features hardened at the memory of the mercenary woman of the letters. Turning a measured gaze on her, he studied her every move.

"How are you feeling?" she asked, her voice lilting.

It reminded him of a bird's call. Or the call of a siren waiting to entrap a man.

"Fine," he answered in a flat tone.

Jacey blinked as if taken aback, then smiled at him almost shyly as she set the lunch tray across his lap. He tensed at the close contact, shifting away from her.

At his sudden movement, a sense of unease skittered across Jacey's shoulders, almost as if someone had shut out the warmth of the sun. She glanced over at the window and at the cloudy sky outside. She hoped it wouldn't rain. She hated dark, rainy days.

When she turned back to Stryker, her smile bright again, he didn't return it. His lips remained in a firm line. His expression was shuttered, closing her out as effectively as if he had slammed a door on her intrusion.

Something was wrong. She could sense it in the depths of her being.

The tender, loving man of the night was gone. He had changed somehow, replaced by the stranger in the bed who watched her closely. Too closely. And without any show of tender regard in his gaze. No, she saw something else there. Something that chilled her to the bone, even more effectively than the eastern winter snow storms back home.

She saw doubt and distrust. Her heart skipped a beat. Had he found the wanted poster? She was certain she had hidden it away carefully.

She studied him from lowered lashes. The problem couldn't be the wanted poster. Stryker was too straight forward of a man, too much of a lawman, not to mention it outright. No, something else was bothering him.

Another moment passed, and her concern grew into actual fear. Had Stryker somehow learned of her deception? Did he know he had married the wrong woman?

The more time she spent with him, the more she came to know about the man behind the badge. Honesty was as much a part of him as the blood running through his veins. He would never be able to understand the twins' reasons for deceiving him and trading places for the trip to Texas, much less for the marriage. She stiffened her back to hold off the shudder prompted by her disturbing thoughts.

She had to know.

She forced her lips to form the question. "Is something wrong?"

As she waited for his answer, she knew she was holding her breath, but she couldn't help herself.

"I think you should move back to the other bedroom," he announced.

"Why?"

When he didn't answer immediately, she rushed on, her inner doubts about their marriage forcing her to prod him. "Are you saying last night was a mistake?"

He met and held her gaze for the space of a heartbeat, and Jacey was certain hers had stopped beating.

"Yes."

His answer was spoken in a voice so low that she missed the agony behind it.

Jacey jerked back as if she had taken a blow. She felt like she had, straight to the heart.

What had happened last night had been wonderful, precious, something to be treasured by both of them. The loving between them had changed her. She knew that fact with all her being. It had bound her to Stryker as surely as if metal chains had been wrapped and fastened around her heart.

To him it had merely been a mistake.

Whirling around, she forced herself to walk, not run, out of the room with all the dignity she could muster. She held her tattered dignity like a cloak against the harsh winter winds. Today the sun hadn't shone in more ways than one. She was chilled clear through, all the way to her heart.

Her pride would not allow her to show him how deeply his answer had cut her. She would never let him know he had sliced clear to her heart, not when he didn't feel the way about her that she felt about him. She knew no one could force another person to love them; it had to come from the heart of its own free will. Exiting with deliberate movements, she shut the door quietly behind her.

Something had happened. And she had to find out what it was before it destroyed her.

She swallowed past the growing lump in her throat. She had thought after last night that her marriage with Stryker had been heaven-sent, that he returned her love, but now she knew differently. Every time she drew close to him, he pushed her away.

Something prevented him from loving anyone in return.

Somehow she knew the reasons behind his actions lay in his past in Braddock. Her suspicions told her they might well lay directly at the feet of Madeline Raines.

She intended to find out one way or another.

Glancing out a hall window, she realized it was too late to go into town for answers. But tomorrow—tomorrow she would learn the truth.

She opened the door to the other bedroom and closed it with a decisive click. The sound woke Tinker from her nap on the bed pillow. Stretching, the kitten ambled to the foot of the bed where she sat down and yawned.

Jacey crossed to the bed and scooped her up. She snuggled the kitten to her chest, needing the soft comfort her pet readily offered.

For today, she would accept Tinker's comfort, think things out, and make a plan. Tomorrow, she would go to Braddock.

One way or another, she would learn the truth before the next day was out.

Brett's day progressed from bad to worse. Once he reached town, he suffered the misfortune of bumping into the two owners of the town's boardinghouse.

"Good afternoon, Brett." Linda spotted him first. "Rosalyn, it's Brett."

He held back his groan. While he cared for the two ladies dearly, they almost always managed to con him into or out of something. He never could figure out how they did it. They always got the better of him. And it bothered him more than he liked to admit to himself. He absolutely refused to admit the fact to anyone else. Even Stryker.

Brett tipped his hat to the women. "Good day, ladies. How are you two doing today?"

"We're fine, but you don't look at all well," Rosalyn observed to his chagrin.

His smile wavered a bit.

Rosalyn hurried to his side and slipped her hand into the crook of his elbow. "Oh, dear boy, come on home with us for a spell." She patted his arm with her other hand. "We'll have a nice chat."

"A cup of our special tea will have you feeling better in no time," Linda told him as she crossed to his other side and slipped her hand through his other arm.

"No time at all," Rosalyn added.

Brett felt decidedly uncomfortable. In fact, he felt like a trapped animal. He glanced from one woman to the other. They both beamed smiles at him. He didn't trust those too-innocent smiles in the least.

The women's reputation for ferreting out any gossip in town disturbed him. He had too much to hide today to dare spend much time in their company.

"Thank you, ladies. But I really have to be—"

"Oh, we wouldn't hear of you refusing," Rosalyn insisted, patting his hand.

Brett had the sudden unexplained urge to bolt.

As if sensing his intention, both women tightened their hold on him. Against his polite protests, they shanghaied him to the boardinghouse.

And for the life of him, he couldn't figure out how they accomplished the feat.

Once settled at the kitchen table with a cup of fragrant, steaming tea in his hand, Brett knew he couldn't hold out against their combined efforts. But he continued to attempt to hide his guilt-ridden secret.

His conscience bothered him. He hadn't told his friend Stryker the full truth about last night. He hadn't forgotten the night of drinking like he had said. Truth was, he remembered everything about it. Even worse, he desperately needed to tell someone who would understand.

Rosalyn and Linda's friendly concern over him and the way he looked was his final undoing. The two women were practiced experts at gently wheedling out the information they needed. With Brett, it didn't take much prodding to learn the facts of the night before.

At long last, he divulged in detail what he had foolishly revealed under Madeline's careful prompting.

Once again, he talked too much.

* * *

The next day Jacey stepped down out of the buggy in front of the mercantile store.

"Thank you, Hank." She smiled up at the ranch foreman.

It had taken her more than ten minutes of cajoling, and finally the promise of a plate of bear sign, to convince him to drive her into town.

"Can't figure what you needed so bad today," he said, hinting at his curiosity.

She merely smiled back at him. "I needed a few woman's things."

His cheeks flushed, and he didn't meet her eyes. She barely suppressed her smile. She had known the answer was guaranteed to put off any further questions.

"I shouldn't be more than an hour," she assured him. "Why don't I meet you at the livery?"

"No, ma'am." He shook his head adamantly. "I'll be back here with the buggy in less than an hour's time."

"Very well."

Apparently a woman wandering into the livery stables wasn't done in Braddock. She shrugged at the thought, then stepped up onto the boardwalk. She hadn't taken more than two steps when someone hailed her.

"Miss Jacey, ah, Mrs. Stryker!" a man called out.

She turned around to recognize the telegraph operator heading for her. He quickly grabbed his hat off his head and smiled at her as he drew even with her.

"Good morning, Matt," she greeted.

"Morning, ma'am." He shifted his feet. "Ah, how's the marshal doing?"

"He's much better."

"Ah, that's real good." He fidgeted with unease.

Jacey felt sympathy for his nervousness. "How are you doing today?" she asked.

The young man swallowed before he answered, "Fine, ma'am." He suddenly thrust out his hand toward her. "I got two telegrams came in for you. Wanted to get them right to you."

Her throat closed off for a moment.

Two telegrams.

She swallowed tightly and forced a smile. At least she thought she was smiling. One of the messages was likely from Jeanette. She cringed at that possibility.

The other message she didn't want to think on yet. She grasped the two folded papers from him and murmured her thanks through stiff lips.

Catching up her skirt, she walked off in the opposite direction, attempting to garner a bit of privacy to read the two missives. Something told her she wouldn't want anyone else to know the contents.

She stopped on the boardwalk in an out-of-the-way spot and read the first telegram. As suspected it was from Jeanette. The words made her catch her breath and let out a groan.

Jeanette would arrive tomorrow.

Jacey squeezed her eyes shut and sucked in a deep breath. Tomorrow her twin would learn that Jacey was married. Jeanette would learn she had in fact married *her* fiancé. The man her twin had asked her to "hang on to" for *her*.

Jacey winced at the upcoming reunion with her twin. Without a doubt, all kinds of trouble would break loose.

Sighing, she turned her attention to the second telegram. Her mouth dropped open immediately. As she read, her sigh turned into a groan.

Could things get any worse? she wondered in dismay.

She stared in frustration at the unwanted message from her cousin Earl.

Have tracked the runaways. Stop. Am coming to take you home. Stop. Such disgrace. Stop.

Somehow he had tracked the twins here. He would ensure everyone within hearing range knew of her disgrace. She could tell that fact by his tersely worded message. Disgusted, she shoved both telegrams into her reticule.

First things first. She needed to locate Madeline Raines and have a little "chat" with her. Raising her chin in silent determination, she felt as if she was readying herself for battle.

As if her thoughts had conjured the woman up, Jacey turned to see Madeline crossing the dusty street. The woman was headed straight for the spot where Jacey stood. That fact made her decidedly uneasy. She had planned to be the one in charge of this confrontation, not Madeline.

There was nothing to do but wait for the other woman to reach the boardwalk. Jacey resisted the urge to tap her foot with impatience.

"Good morning, Mrs. Raines." Jacey made certain she got out the first greeting. It would give her the advantage of striking first.

Madeline's lips turned up into a sneer. "Yes, it is a good morning, isn't it?" She gestured to the cloudy sky above them. "Would you care to get out of the dust and talk civilly in the restaurant?"

The offer put Jacey instantly on her guard. She didn't particularly want anyone eavesdropping on their conversation.

"Why don't we just walk a bit?" Jacey's firm voice ensured the suggestion would be taken as an order. She took a step forward, forcing the other woman to accompany her or be left behind with her mouth hanging open.

Madeline's sigh of disgust left no doubt as to her opinion on the suggested walk. "Yes, I do suppose you'd like to keep my news quiet."

Jacey nearly stumbled on the uneven wood planking. "Your news?"

The other woman lightly touched her arm, and Jacey felt the chill clear through to her bone. The smile Madeline fastened on her was cruel and triumphant, causing Jacey's stomach to knot uncomfortably.

"Yes, I do suppose you're curious. Such a distasteful trait," Madeline observed.

As Jacey opened her mouth to retort, the other woman cut her off.

"Don't be too hasty to speak. That is, before you hear that I've learned your little secret. I truly must admire Stryker for thinking up the plan. It's positively ingenious. Bertram would never suspect a thing."

Jacey resisted the overwhelming impulse to prompt the other woman. Instead, she merely raised her brows at the woman's insult of her banker husband.

"Why, yes. I heard all about it from Brett. You do know of Brett Mason? Stryker's best friend."

Jacey merely nodded in affirmation.

Madeline smiled widely. "Dear Brett. He does have a problem when he drinks of talking too much." She laughed gaily. "Everyone knows he can't keep a secret to save his soul."

"I do hope you have a point," Jacey prompted.

"What a sense of humor you possess. But then, I guess you needed one to go through with this. I admit it is funny." She paused a moment, savoring her revenge. "A temporary marriage bargain. What a marvelous idea."

Jacey heard the words and then a roar in her ears, shutting out everything around her.

Temporary?

She stared at the other woman. It couldn't be true. It couldn't, she denied. But the smug look of triumph on Madeline's face told her it was true.

Jacey bit her lower lip until she tasted the sharp, coppery sting of blood. Smoothing her tongue over her lip, she drew in a bracing breath.

"No—"

"Ohh, yes, my dear. I heard it all straight from Brett. It seems Stryker confided his little plan to him. Send for a mail order bride to get the town husbands off his back." She paused to ask, "You did know he was a womanizer?" With a dismissing wave of her hand, she continued, "Then shortly after the wedding he'd send the little wife packing with no one the wiser."

Disbelief and shock warred in Jacey. She clenched her hands around her reticule. Her hands felt cold; then the sensation crept through her entire body. She felt rooted in place. No, she had been frozen into place, she corrected.

Frozen by the cold, calculating plan that Stryker had devised. Her blood turned to ice, and her heart surely shattered into a hundred pieces.

"You're lying," Jacey said, her voice wavering.

Madeline merely smiled.

"Brett wouldn't—"

"Oh, but he did."

"No."

"Brett doesn't lie well at all. The young man was too drunk to tell me anything but the truth. The absolute truth." Madeline brushed a curl back from where it had fallen to her low-cut bodice.

Jacey knew she shouldn't believe the woman. Madeline would likely say or do anything to get Stryker back or persuade Jacey to give him up. But she couldn't forget that he had called out for Madeline when he was ill, not for her.

Madeline's words rang too true. She remembered how many times he had mentioned their bargain, and always with the hint of something else. Could Jeanette have agreed to such a thing? If so, how could she have kept it from Jacey and sent her to Texas anyway?

Jacey faced the truth about her twin. Jeanette would keep a secret from her if it was the only way she could talk her into doing a favor.

A temporary marriage.

Her usual confidence shaken, the other woman's insinuations took root.

This was the "bargain" he kept reminding her about.

Pain hit her so hard it nearly took her to her knees. His bargain had been a temporary marriage to her to solve his problems. But in the course of seeing to himself, he had practically destroyed her.

He had broken her heart as surely as if he had reached out and cruelly snapped it into pieces.

She had been wrong about him. Not only couldn't he love, but he didn't even want to.

Jacey forced herself to raise her chin, although it was the hardest thing she had ever done. But the worst was yet to come.

She had to leave Braddock. And Stryker.

Today!

The message in her reticule crinkled, reminding her of her twin's pending arrival. She nearly groaned aloud on the boardwalk. She couldn't leave yet. Jeanette was coming. She didn't care a whit if Cousin Earl arrived to find her gone. But she had to be here for her twin's arrival, and to explain everything to her.

Right then she could most assuredly use her sister's

shoulder to cry on. Instead, she stiffened her spine and tightened her fingers around the strings of her reticule until they left marks on her palms.

She would stay with Stryker, but only as long as necessary to wait for her twin.

Then she would leave Braddock and Logan Stryker behind so fast, the dust would never settle.

Chapter Seventeen

The train pulled into Braddock without any fanfare. The conductor dropped off the mail pouch and assisted down one passenger.

The woman was clothed in a somber gown and wore a matching hat with a heavy veil. No matter what angle he used to glance at her, he couldn't see through the veil to the features hidden behind it.

A most curious woman, he thought to himself. However, she wasn't any of his business, and he had a schedule to keep. Dismissing the woman from his mind, he climbed back aboard the train. Moments later, the locomotive chugged away from the wooden platform.

Jeanette Forester picked up her single piece of luggage from the train platform. Gripping the handle of the valise tightly in one hand, she threw a cautious glance around the surrounding area.

She didn't see another person close in sight.

It was safe.

She lifted one corner of the heavy veil and peeked out. Still not spotting anyone close enough to notice her actions, she lifted the veil a bit higher and surveyed the town. Her mouth dropped open.

Good heavens, the place was in the backwoods of nowhere. How could Jacey stand this wilderness?

Hearing the sound of a wagon down the street, she hurriedly lowered the veil, adjusting it into place so no portion of her face showed. She patted the back of the veil down over her giveaway blond curls, ensuring not a tendril showed for anyone to see. To any onlookers, she appeared like a widow woman of indiscriminate age, wearing widow's weeds. She wrinkled her nose in distaste. Her personal tastes ran to much brighter colors.

Maybe the disguise was a bit much, but back in Baltimore Jacey had ordered her to come to town "discreetly." The widow's disguise was about as discreet as she could devise. Not to mention nearly foolproof.

She inched up the veil again and threw a cautious glance around. She was also trying to lose Franklin Prescott's odious presence. The scoundrel had been penniless, she learned.

Penniless!

He had intended to spend her dowry. The moment Great-aunt Cordelia had unearthed this distressing news, Jeanette had sent him packing but good. No amount of cajoling on his part could convince her to retain their engagement.

Her insistence they were through had done little enough good. Franklin had persisted in giving her excuses to discount Great-aunt Cordelia's information. However, Jeanette knew better than to disbelieve or cross her aunt, since the woman was highly displeased with her anyway.

The telegram to Jacey had been an act of desperation to get away from both her disapproving aunt and Franklin.

She was nearly broke. Marriage to Logan Stryker would be her only salvation. So, here she stood in a poor excuse for a town.

Sniffing in distaste, Jeanette picked up her heavy skirt with one gloved hand and walked off down the street toward the building she had seen with the sign *Braddock Hotel* in front of it.

The small hotel missed meeting her expectations by a long shot, but it would have to do, she supposed, until Jacey could arrange for them to switch places. She registered as Jenny Harvey, secretly delighted at her choice of alias. Wouldn't Uncle Harvey be furious if he knew?

Jeanette sniffed with the onset of tears. She was homesick for her twin. She could hardly wait to see her again. Since the town possessed only one hotel, Jacey would know where to find her, but she had no idea where Jacey was staying. Perhaps she had better learn her whereabouts before she made a slip.

Smiling at the desk clerk, she fluttered her eyelashes. He didn't respond. In fact, he turned his back on her. She sniffed with indignation. This had never happened before with any man. She blew out a frustrated breath, lifting the veil slightly. It settled back down with a tickle against her chin, and she remembered the man couldn't see her face clearly enough.

Well, at least he hadn't been ignoring her.

Jeanette cleared her throat to get his attention. When he turned back around, she asked, "I am looking for Jacey—"

His instant smile cut off her question. "Yes, ma'am. You a friend of hers? She sure can cook."

"Do you know where could I find her?"

"Why, she's out at the ranch."

"Thank you." Dismissing him, she turned away and sauntered up the stairs to her room.

Once inside, she tossed the veiled bonnet on the bed

and sneaked a peek out the curtained window of her second-story room at the town laid out below. She nibbled delicately on her upper lip. Her innate curiosity prodded her into rashness.

She wanted to see the town. And her fiancé.

Tilting her head, she had a sudden thought. Jacey was at the ranch, not in town. Her twin couldn't be in two places at once. Since Jacey was safely ensconced at the ranch, it was harmless for her to go out for a little stroll. What could it hurt?

Dumping the contents of her valise on the bed, she dug through the items until she found her favorite turquoise gown. She shook it out and held it up with a giggle. As an afterthought she caught up a fan. It would feel so good to dispose of her widow's weeds.

Within a half hour, Jeanette descended the hotel stairs, the fancy fan hiding a portion of her face until she stepped outside. Snapping the fan closed, she let it swing from her wrist and adjusted her turquoise feathered bonnet before she set out down the boardwalk.

As she neared the mercantile store, she spotted a restaurant across the street. Pausing to daintily pick up her skirt, she stepped down off the boardwalk. She hadn't taken more than a few steps when a man grabbed her and yanked hard enough to swing her around into his arms.

"What!"

Jeanette's startled yelp was drowned out by the roar of a wagon lumbering by within inches of her. She sagged against the male chest, her arms going around her rescuer.

"Why, you saved my life," she exclaimed, tilting her head back.

She stared up into the greenest eyes she had ever seen and continued to hold on to him. Was this wonderful man her intended, Logan Stryker? Oh, she dearly hoped so. He would do just fine.

"Oh, my," Jeanette whispered, instantly smitten.

Brett stared down into Jacey's upturned face. For the first time he felt the stirring of attraction for her and kept his arms around her.

"Stryker?" she said hesitantly.

His best friend's name on her lips reminded him he was holding his friend's wife. Forcing himself to do so, he slowly eased his arms away from her.

"I'll take you to him at the jail. But first, are you all right, Jacey?"

Jeanette gazed into his eyes. He had the most beautiful eyes, and it had felt so wonderful while he had held her. Then his words penetrated her mind. He thought she was Jacey. The spark of attraction in his gaze had been for her twin, not her. Her pride injured, she recalled the remainder of his words. He was taking her to Stryker.

Oh, pooh. This man wasn't Logan Stryker. Worse the luck. She could definitely tolerate being married to this man. She had to find out who he was and what he was doing in town. Maybe she could lure him away from her twin.

Her interest piqued, she smiled up at him and fluttered her lashes in her practiced way. His return smile proved he wasn't immune to her charms. She looked down, then back up at him. This time he appeared to become decidedly uncomfortable. In fact, he looked as if his collar was too tight, except that his shirt was open at his neck, the deep vee revealing his suntanned throat.

"Yes, I'm alive and well, thanks to you." She sighed at him.

Jeanette barely resisted the impulse to run her hands up to his neck. It took all her effort to not do so. Regrettably, he wasn't her fiancé. She sighed again, this time the sound a soft flutter of air. Her twin was going to be very upset over this meeting, but she didn't regret it one whit.

Stepping back with reluctance, she linked her arm with his and placed her other hand over his. She wasn't ready to let him go yet.

"Ah—" He cleared his throat. "I'd better take you to Stryker."

"I suppose so."

Brett looked at her in askance. That hadn't sounded at all like Jacey. "Are you sure you're all right?" he asked with growing concern.

She smiled at him with a slight lifting of her delicate brows. "Why, I'm nearly perfect." With a tinkling laugh, she leaned closer.

Swallowing down his sudden desire to kiss her parted lips, he led her across the street, keeping her arm in his.

Jeanette and Brett's lengthy embrace and conversation didn't go unnoticed by three citizens of Braddock. Rosalyn and Linda stopped in their tracks on their way out of the mercantile store. They stood close enough to see every movement and hear every word.

Not more than two feet away, Madeline Raines had also watched the scene with growing interest. When the seemingly loving couple crossed the street, she grinned like a cat who had been given all the cream she could ever want. Sauntering forward a few steps, she stopped and stared out across the street in contemplation.

"Oh, my," Madeline spoke aloud to herself. "So Stryker's little wife is occupying herself with Brett now." She held her hands together against her lips for a moment. "I think I'd better console Stryker tonight. And I know the perfect place to do so. I dearly love the smell of hay and sweat."

As she whirled away and walked off toward the livery stables, her self-satisfied laughter floated over to Rosalyn and Linda.

"Oh, dear me. Did you hear that!" Linda whispered to her companion.

"I'm afraid I did. We've got to do something." Rosalyn planted her hands on her hips and stared after Madeline Raines. "If that woman succeeds, everything we've done will be for nothing. If Stryker meets that *creature* for a roll in the hay, he'll wind up losing his ranch and job for sure."

"You take care of her, and I'll put a stop to Brett's interest in Jacey," Linda said, glaring at Brett across the street. "I'm sure he'll listen to reason, but I didn't like the way he was holding her at all."

Rosalyn looked after the couple and nodded. Then she glanced back to where Madeline was entering the livery stable. A smile slowly lit up her face. "You see to him. I've got an idea that will fix Mrs. Raines and her intimate evening plans but good."

Their tasks set, the two women hurried down the street back to the boardinghouse to set their plan in motion.

As Stryker walked out of his office, he spotted Jacey walking with Brett toward him. He watched their approach with increasing interest. She held his friend's arm as if she couldn't let go, and Brett's gaze kept straying to her smiling face.

A rush of anger hit him hard like a solid punch to the gut. He attempted to shake off the blow, telling himself he didn't care who she walked with, but his jaw clenched involuntarily.

Without realizing it, Stryker took a menacing step forward, nearly grabbing Brett by the shirtfront. Only by tightening his hands into fists did he stop himself in time.

"Stryker, look who I found," Brett announced to him.

Stryker narrowed his eyes on his friend. "I see." He left the words hanging in the air with their unspoken meaning.

Brett had the decency to look chastised. But Jacey was another matter. She appeared to miss the tense interchange completely. Instead, she persisted in blessing both of them with her smiles.

"Good afternoon," she greeted him, in a voice that didn't hold its usual warmth and life.

Stryker tipped his hat to her, but felt uneasy doing so. She fluttered her lashes again, then looked away coyly. She wasn't acting like herself at all.

"Are you sure you should be back working so soon?" Brett asked.

Was he pointing out he was an invalid? Stryker shifted his weight and met his friend's gaze squarely. "I'm fully recovered."

Brett cleared his throat in a nervous gesture. "Ah, I can see that. I guess I'll be going."

"Oh, do you have to leave yet?"

Stryker tensed at Jacey's flirtatious remark. He found himself gritting his teeth to hold back his response. He admitted to himself he hadn't treated her right the last time they had spoken, but he hadn't told her to go to someone else. It looked like that was what she was planning on doing.

He didn't like the way she kept eyeing Brett and fluttering her lashes at him. Not in the least.

She looked especially pretty today in a brightly colored turquoise gown. He didn't recall seeing it in the wardrobe and wondered if it was new. The dress was pretty enough, but it outshone her, turning her normally deep blue eyes a soft, pale blue. He didn't like the change at all. She didn't look like *his Jacey*.

There he was, thinking of her in that way again.

If Brett wasn't his friend, Stryker would call him out. He might even do it anyway if he caught him looking Jacey's way one more time.

"Brett, don't you have something else to do?" he asked pointedly.

His friend took the hint and stepped away from Jacey. Stryker nearly sighed in relief.

"Yeah, I'd better be going." He tipped his hat to her, and added, "You be careful."

"I surely will," she answered with a sigh.

Stryker stiffened and reached out to clasp her arm. She looked from his hand to his face and back to his hand. Gritting his teeth again, he released her.

"Jacey, we need to talk—"

She quickly stepped back. "I have some shopping I need to do." Whirling away from him, she started off down the boardwalk. "I'll see you later," she called back over her shoulder.

He watched her in amazement. She had walked off on him. He stared at her, noticing this time her bustle didn't sway like it usually did. A frown settled on his face.

Something wasn't right.

And he intended to get to the bottom of it.

Two hours later, Stryker stormed into the ranch house, slamming the door behind him. Jacey nearly dropped the pie she was carrying to the table.

She set it down carefully, then turned to face him. She knew immediately he was angry. And it seemed to be directed straight at her. Her own temper had been simmering too long. It blazed to life, rising to meet his.

"Did you finish your *shopping*?" Stryker asked, his voice strained.

Jacey looked at him blankly. "Shopping?"

"So it was an excuse to avoid talking."

"What are you—"

"Don't play me for a fool, Jacey," he snapped, the rein on his temper fraying.

If anybody was acting like a prime fool, it was him. She planted her hands on her hips and stared at him with haughty indignation. "From the way you're acting, I don't have to do anything. You're doing a wonderful job of playing the fool on your own," she snapped back at him.

"Tell me the truth."

She tensed at his order, suddenly apprehensive. What was he talking about? What had he found out?

When she didn't answer straight off, he pressed, "Was the shopping a ploy to meet Brett again?"

"Brett?" she repeated, confusion overlapping her irritation.

She stared at Stryker in bewilderment, struggling to make sense out of his words. She had only seen his friend Brett for moments when Tinker had pounced on his feet on his way out of the house that last time. He had scarcely said a repeatable word, then stormed up the stairs to yell at Stryker.

"I don't know what you're talking about. Are you—"

"Don't change the subject."

"Then, tell me exactly what we're talking about."

"Dammit, are you denying you were playing up to him today in town?"

"I was not!" She raised her chin in defiance, then blinked. "Today?" she repeated.

"Yes, today," he shouted.

Jacey opened and shut her mouth. Oh, heavens, Jeanette must have arrived in town earlier than expected. They were supposed to meet this evening. What had her twin been up to? It was just like Jeanette to try to attract Brett. Especially when she didn't know who he was.

Why couldn't her sister have been discreet like she had told her!

"Ah." Jacey rubbed her forehead. She needed time to think. "Can we discuss this later? I don't feel well."

It was only a partial lie. She was feeling sick with worry over whatever possible chaos her twin had caused. If she didn't get to her soon, who knew what trouble she would stir up for both of them.

"No!" he shouted at her.

"Yes," she snapped back.

"Jacey."

His voice held a warning she chose to ignore.

"I'm not going to dignify your insinuations with an answer," she announced with a defiant toss of her head.

"I'm not insinuating anything. I'm stating facts."

"No, you're not. You're yelling at me!" she shouted back at him.

Stryker closed his eyes and sighed deeply. He didn't remember the last time he had raised his voice to a woman. Jacey could make him forget his manners, his good intentions, and his temper faster than anyone he had ever met.

"I—" he began.

"We'll discuss this later," she announced with a firm lifting of her chin.

Stryker nearly groaned aloud at the too-familiar gesture. When she did that, he knew there would be no reasoning with her. She had stubbornly set her mind not to "discuss" it now. He knew no amount of questioning or demanding would get her to agree right then.

Without giving him a chance to protest further, Jacey swept up her skirt and walked across the room to the stairs. She held her breath, fearful he would stop her.

She was halfway up the stairs before Stryker came out of his shock at her action. She had walked off on him again.

"Jacey."

"Later," she called down over her shoulder, without pausing in the slightest.

He stared after her, watching her in disbelief. What was wrong with her? She was behaving very strangely. As he watched her, he frowned deeply. This time her bustle swayed with each step she took. He shook his head.

Suddenly another thought occurred to him. She had changed her clothes. She was wearing a lavender gown instead of the turquoise-colored one in town. Her eyes had lost the pale look of earlier and returned to their deep, fiery blue color.

How odd, he thought, rubbing the back of his neck.

Something was going on, and she was definitely smack in the middle of it.

Chapter Eighteen

Jacey shut the bedroom door behind her, resisting the urge to slam it. Hard!

What a mess her twin had made of things! She leaned against the door, needing the support for her shaking knees. Her temper still raged at Stryker. He had arranged a temporary marriage to suit his needs, then had the audacity to get angry when he thought he saw her flirting with Brett.

A sudden thought struck her. Had his anger been a screen for jealousy? No, it was foolish to even entertain such a ridiculous thought. Or hope. His emotions were too securely locked away for something like jealousy to slip out.

How long could she continue to put off the confrontation with Stryker? Near the end of their angry exchange, he had had an odd look on his face, almost as if he were attempting to put together the pieces of a puzzle and nearly had it finished. If she didn't know better, she would think he suspected something was wrong. But he couldn't, could he?

She had to get to Jeanette. Before she created more havoc for them both. There was nothing else to do but go see her twin as soon as it was dark enough to leave unseen.

Jacey paced the room, deep in thought, ignoring Tinker's playful attacks on her feet. She dared not ask anyone to drive her to town in the wagon. She would have to sneak a horse out and ride into town herself. Thankfully Uncle Harvey had insisted the twins have riding lessons.

Rummaging in the bureau, she pulled out a dark cloak. She had always hated secret rendezvous. She dropped the cloak on the bed in readiness. At her step, Tinker scampered to her, and Jacey scooped her up. Sitting on the bed, she absently petted the kitten and waited for the cover of darkness.

"Did you find it?" Linda asked the moment Rosalyn came in the door.

Smiling, Rosalyn held up a folded sheet of paper.

"Thank heavens." Linda laid a hand over her heart in obvious relief.

"Would you believe it was lying right in the middle of Stryker's desk?"

"The woman has some nerve."

Rosalyn gave her a steady look. "Nerve is not what I would call it."

"Now—"

"Madeline Raines has the morals of a prowling tomcat, and you know it, too."

"Shame on you, Rosalyn. You really shouldn't talk like that about a tomcat. It's an insult to the poor things to be compared to that woman."

They looked at each other and burst into laughter.

"Come on, we've got more work to do." Rosalyn linked her arm with Linda's arm, and they headed to the rolltop desk across the room.

In no time, they had recopied the missive from Madeline, carefully tracing over the words on another sheet of almost identical paper. Studying their handiwork, they decided it was so close to the original that anyone reading it would be certain to believe it was Madeline's handwriting, if they didn't give it too close a look. They knew Bertram wouldn't bother examining it too closely.

Next they wrote out a response and signed it from Stryker, carefully copying his signature from a second paper they had "borrowed" from his desk.

"Now to finalize our plan," Rosalyn said, replacing the pen on the desk with a triumphant flourish.

Linda grinned back at her. "I'll see those are delivered to the proper parties right away." She winked before she gathered up the sheets and walked out the door, humming a cheerful melody to herself.

Stryker watched Jacey ride away from the barn. He stepped back behind the side of the building, then looked out across the dark yard. Assured she was far enough away not to hear him, he returned to where he had tied his horse.

Swinging up into the saddle, he headed out after Jacey. He was reasonably certain he knew where she was riding, but he didn't want to risk being wrong and losing her.

He felt as if a band had tightened around his heart. If he lost track of her on the horse, he feared he might lose her in another way as well. Kneeing his horse, he closed the distance enough to keep her in sight.

In his mind, he imagined all sorts of things. When she drew her mount to a halt at the hotel, then dismounted and walked calmly inside, his worst fears were confirmed. She had come to town for an illicit rendezvous.

Fury held him in its fiery grasp. He tightened his hands on the reins until the leather strips cut into his palms. He almost welcomed the physical pain. It was much better than the feeling of his heart being sliced into ribbons.

He gave in to the fury, letting it sweep through him. He was going to enjoy taking Brett Mason apart, right in front of Jacey. Then he wouldn't—

"Marshal!"

Stryker turned at the shout to see his deputy running toward him. He swung down out of the saddle, tied his horse to the hitching post, and faced the other man's approach. This better be important.

"What is it?" he asked, irritation roughening his voice.

"You need to come to the jail right away. There's something you need to see. Came in the mail pouch." The deputy stopped to draw in air.

"Can't it wait?"

"I don't think so."

As Stryker hesitated, glancing over at the hotel, the deputy added, "You need to see this."

"Sure," Stryker muttered under his breath, hating the notion of duty at that moment.

He turned a narrowed glare at the hotel entrance. If his suspicions were correct, Jacey would still be inside when he finished at the jail.

If not, he would hunt her down.

Jacey stood inside the hotel and glanced around in apprehension, then sighed in relief. At least Jeanette wasn't entertaining men in the hotel lobby. Although, right then she wouldn't put it past her.

Marching to the desk, she greeted the owner. "Good evening, Mr. Matthews."

"Miz Jacey." He beamed a smile at her. "You here to visit with the widow lady?" He nodded his head. "I been expecting you'd be in to call on her soon. What with her asking 'bout you and all."

Widow lady?

Jacey closed her eyes for an instant. Jeanette's idea of discretion, she supposed. But a widow lady? She bit her cheek to hold back her grin. That she would have liked to see.

She snapped her eyes open with a start. Jeanette had been asking about her? It took an effort to suppress her groan at the news. Exactly what had her twin been asking? And what had she found out from the friendly, talkative hotel proprietor?

"Miz Harvey is in room two ten," he told her with a smile.

Thanking him, Jacey almost laughed at her twin's choice of name as she climbed the stairs to the second floor. Excitement licked along her veins. She was going to see her sister again. Quickly, she located the room number and then tapped on the door three times in the old childish code she and her sister had devised years before.

The door swung open almost instantly, and Jeanette pulled her inside. Without a pause, Jacey hugged her twin in sheer happiness to see her again. Then she remembered she was supposed to be angry with her.

Jacey ended the hug reluctantly. Stepping back, she surveyed her sister. "What have you done now?"

Jeanette tossed her head. "Well, that's a fine hello. Did you miss me?"

"Of course. Don't I always?" Jacey planted her hands on her hips. "When did you get in?"

"Early this afternoon on the train."

"The train?" Dismay edged Jacey's voice as she stared at her sister with trepidation.

"Don't worry. No one paid a whit of attention to me. See." With a dramatic flourish she swept up the widow's hat and set it on her head, pulling down the veil.

Jacey couldn't stop the laugh from slipping out.

Jeanette raised the veil and stuck her tongue out. Then she tossed the hat to the bed and announced, "I met the most handsome man today."

"Yes, I know. Stryker told me that he saw *me* in town today. Care to tell me how that happened?"

Jeanette waved a hand. "Oh, pooh. You can blame the desk clerk—"

"Hotel proprietor," Jacey put in.

"Really? Imagine that."

"Go on," Jacey prompted.

"Where was I? Oh, yes. The desk clerk . . . owner told me you were at the ranch. So, I figured it was safe for me to take a stroll. Can you believe this place? Why, I—"

"You were wrong. It wasn't safe."

"Oh, pooh. No harm done."

That was what her twin thought. Heaven only knew what trouble she had stirred up, Jacey thought to herself. She sent her sister a quelling glance, but it bounced right off the enraptured expression on her face. Jacey wanted to groan. She had seen that look on her twin before. It always boded no good.

"Who is it this time?" she asked.

"Oh, where was I?" Jeanette stared at her, clearly distracted. "Oh, yes. I met the handsomest man today. I swear he nearly took my breath away. And when he held me in his arms." She stopped to stare off across the room.

A flare of jealousy consumed Jacey. Couldn't her sister leave one man for her? No, she had to go after every man who so much as looked at her. Well, she wasn't getting Stryker! He belonged to her.

"Stryker is—"

"I'm talking about Brett Mason," Jeanette informed her.

Jacey knew her mouth had dropped open, but for the life of her she couldn't manage to stop it.

Jeanette continued on as if she hadn't said anything of surprise. "Did you know he saved my life today? I was nearly run down by a wagon, and he pulled me back in time. And right into his arms." She sighed deeply.

"What about Franklin Prescott?"

"Don't even mention his name to me again," Jeanette suddenly snapped at her. "Aunt Cordelia found out he's penniless. Penniless, can you imagine that?" She tossed her head. "Well, I sent him packing and without my dowry, too."

"Did you already marry him?" Jacey asked in horror.

"No, silly."

Jacey released a sigh of relief.

"But I think he may have followed me here," Jeanette leaned forward and whispered.

Jacey didn't know whether to laugh or scream at the look of distress on her twin's face.

"Forget about him," Jacey reassured. "I'm sure he's moved on."

"Good." Jeanette smiled at her. "I also met my fiancé today."

"Your what?"

"Fiancé. Remember the marriage contract? You did hang on to him for me, didn't you?"

A rush of guilt flowed over Jacey. She would have to tell her sister she had not only held on to him, but she had married him. She wanted to ease into the explanation, so she would understand.

Jeanette continued talking, not noticing Jacey's sudden

quiet. "He is handsome. But not as handsome as Brett. But no matter, Stryker owns a ranch. Did I tell you that?"

"No."

"I didn't?" Jeanette asked, the picture of feigned innocence.

"You know you didn't."

"Sorry." She shrugged her shoulder daintily. "Well, anyway, he owns a ranch, doesn't he? And a ranch means money. And that means I can buy a new wardrobe. I left almost everything back in Baltimore, and it will take forever to get it here. Meanwhile, I can't keep wearing the same gowns, can I?"

Jacey stared in disbelief. Her twin planned on marrying Stryker to acquire a new wardrobe! This was by far the worst thing the woman had ever thought about doing. What about love? Jeanette didn't care a whit about him.

They had never fought over a man before, but Jacey knew there was about to be a first time. She wasn't simply handing Stryker over to her sister to use. Jeanette would ruin his life and make him miserable.

She wasn't about to let that happen. Not even for her own twin sister.

"You're not marrying him," Jacey said in a deceptively low voice.

"Why, of course I am." Jeanette laughed. "Brett is more handsome, but I learned he's not rich. I learned my lesson with Franklin. From now on I'm only interested in men with money of their own."

"Leave Stryker alone."

Jeanette laughed out loud at the order. "Give me one good reason why I should."

"Because he's my husband!" Jacey announced in a near shout. She hadn't meant to let it slip out that way.

"Husband," Jeanette shrieked. "You married him!" Tears welled up in her eyes. "How could you?"

"I didn't have a choice. Especially since you didn't tell me he had to be married *fast*."

Her sister had the grace to look at least slightly chagrined. "Oh."

"You also left out the part about your 'bargain!' " Jacey shouted back at her.

"Never mind that. It doesn't matter."

Jacey's temper flared to full life. How could her twin dismiss it so casually when their bargain had broken her heart?

"What in heaven do you mean it doesn't matter?"

"After we've switched places, I'll just tell him I've changed my mind."

"You can't do that," Jacey informed her with conviction.

"Of course I can. I'm always changing my mind." Jeanette waved her hand in the air.

The dismissing action only served to inflame Jacey's already soaring temper. "I couldn't care less about your mind. And we're not switching places!" She planted her hands on her hips.

Across from her, Jeanette made the identical gesture. "Oh, yes we are."

"No!" Jacey narrowed her eyes in warning.

"You promised."

"You lied."

"I did not." Jeanette stomped her foot in a Jacey-like gesture. "I merely left out some details."

Jacey stepped forward until they were nearly standing toe to toe. "You lied to me."

"Oh, pooh." Jeanette glared back. "I want to marry Stryker."

"You what?" Jacey nearly stepped back in shocked surprise at the sudden announcement.

"You heard me."

Jacey clenched her teeth until her jaw ached. "You cannot marry him. I'm already married to him." She enunciated each word slowly and clearly, anger coloring her tone.

"You stole him from me! Give him back."

"Stop it, Jeanette." For the first time in her life, Jacey completely lost her patience with her twin.

Jeanette's lower lip came out; then she grabbed up her reticule and threw it at Jacey. "How could you?"

Jacey sidestepped the bag and grabbed up the hairbrush from the dressing table and threw it back at her twin. It missed, clattering to the floor. "You're the one who sent me out here. Remember?"

"But I didn't tell you to steal him away," Jeanette yelled, grabbing up the water pitcher and throwing it. "He belongs to me."

Jacey ducked her sister's aim, and the pitcher smashed against the wall, splashing water over the flowered wallpaper. The broken pieces of the container fell to the floor with a crash. She merely spared them a glance, before she turned a glare back on her sister. "He's my husband."

"But I signed the contract." The matching water bowl hit the wooden door as if to punctuate Jeanette's statement.

"With my name." Jacey caught up her sister's scent bottle in growing anger.

"Not that," Jeanette cried out, stretching out her arm to stop her.

Jacey ignored her and flung the bottle. It landed at Jeanette's feet.

Someone pounded on the door.

"Go away," Jacey and Jeanette yelled at nearly the same time.

"What's going on in there?" Mr. Matthews shouted back. "Stop it this minute."

Neither Jacey nor Jeanette paid him any attention.

At the next sound of breakage, he turned and took the stairs two at a time. He was going for help in dealing with the two women. This was Stryker's job, and it was best left up to him. Not caring that he left the hotel unattended, he ran straight for the marshal's office.

"Stryker!" Nathan Matthews dashed into the jail office, out of breath.

Stryker looked up from the wanted poster of his wife. His wife. Wanted for theft. The poster explained so much. He scarcely gave the attached retraction of the charges a second glance. What mattered to him was she had deceived him, hidden the truth from him, and used him to hide her out from the law. Hell, he was the law.

He rubbed the knot of pain at the back of his neck and, sighing, turned his attention to the hotel proprietor.

"What's wrong, Nathan?"

The short, stocky man leaned forward and planted his hands on the desk. "You gotta come quick, there's trouble at the hotel."

Jacey. Stryker knew it for a fact.

He forced himself to ask, "Jacey—"

"It's the biggest fight I've had at the hotel in years. They're tearing the place apart."

Stryker crumpled the poster with his fist and surged to his feet in one sure move. Wanted poster still in hand, he strode out the door. With long strides, he closed the distance to the hotel in record time.

As Stryker strode into the hotel, Earl Forester stepped back into the shadows of the building and rubbed his chin thoughtfully. He ran over in his mind the facts he had unearthed that day. Jacey had married a lawman, and without her uncle's knowledge, much less his consent.

In fact, she hadn't even bothered to let him know she was going to travel to Texas. His father would not be pleased with her. Earl grinned so hard, it hurt his cheeks.

His father had always sworn if either of the twins married without his approval, he would disown them. Well, it appeared Jacey had done that very thing. Now all Earl had to do was ensure Jeanette followed the same fate. She was already supposed to have wed the fool Prescott.

The twins had outfoxed him for the last time. Here he would be the one in control. Anger at his earlier failures prodded him, and he slammed a fist against the wall beside him. He blamed Jacey for slipping out of his grasp in Baltimore.

If everything had gone as planned, she would have been sitting in a jail cell when his father returned from his business trip. Gregory Canefield had cooperated fully when Earl had suggested to the fool that he would be the laughingstock of Baltimore society when word leaked out about Jacey jilting him, and slapping him soundly, too. With only a little coaxing, Canefield had gone to the police, claiming she had stolen the necklace.

But no, she had fled, barely in time. With both twins missing, his father had laid the blame squarely on *him*. It wasn't fair. He wouldn't fail this time.

Narrowing his eyes, he rubbed his hands together. He had it all worked out down to the last detail, even wiring his father. Everything would be in place for his dear father's arrival in town. Soon he would have his revenge on his cousins and everything that rightfully belonged to him. He let a gleeful chuckle slip free. It echoed eerily off the wooden wall of the building beside him. He sobered quickly. He wasn't finished yet.

Only one thing left to do. Then both Jacey and Jeanette would be disowned and out of his way for good.

He stepped out and headed for the livery stable and his waiting horse. When he reached the livery, no one was about. Not willing to wait for the owner, he lit a lantern and started down the stalls, looking for his horse.

Madeline heard footsteps and giggled with anticipation. "Back here," she called out, invitation in her voice. "Leave your boots outside the stall if you don't mind."

A man's figure appeared at the open door of the stall. He held a lantern high, its beam shining on her. She stretched in the glow of the light, knowing she looked her best tonight with her hair carefully arranged around her shoulders. She hoped he appreciated her efforts, but couldn't see his expression behind the light of the lantern.

"Well, set the lantern down and come on," she ordered.

Earl stared in shock at the naked woman lying in the pile of hay.

"Darling, do come join me," Madeline called out in a seductive purr.

Earl wasted no time in stripping off his coat, shirt and pants at her invitation. He paused only long enough to lay his clothing carefully over the stall rail. No sense in getting them hay-covered for a little trollop.

He positioned himself over her, and she opened her eyes and shrieked in the most awful voice he had ever heard. "Who are you?"

"Earl Forester," he announced, smashing his mouth down on hers, before she could say another discordant word.

Madeline shoved at his shoulders until he moved back from her. "Where is Stryker?" she asked, slightly dazed by his kiss.

"The lawman's busy at the hotel with his wife."

He saw her eyes glitter with anger a minute; then she reached up and pulled his head down to hers. Halfway through the kiss, the stable door creaked open. The hay muffled the approaching footsteps.

"Madeline!"

She turned her head to look into the eyes of her husband.

Bertram stared down at her in disgust. "What they said about you is true."

"Bertram?" Her voice rose in surprised dismay.

"How many notes did you send out?" he asked, his face reddening with anger. "You can keep mine."

Bertram flung the folded note and the bouquet of flowers to the stable floor. Turning away, he said over his shoulder, "Don't bother coming home. I'll be formally ending our marriage first thing tomorrow." He swung the door firmly closed behind him.

He shook his head in combined disbelief and disgust. He had been expecting to find Logan Stryker, but he had been wrong. Seemed getting the lawman married hadn't helped him a bit. He hoped Marshal Stryker's marriage would be better than his had been.

Stryker could hear the commotion as soon as he entered the hotel. The fight came from upstairs. He took the stairs two at a time, determined to put an end to the disturbance in short order. Then he would find Jacey.

He pounded on the door. At the sound of breaking glass, he drew his gun, then put his shoulder to the door panel and forced it open. The door gave, swinging open and crashing against the wall.

Jacey whirled around and met the startled gaze of Stryker. He looked from her to Jeanette, and back to her.

"I'll be damned," he muttered under his breath.

From the look on his face Jacey figured she was the one who would be that.

His gaze flicked from one woman to the other again. "Twins."

His gaze settled on Jacey after a moment, and it hardened. His dark eyes told her he knew it was her. She stared at him in amazement. He was the only man who had been able to tell them apart, and she hadn't even had to say a word.

Their eyes locked, each searching the other for something, but not finding it. Stryker was the first one to break the contact.

"And I thought Madeline had the market cornered on deception," he said, scorn roughening his voice. "I was wrong."

"Stryker, let me explain."

He looked her up and down, his eyes dark and infinitely cold. Jacey felt frozen in place by the look in his eyes.

"Don't worry, I'm not going to arrest you two." His voice hardened, shutting out all traces of emotion.

"Stryker, listen—" Jacey moistened her lips.

He threw the wanted poster at her feet. "Pick it up," he ordered.

Jacey did as he said. Smoothing out the paper, she stared down at her likeness on the wanted poster. Her breath caught, lodged in her chest.

"Read it," he snapped.

She didn't need to. She knew exactly what it said. She looked up at him.

"Was it a joke to you living with a lawman while you were wanted?"

"No, I—"

Not giving her a chance to answer, he cut her off. "You've played me for the fool for the last time."

He turned away from her. For good.

Chapter Nineteen

"Stryker, let me explain." Jacey took a step toward him. "Please."

The stiffening of his back was the only outward sign he had heard her. He didn't turn back to face her. Instead, he walked out of the room, ignoring her plea.

Jacey stared at the empty doorway. She had to go after him, make him listen to her, somehow reach him. She couldn't let it end like this between them. And she knew with certainty as far as Stryker was concerned right then, their marriage was good and over.

Temporary or not, she knew from the look of pain in his eyes in the instant before he had turned away that he had felt something for her. She grasped at the tiny flicker of hope and held on to it. The lovemaking they had shared had been too wondrous to merely be part of a plan.

No, she refused to accept it was over. She would find *some* way to make him listen.

If he thought he was just going to walk away and dismiss

her without even giving her a chance to explain, he had another thought coming. She crossed the room after him.

"Jacey?" Jeanette caught her arm, stopping her.

Jacey shook off her twin's hold. "Not now. I have to catch him."

"Let him go."

"Jeanette, shut up!"

Jacey ran out the door and down the hall. At the top of the stairs she caught up her skirts for added speed and started down. She had to stop him before he left the hotel.

"Stryker!" she shouted from halfway up the stairs.

He jerked around and spotted her, then once again turned his back on her. She didn't catch up with him until he was halfway across the hotel lobby. She grabbed his arm and felt him stiffen beneath her hand. Determined, she held on.

He turned around slowly, then stared pointedly at her hand on his arm. Even under his demanding gaze, Jacey refused to release her hold on him. She knew her hand on his arm was the only thing keeping him from walking out of the hotel.

And out of her life.

"Will you listen to me!" she demanded.

"There's nothing you can say I want to hear," he stated in a flat, cold voice.

Jacey's temper rose along with her sense of desperation. "Did Madeline hurt you so badly that you see every woman as her?"

She knew she had made a mistake in asking the question the instant he jerked back from her.

"Madeline was an innocent in the art of deception compared to you."

"I—"

He glared at her, his anger raging. "I've had enough deception to last me a lifetime."

"I didn't deceive you—"

"Didn't you?" he challenged.

She opened her mouth, but he cut her off.

"Did you tell me you were wanted for theft?" He raised an eyebrow at her, waiting for her to deny her lie of omission.

"No, but I didn't steal that necklace," she insisted.

He continued as if what she said didn't matter. "Did you tell me you had a twin sister?"

"No, I couldn't. She hadn't mentioned it in the letters." The moment the condemning words left her mouth, Jacey knew she had made an unforgivable slip.

"*She* wrote the letters?" Stryker took a menacing step forward.

Jacey backed up a small step before she could stop herself. Her hip bumped up against a chair.

"Let me get this straight." He narrowed his eyes. "Your sister wrote the letters, and the marriage contract was hers, too. Wasn't it? Tell me, where did you come into the picture?"

Jacey gulped. "I came in her place."

"So I even married the wrong one." His laugh was hollow and chilling.

"No."

"Is your name even Jacey?"

"Of course it is."

"That's the only honest thing about you. And about our marriage," he added cruelly.

Jacey reached out to catch his arm. "Our marriage—"

"Our marriage was a mistake. One I mean to rectify." This time he forcibly shook off her touch.

Her face paled at his announcement. Pain robbed her of speech for the space of a broken heartbeat.

As she stared at him, Stryker turned on his heel and stormed out of the hotel.

The sound of the lobby door slamming spurred her into action. She started after him.

"Miz Jacey?" Mr. Matthews stepped in front of her, blocking her path. "Ah, about the breakage upstairs?"

She attempted to sidestep him, intent on catching up with Stryker.

"Miz Jacey."

"Not now." She barely spared the proprietor a glance before she shoved him out of her way.

Clenching her hands tightly on her skirt, she hurried across the lobby to the door Stryker had exited through. She had to make him listen.

She had to.

Outside, she looked up and down the street, searching for his tall figure. She didn't see him anywhere. Stepping off the boardwalk, she raced across the street and headed for the jail office. Surely she would find him there.

She was wrong.

When Jacey reached the office, the only person she found inside was the deputy. She tapped down her frustration at the discovery.

"Ma'am." The deputy nodded to her with a curious glance.

She didn't have time to spare to exchange pleasantries. "Where's Stryker?" she demanded.

"Last I knew he headed over to the hotel to quell a disturbance."

Jacey barely stopped herself from stomping her foot in anger.

"Anything I can help you with, ma'am?" he asked.

Not even taking the time to answer him, she whirled around and dashed out the door. Out on the boardwalk, she paused, trying to think of where to look next.

As she recalled, Stryker had most assuredly been upset.

Would he go to the saloon? Her cousin Earl tended to get roaring drunk when upset over something.

Once again, she turned and headed off down the uneven boardwalk. At the saloon door, she paused only long enough to take a bracing breath for courage, then shoved the batwing doors open. Stepping inside, she noticed how, just like the last time, the room fell silent for the space of a heartbeat.

She only took three steps into the room before the bartender raced around the bar to plant himself directly in front of her. She knew she didn't stand a chance of moving his bulk aside.

"Ma'am, you can't come in here no more," he told her in a firm voice.

She dismissed him with a look. Then she peered around his side to search the room. She didn't see either Stryker or Brett sitting at a table or leaning against the bar. Instead, every man there returned her perusal.

She returned her attention back to the bartender. "Is Stryker here?"

"Ah, no, ma'am." The burly bartender shook his head vigorously. "Pardon me, ma'am, but will you *please* leave?" he pleaded, wiping his hands on the wide apron spread around his waist.

"All right, I'm going," she informed him with an indignant sniff.

Whirling around again, she walked to the doors with all the dignity she could muster, knowing every eye was firmly fixed on her departure. She pushed the doors open and stepped outside. Breathing in deeply of the fresh air, she looked up and down the street again.

Where was Stryker?

Maybe he had gone back to the ranch. She decided she would go there next. She walked back to the hotel where she retrieved her horse and headed to the ranch, her heart growing heavier with each passing minute.

Stryker walked through the door of the ranch house, and memories of Jacey struck him so hard he took a step back. It was as if her presence filled the very air around him.

Groaning, he closed his eyes and released a ragged breath. It felt as if it had been torn from his chest. How could she have deceived him this way?

He thought he was through being played for a fool, but it seemed it had only just begun.

Jacey had never cared for him, never loved him. For her and her twin sister, it had simply been a ruse. He had been a fool to trust again. To begin to care again.

Pain crushed his chest, making it hard to breathe. The hurt of Madeline's betrayal years before was nothing compared to the pain inflicted by Jacey and her twin's ploy.

A twin?

Who would have believed there could be two of them?

No, he shook his head sadly. There was only one Jacey. His Jacey, the little voice reminded him. He shoved the thought away. She would never be his again.

He was through with her lies and deceptions.

He was sending her away. It was the only thing he could do to save his sanity. His heart was already past salvation, and he no longer even cared.

Nothing mattered anymore except getting her out of his life. He walked up the stairs slowly and into the bedroom. Shutting his mind and heart against the memories, he crossed to the bureau. With jerky movements, he opened the bottom drawer and withdrew an envelope. He stared at it a moment in resignation, then tightened his fist around it until it crumpled in his hand.

With purposeful steps, he walked back downstairs, not stopping until he reached the dining room table. He tore open the envelope with one vicious rip and pulled out the train ticket to Baltimore, then dropped it on the center of the table.

By this time tomorrow Jacey would be gone.

One thing left. After writing out a note, he set it upright beside the train ticket, then walked out of the house.

Swinging up into the saddle, he knew he couldn't remain at the ranch that night. He turned his horse in the opposite direction and took the circular route to town. He would spend the night at the boardinghouse.

He couldn't face seeing Jacey again.

Jacey rode into the ranch yard nearly a half hour later. She stared at the darkened house. It had never felt so unwelcoming.

Suddenly weary, she led the horse to the barn and cared for it before she walked across the yard to the house. Unshed tears burned her throat, and she turned toward the kitchen for a drink. She felt as if she moved with heavy, wooden feet.

At the door of the dining room, a lantern on the table drew her attention. She stared at the folded piece of parchment with her name written boldly on it. She knew without looking that it was from Stryker.

For a moment, she couldn't swallow and couldn't move a step. Her mouth turned dry with fear. Slowly, she crossed to the table and picked up the message. She closed her eyes, savoring the uncertainty for a moment longer.

Once she unfolded the note and read the words Stryker had written to her, it would all be over. She knew it with an absolute certainty that shook her to her toes. Tears stung her eyes behind her closed lids, and she drew in a ragged breath and forced them back into their hiding place.

Opening her eyes, she swallowed, then focused on the words on the page. A minute later, she closed her eyes against the pain. Stryker's words had been cold with an undeniable finality no amount of hope could survive.

She dropped the paper to the table and clenched her hands into fists to remain upright. He was having their marriage annulled, and he wanted her gone. On tomorrow's train out of town. He had even provided her a return ticket to Baltimore.

Staring at the ticket on the table, she turned cold inside. He had bought the train ticket long before today. He had always planned on her using it. A sense of finality hit her with enough force to make her grip the corner of the table to remain upright. She faced the truth. Stryker wasn't going to listen to her, even if she could manage to find him and talk to him. And that chance was unlikely, since he was taking great pains to avoid her.

Jacey wrapped her arms around herself, trying to hold herself together. She felt as if she might shatter into pieces. She knew for certain her heart had. If she had had any chance of working out her marriage with Stryker, it was gone now. She had had a hard enough time before trying to reach his heart, before she had destroyed his trust in her. And any hope along with it.

Sinking down onto the chair, she leaned forward and crossed her arms on the table. The pain and despair swept over her, and she laid her head on her arms. She let the tears flow, sobs wracking her body.

There was no one else to see them. No one else to care.

Jeanette stared out the hotel window and sniffed at the threatening tears. The fight with Jacey had been awful.

How could Jacey have left her here without so much as a good-bye? She sniffed again. Everything had turned into such a mess. Even the hotel room.

It had taken her almost an hour to clean up after their fight. She shivered in remembrance and began to pace. Although they had disagreed in the past, she and Jacey had never had a real fight before.

She crossed back to the window and looked out, hoping to see some sign of her twin. She missed her.

Unexpectedly a sensation of weakness and complete despair came over her. She closed her eyes, welcoming the empathic link with her twin, and sharing her pain.

Softly she whispered, "Jacey." She knew the hurt and tears were her sister's.

At a knock on the door, the sensations vanished, leaving her feeling disoriented. And alone.

"Coming," she called out, crossing the room.

Jeanette swung the door open without stopping to think of possible consequences, and her mouth dropped open.

"What are *you* doing here?" she demanded.

Franklin Prescott pushed his way into the room before she could think to stop him. He reached for her, and she sidestepped his arms.

"I've come for you, dear," he announced with a dramatic swing of one arm.

"You've what?" She burst into laughter at his effrontery.

His smile vanished, and his eyes hardened on her. "I said I've come for you."

"You could have saved yourself the trouble." She tossed her head. "I'm through with you. I told you that before. At Aunt Cordelia's."

"Listen, Jeanette, you know how I feel about you," he implored, with a practiced tender regard in his voice. "Come away with me."

She started to open her mouth to refuse, but he rushed on before she could get her denial out.

"With your rancher's money we won't ever have to worry about anything but each other." He took her in his arms.

Thoroughly shocked at his assumption, Jeanette didn't fight him. He thought *she* had married Logan Stryker. He thought she would run off with him and bring Stryker's money with her. Shock gave way to fury.

Shoving him with all her might, she sent him staggering backward. She sidestepped him deftly and yanked the door open.

"Get out." She pointed to the hall. "Before I scream this place down around your ears."

"But, Jeanette. Dear," he coaxed.

"Out!"

His eyes narrowed on her. "You'll regret this." Turning, he stomped out the door.

Jeanette slammed it shut behind him and locked it.

Franklin stood on the other side of the door and heard the click of the lock. She thought she could lock him out of her life? Silly woman. He had hoped he could do this the easy way, but it looked as if Earl's plan was the best one after all.

Now he would bide his time and wait for the right moment.

Pretending nothing had gone wrong, he walked back down the stairs and out the door. He paused outside and reached in his pocket and checked his remaining funds. Sighing, he replaced the meager amount. It wasn't enough for a night's lodging.

He sighed again and looked up and down the street cautiously before he strolled to the livery stable. Sneaking inside without making any giveaway noise, he headed for his horse's stall. Tonight he would be sleeping with his horse. It wouldn't be the first time, but hopefully it would be the last. All he had to do was convince Jeanette of his devotion to her.

His opportunity came quicker than he had hoped. Sometime later, after he had dozed off, the approach of a rider woke him. He lay still and listened.

"Stryker, is that you?" Chet called out. "What are you doing here? Thought you'd be out at the ranch with your new bride." He chuckled to himself.

"Well, you thought wrong."

"You staying in town tonight?"

"Yeah," Stryker answered with uncustomary abruptness.

Chet threw a glance to the door. "Is your new bride waiting outside?"

Stryker jerked as if he had been struck. "No, she'll be staying at the ranch tonight."

Chet wisely didn't ask any further questions, merely raising his eyebrows and taking the reins to Stryker's horse from him.

Stryker clenched his teeth, then tried to relax. He wasn't likely to get any sleep tonight. Or for many nights to come. He walked out of the livery, his footsteps as heavy as his heart.

Franklin listened to the footsteps fade away. He had learned plenty from eavesdropping on the two men. He rested his hands under his head and thought about what he had heard. And what to do about it.

So, Jeanette had packed up and left the hotel following his visit. She had run straight to the new "husband" he had heard about from Earl. However, all didn't seem well between the newlyweds if the rancher was staying in town. That meant Jeanette was out at the ranch alone. He didn't stop to question why she had been at a hotel. There was nothing to do but go after her. He hadn't followed her all the way to Texas to give up on her easily.

Pushing himself to his feet, he dusted the hay from his

clothes and readied his horse. Thankfully he had already informed himself of the way to Stryker's ranch in case he needed to visit. Checking his saddlebags for the items he would need, he set off for the ranch.

Franklin followed the directions he had been given and arrived at the ranch without fail. He dismounted, withdrew the necessary items from his saddlebags, and tiptoed to the door.

Trying the knob, he was pleased to find it conveniently unlocked. He slipped inside and crept through the house, carefully searching. He found her in the dining room, asleep at the table.

He paused to smile in satisfaction and crept closer. Withdrawing the bottle and a cloth, he held them at arm's length as he poured the liquid onto the rag. He reached her side in three steps. Leaning forward, he pressed the rag over her mouth and held it there with one hand while he pulled her back against him with his other arm.

She jerked her head up, fighting against the suddenness of his attack. She mumbled against the cloth, but her cries were nearly inaudible. A moment later, she sagged forward limply.

Franklin tossed the rag to the floor and shifted her unconscious body in his arms. Pulling a note from his pocket, he propped it up against the lantern where anyone entering the room would be sure to see it.

Smiling to himself, he lifted her up into his arms and carried her from the house.

Chapter Twenty

Jacey opened her eyes and blinked against the harsh glare of the sun. Her eyes felt dry and scratchy, and her head hurt like the devil.

She swallowed, and her mouth tasted dreadful. Suddenly the night's events came rushing back to her. She had foolishly cried herself to sleep at the table. She remembered being grabbed from behind, and the acrid smell pressing against her nose, then blackness.

She fought back the terror that threatened to overwhelm her. Sitting straight up, she bumped her head on . . . someone's chin. She jerked around to look into the amused gaze of Franklin Prescott, sitting propped against a tree trunk.

Blinking in shock, she stared at him. He smiled back at her. For an instant she couldn't speak if her life depended on it.

She had been kidnapped by Franklin?

The very idea was preposterous. She looked around

them and realized they were camped near a streambed. One lone horse grazed nearby. The realization of riding double with him sent a shiver down her back. Red-hot anger followed right on its heels. How far had he taken her from the ranch? And why?

"Good morning, dear," he said in a cheerful voice.

Jacey opened her mouth to respond with a blistering retort, but nothing came out.

"Thirsty?"

She glared at him in response to his foolish question. What did he think?

He reached over and picked up a canteen. She thought about using it to hit him over the head with if he handed it to her, but he held the water to her lips. She clasped hold of the canteen and tugged, but he retained his hold. Disgusted, she realized he had too firm a grip on the thing for her to use it as a weapon. Glaring at him the whole time, she took several swallows of the metallic-tasting water, letting it soothe her throat.

"He warned me you'd wake up feeling bad. I'm sorry."

"Who?" Jacey forced the question out in a hoarse whisper.

"Never mind, dear. I—"

"Don't call me 'dear,' " she snapped in a voice that had gathered strength and now carried slightly above a whisper.

"Now, Jeanette, calm yourself."

Jacey shoved the canteen into his chest. "I'm Jacey," she said in a low voice.

Franklin's mouth worked, but not a word came out. He stared at her, shaking his head back and forth. "No. No, it can't be. You're—"

"Yes, it can. You got the wrong woman, you simpleton," she informed him. Her voice gathered strength along with her anger.

"Oh, no," he moaned. "What am I going to do?"

Jacey planted her hands on the hard ground and shoved herself to her feet. She wobbled unsteadily a moment. "Let me go," she ordered.

"I can't," he answered in distress. "He'd kill me if I did."

The question of who plagued her. Knowing someone else was behind Franklin's botched attempt scared her more than she wanted to admit. She had to get free.

Steadying herself as best she could, she reared back and kicked him. Her foot connected with his knee—not where she had been aiming.

"Yeow!" Franklin yelled in pain and jumped to his feet, hopping on one foot and rubbing his other leg.

She stepped away from him, whirled about, and ran for his horse. Before she had taken more than half a dozen steps, Franklin caught her, dragging her to the ground with a *thud* that knocked the wind out of her lungs.

"I don't want to hurt you, but I will," he told her. As he rolled her over, he asked, "Understand?"

Jacey glared her answer at him, a threat of her own shining in her eyes.

"Now see what you've done. I'm going to have to tie you." He yanked up a length of rope from beside the saddlebags and wrapped it tightly around her wrists.

She tried to kick him again, but he held her legs down with his. Then he tied a bandanna around her mouth as a gag.

"Now I know why I wanted Jeanette," he muttered beneath his breath.

Finished tying her, he pulled her to her feet and stared at her in confusion.

"I don't know what to do now, Jacey." He blinked several times and glanced around the area. "It wasn't supposed to happen like this."

Jacey's look spoke volumes. She had even more to say

if he ever took the gag off her mouth. He looked away, uneasy under her contemptuous stare.

"I was told if I could only get Jeanette away, she'd marry me for sure this time."

Jacey responded with a muffled snort.

Franklin grabbed her arm roughly and pulled her toward the horse. "I have to take you to the boss. He'll know what to do next."

She should have known Franklin didn't have the intelligence to think up a kidnapping, only to botch one. Someone else was the mastermind behind this. The fear of the unknown ate at her, destroying her courage bit by bit.

Attempting to hold her growing fear at bay, Jacey swore then and there she would repay him for this.

If she ever got free.

Stryker, she called out silently. *Help me.*

She concentrated on Stryker as hard as she could, hoping to somehow send a message to him.

Stryker would come after her, she told herself.

He had to.

Stryker waited until he heard the train pull out of the Braddock station before he left the boardinghouse. He was tired and in a foul mood. He refused to even consider the state of his heart. He had spent a sleepless night, lying awake and remembering every moment of his marriage.

Striding toward the jail office, he forced himself not to glance across the street to the departing train as it pulled away from the platform. Jacey was on the train headed back to Baltimore where she belonged. This was the way it had to be.

A band of pain constricted in his chest, and he swallowed fighting against it. It was best this way, he told himself. No good-byes. No recriminations.

Nothing said that could be regretted.

In truth, it wasn't what might have been said that worried him; it was the possibility that he might have listened to her soft words of explanation. Might have believed her fabrications again.

He shook his head, shaking off the possibility. She was gone now.

Gone from his life for good. Why didn't that fact make him feel better?

He strode past the jail, instead going to the livery stable for his horse. He might as well go out and check the ranch, make certain nothing there needed his attention.

Like Jacey for instance, a little voice prodded.

He ignored it, swinging up onto his mount's back and turning toward the ranch.

Stryker rode at a gallop, letting the warm air blow in his face, hoping it might blow away the persistent thoughts and memories of Jacey. He told himself he had planned on the marriage being temporary, and he had gotten what he wanted. His plan had succeeded exactly as devised. It didn't lift his heavy heart in the least.

Drawing his horse to a stop, he dismounted at the door of the ranch house and tied the reins to the railing. He might as well check the house. He was merely making certain she had left as ordered, he told himself. He wasn't hoping she was still here. No, not at all.

Liar, the little voice whispered. The word echoed over and over in his mind.

He threw the door open and stepped inside. Striding from room to room, he quickly checked for any sign that she had left. Or stayed. He didn't speak until he reached the bedroom.

"Jacey?" he called out before opening the door.

Empty.

He turned and walked across the hall to the second bedroom. For an instant, he held his breath in anticipation. Throwing the door open without knocking, he strode inside, coming to a stop at the foot of the bed. The ocelot kitten arched her back from her spot curled up on the bed. Then he noticed the bed hadn't been slept in, except for her pet.

The kitten blinked its big blue eyes at him plaintively. He stared in disbelief as it bounded toward him. Absently, he rubbed the kitten gently behind the ears. The little thing leaned against him and purred so softly he almost didn't hear it. Jacey had left her pet behind and alone?

No, Jacey wouldn't leave the kitten unattended for long. A faint hope took root in spite of his efforts to keep it away. He was being a fool, he told himself harshly. It was better if she was gone.

The back of his neck knotted. His lawman's intuition intruded and prodded him to check the room closer. He walked to the wardrobe and opened the door. It was filled with her gowns.

Stryker swallowed down the bad taste in his mouth. Something wasn't right. He could sense it.

Uneasiness ate at his gut, and he turned and took the stairs two at a time. A thorough search of the house failed to turn up anything until he reached the dining room.

Suddenly he spotted a note sitting propped up on the table, his name sprawled across it. He reached for it, his stomach forming a knot of tension. The paper crinkled loudly in his hand as he unfolded the note.

At sight of the words scrawled across the paper, his blood ran cold in his veins. Rooted in place, he gripped the paper so tightly he thought his fingers might snap. The brief message shook him all the way to his boots.

Someone had kidnapped Jacey.

He leaned his head back and squeezed his eyes shut. Guilt rushed over him, flooding his senses. He never should have left her alone. He had known both Hank and

Mrs. Carson were gone for the night. He shouldn't have left her.

He slammed his fist down on the table, rattling the unlit lantern. The words of the message were branded in his mind. He couldn't shut them out. Not even for an instant.

The kidnapper demanded a ransom for his *wife*. Stryker swallowed down his impotent fury at the man. The kidnapper ordered him to get the money, then go to the jail and wait for further instructions. He glanced down at the note. The high amount of the ransom jumped out at him. It would cost him his ranch. He lowered his head until his chin almost rested on his chest.

The ransom price would cost him his ranch. He knew it for a fact, but Jacey's life was at stake. It was his fault. If he hadn't planned the foolish temporary marriage to a mail order bride in the first place, she wouldn't be here now.

Did he have a choice? He couldn't let Jacey. . . .

He snapped his head back up. Staring hard at the note, he reread it, searching for what suddenly bothered him. There! He found it.

If you want to see your wife Jeanette again . . .

Stryker stared at the name. The note said Jeanette, not Jacey.

His wife Jeanette?

He hadn't married Jeanette. He had married Jacey!

The kidnapper had taken the wrong woman. He had taken Jacey's twin sister. But what had Jeanette been doing here alone? Unless the twins had been up to their trick of trading places again.

He now knew the woman he had met in town with Brett had been the twin sister, not Jacey. It all made perfect sense now. The pieces fit together like a completed puzzle—the pale blue eyes, the coy smiles, the way her bustle had lacked that special way of swaying—that woman had been Jeanette.

Yesterday in the hotel, he had known Jacey in a glance. He hadn't had to look twice. He just knew.

If the kidnapper had taken Jeanette, then where was Jacey? Likely as not he would find her where he had expected to find her twin sister—at the hotel.

What game were the sisters playing now? Were they scheming together to get rich off of him? If that was their plan, he had a surprise for them in the form of a pair of handcuffs and adjoining jail cells.

Swearing, he strode back out the door. He had had enough of their deceptions. He intended to let Jacey know that fact in no uncertain terms.

Stryker reached the hotel in less time than he had thought possible to make the trip. After tying his horse to the rail, he stormed into the hotel and up the stairs without ever stopping in spite of the curious stares and overheard remarks he drew.

He pounded on the door, and the instant it opened a crack, he shoved his way inside.

"What game are you playing this time, Jacey?" he demanded, advancing on her.

She scurried back from him. He had only taken a step when he realized his mistake. This woman wasn't Jacey. Her twin Jeanette faced him in open-mouthed amazement.

"Jeanette," he whispered the name.

Across from him, she nodded in acknowledgment, too startled to speak.

"If you're here, where is Jacey?" he asked, his voice filled with dread.

"I—" Jeanette started, then stopped.

She wrung her hands together, then bit her lower lip in a gesture that was so like Jacey it made his heart constrict.

"Jeanette, if you know where she is, tell me." Desperation edged his voice, making it ragged with the sudden need to know.

She tightened her hands together and faced him. "I don't know." She sniffed at approaching tears. "I haven't seen her since she ran out of here after you last night."

Stryker felt real fear deep in the pit of his stomach. It wound itself around him, tightening its hold.

Jacey had been the one kidnapped!

His gut formed into a cold knot, and he fought down the terror edging at him. He didn't even know where to start looking for her.

His training and natural skill took over, calming him. First things first; he had to gather up the ransom money, then to hell with waiting for further instructions as the note had ordered. He was an expert tracker, and he would track whoever took her to the ends of the earth if he had to.

"Stay here," he ordered Jeanette.

Turning on his heel, he strode out the door. As he reached the stairs, he heard her footsteps behind him. He should have known she wouldn't meekly obey if she was related to his Jacey.

His Jacey.

The thought nearly stopped him in his tracks. This time he didn't deny the truth. She was his. And he wasn't about to let her go this way. Whoever took her had better pray she wasn't harmed.

No one took what was his. Much less *his wife.*

And the woman he loved.

Instead of hurting, the realization brought him a sense of rightness and of peace. He knew it wouldn't do any good to try to deny he had fallen in love with her. He had fallen in love too completely for denials.

Too completely for anything else but to make it up to

Jacey. He would tell her he loved her; then he would never let her go.

If he got to her in time.

Fear held him in its punishing grasp. He had to get to her.

A hesitant touch on his arm jerked him around. Jeanette stepped back, her eyes widening in alarm.

"Stryker?" Her voice wavered; then she made an obvious effort to go on. "Will Jacey be . . . will she be all right?"

He nodded, not trusting himself to speak.

"You're sure?" Jeanette prompted.

His eyes hardened as he promised, "I'll find her and bring her back safely."

The words of his vow branded themselves in his heart. He wouldn't return until he had found her, and he wouldn't return without her.

"What should I do?" Jeanette asked, her voice trembling with the approach of tears.

He knew he needed to give her something to do before she started crying. "Go back upstairs and get your bag, then go to the jail and wait for me there."

He didn't give her time to refuse or ask him any further questions. Taking the remaining stairs two at a time, he hurried out of the hotel and headed straight for the bank.

Halfway to the bank, he heard someone call his name. He whirled around to spot Brett several feet away. He didn't have time to visit with his friend.

"Hey, Stryker, wait up," Brett yelled.

Stryker ignored the order, focused on reaching the bank and convincing Bertram Raines to loan him the ransom money.

Brett caught up with him, grabbing his arm. Stryker jerked away.

"Hey, what's wrong?"

"Jacey's been kidnapped." Stryker realized saying the

words out loud made the sitation even more real than before. Even more frightening.

His friend paled at the announcement. "What can I do to help?"

Stryker sighed and rubbed the back of his neck. "Go to the jail and take care of things there. My deputy is over in Webster today. I'll meet you there in a bit."

"Done." Brett dropped a hand on his friend's shoulder for a moment, then stepped back.

Less than thirty minutes later, Stryker strode out of the bank with the ransom money. Bertram had been uncommonly understanding, loaning him the money without making him sign over the deed to his ranch on the spot. Instead, he gave him thirty days to pay. Stryker shook his head in disbelief. The banker was a changed man. Whatever had happened, he thanked heaven for it.

Stryker stepped into his office to find a small crowd waiting for him. Rosalyn, Linda and Brett stood anxiously beside the desk.

"What are you all doing here?" he asked in surprise.

"We heard Jacey's been kidnapped," Rosalyn told him.

"We came to help," Linda said in the next breath.

"Brett." He shot an angry glance to his friend standing beside the two women.

"Don't blame the dear boy."

The door creaked open, and Stryker whirled around, hoping against hope it was Jacey. For a brief instant relief rushed over him, then fled as he recognized Jeanette.

At her gasp, he smiled in reassurance. He glanced behind him to see the other three occupants of the office staring in openmouthed amazement at Jacey's mirror image.

"Folks," Stryker spoke into the dead silence, "I'd like you to meet Jeanette. Jacey's twin sister."

"Twin?"

"Sister?"

"Jeanette?"

Everyone spoke at once. He noted the smile light up Brett's face in the minute before he turned to Stryker again.

"I'll ride with you."

"No, I can track her faster alone. You wait here for the kidnapper's instructions."

"But, Stryker—" Brett hesitated only an instant. "The ransom money—"

"I got it from Bertram," he stated flatly.

"But won't that cost you your ranch?"

"It will if I can't pay it back in thirty days."

"But that's impossible," Brett muttered.

Stryker nodded once before he stepped out the door, slamming it behind him. He mounted up and rode off at a gallop for the ranch to pick up their trail.

"Well, he's finally realized he loves her," Rosalyn announced with a sigh.

"It's about time," Linda added.

Jeanette turned her full attention on Brett. He held out his arms to her, and she walked into his embrace.

A moment later, the door swung open, and an older gentleman walked inside. He paused to look around at the group and pounded his cane on the wood floor to catch their attention.

"Uncle Harvey," Jeanette exclaimed in joy. "When did you get into town?"

He seemed taken aback by her effervescent greeting. "I . . . I just arrived."

"I'm so glad you're here." Jeanette flung herself into his arms and hugged him tightly.

Shocked, he hugged her back; then his shoulders sagged. "Jeanette, what have you done now?"

She stepped back to stand at Brett's side. Raising her

chin in a gesture she learned from her twin, she said, "I haven't done anything. Jacey's been kidnapped."

Fear for her sister gripped her hard, and she reached down and clasped Brett's hand.

Brett slipped his arm around her shoulders. "There, there. We'll find her."

As she sniffed with pending tears, he rushed to add, "I promise."

"What do you mean Jacey's been kidnapped?" Harvey Forester shouted. He stared at Brett's arm around his niece and added, "And who are you?"

Everyone rushed to explain at once.

Rosalyn held up her hand, and silence fell over the room. She stepped up and slipped her hand into the crook of Harvey's elbow and proceeded to tell him the latest events. Linda added details as she saw fit.

Rosalyn ended with, "Well, let's not stand around here jawing and doing nothing. Stryker might need our help."

"Chet has a wagon. Let's get him and go after Jacey," Linda suggested, already turning and grabbing a rifle from the rack.

She led the way out the door. Rosalyn caught up the remaining rifle, then followed Linda. Everyone fell into step along with her, and they headed for the livery stable.

Without knowing it, Stryker had his posse riding after him with Brett, who was almost as good a tracker as he, at the head.

Franklin shifted in the saddle, swinging his leg out of the way of Jacey's foot. She had kicked him for the last time.

Long before they could reach their destination, he regretted ever daring to kidnap the wrong woman. He even began regretting meeting either of the twins. He would be glad to be rid of Jacey. Suddenly he leaned to the side to dodge her elbow for what must have been the hundredth time, and nearly fell off his horse. He swore at her until his throat hurt.

Sitting in front of him, Jacey merely smiled. Until she could escape, she intended to see Franklin Prescott was very sorry he had ever taken her.

Waiting for the right moment, she shifted her weight and once again thrust back with her elbow, using all her strength. Franklin let out a muffled oath before he rolled backward off the horse and hit the ground with a loud *thud*.

Jacey smiled around the gag in satisfaction, then kicked the horse into a canter. Concentrating on attempting to grab hold of the reins with her bound hands, she didn't see the man standing in the path until it was too late.

He snatched the horse's bridle and dragged the animal to a stop, nearly unseating Jacey. She tried to pull the horse back, but couldn't. Rough hands reached out and yanked her off the saddle and dumped her onto the ground.

Jacey hit the dirt with a bone-jarring thud of pain. She blinked and attempted to get her breath. Looking up, she stared into the eyes of the mastermind.

Cousin Earl.

Shock and fury hit her as solidly as she had hit the ground. As he leaned forward, hatred in his eyes, she tasted real fear.

Heaven help her.

In that instant, she knew he would never set her free alive.

Chapter Twenty-One

"You fool!" Earl turned on Franklin as he limped up to join them. "What did you bring her here for? You were supposed to marry her."

"I couldn't marry her."

"Why not?" Earl shouted, obviously out of patience with his cohort.

"Because she's Jacey, not Jeanette," Franklin yelled. "I took the wrong one."

"You idiot!"

"Now what do we do?" Franklin looked from Earl to Jacey and back again in indecision.

"Shut up and let me think," Earl ordered.

Jacey watched the two men from under lowered lashes. As a rock dug into her behind, she shifted her weight and suddenly realized the ropes binding her wrists had slipped down. They must have loosened in her fall. If the men would only keep their attention off her for a few more minutes, maybe she could slip free of her bindings.

When she did, she would make them both pay.

She twisted her wrists, pulling at the ropes. Bit by painful bit, she tugged at the restraints until she finally could slip her hands free. Then she removed the gag.

"Earl, what are you planning?" Franklin asked.

"Well, I'm not going to let my father simply hand over a third of the business to her," Earl said with a sneer. "It all belongs to me."

Jacey forgot the need to remain silent. She stood to her feet in a rush of anger.

"Earl, is that what this is about? If you think Jeanette or I want the business, you have less sense than Franklin."

"She's untied," Franklin shouted.

"You idiot," Earl told him. "Tie her back up."

If these two fools thought for one minute that she would meekly sit down and allow herself to be bound again, they had a big surprise. Jacey grabbed up a rock, and when Franklin reached for her, she hit him square in the forehead with it.

Franklin fell over backward onto the ground, out cold.

"What did you do?" Earl shouted in disbelief.

"You want to come closer and I'll show you." Jacey grabbed up another rock and hefted it in her hand.

With a roar of rage, Earl lunged for her. She panicked and threw the rock. It hit his shoulder and bounced off.

Earl yelped in pain and grabbed her arm. Yanking her toward him, he raised up his fist.

"Do it and I'll drop you where you stand," Stryker spoke in a deadly cold voice.

Earl turned to stare down the barrel of a gun pointed right at him.

"Just give me an excuse," Stryker said in a low growl. "Please." He cocked the gun, never wavering in his aim.

"Stryker, you came." Jacey jerked free and ran toward him.

He caught her in one arm, shifting her to his side and away from his gun.

Earl stared at them. His mouth worked, and it took two tries to get a sound out. "Where did you come from?"

"I walked up while you were attacking my *wife*."

Jacey smiled at the added emphasis he had placed on the word *wife*.

"She attacked me!"

"He's right, you know." Jacey laughed softly, tucked against Stryker's side.

"What—"

Stryker didn't get to finish his question. The rumble of a wagon drowned out his words. Looking cautiously to the side, he saw the approaching vehicle. Identifying its passengers, he simply stared at the unlikely rescuers.

"Aw, hell," Stryker muttered beneath his breath.

Jacey giggled softly beside him.

"Ahh, we're too late," Rosalyn complained, with a thump of the rifle butt on the floor of the wagon.

"I told you to hurry," Linda turned and scolded Chet.

"I got him covered," Brett shouted out, springing to the ground.

"I got the other one," Chet announced, hurrying out of the wagon and leaving the remaining four to disembark on their own.

"What do I get to do?" Rosalyn grumbled.

"Jacey!" A squeal from Jeanette signaled her arrival a second before she threw herself at Jacey, nearly taking both her and Stryker to the ground.

"Give them a chance to breathe, girl," an older man scolded gently.

Jacey disentangled herself from her twin's exuberant hug to see her uncle walking toward her.

"Uncle Harvey? What are you doing here?"

"What are any of you doing here?" Stryker grumbled as Jacey pulled free from his arm.

"We came to help you," Rosalyn announced with a grin, the rifle held in the crook of her arm.

Harvey Forester swept Jacey up into a bear hug that nearly squeezed the breath out of her. When he finally released her, he patted her shoulder.

"Fine-looking man you got yourself for a husband," he whispered.

"I think so, too," she whispered and hugged him.

"And your dowry—"

"That's my surprise. A wedding gift." Jacey stepped back from her uncle's embrace.

He nodded his agreement and leaned on his cane.

She looked over to where the men were tying up Earl and Franklin for the ride to the jail. She reached out and rested a hand on her uncle's arm. "I'm sorry about Earl."

He nodded, looking down at her. "Maybe some time behind bars will straighten that boy out." He pounded his cane on the hard ground. "I don't want him back until then."

Reluctantly Rosalyn and Linda handed their rifles over to Chet, then came up to hug Jacey, checking for themselves to see she was unharmed. Stryker stood on the sidelines, watching the commotion. Where had the self-appointed posse come from? And how was he going to round them up and disarm them?

Another more important question disturbed him. How was he going to get Jacey alone now from the persistent well-wishers?

Jacey solved the problem for him when she declined to ride back in the wagon, instead suggesting she ride back with Stryker.

Brett stopped by to slap him on the back. "Looks like you won't lose the ranch after all." He grinned and winked.

"Want me to return the ransom money to the bank for you?"

"I'll take care of it," Stryker answered.

As the wagon load of the civilian posse and two prisoners drove off, he turned and eyed Jacey warily.

She returned his look with a wary one of her own. Dared she blurt out now that she loved him with all her heart? What if he didn't care in return?

They stood for endless seconds, like two opponents sizing each other up, each too uncertain of losing to speak the words that had to be said aloud.

Stryker wasn't sure what to say, or how to begin. He had never been tongue-tied before in his life.

"Ransom money?" Jacey asked. "You risked the ranch for me?"

Stryker stared down at her upturned face. "Of course," he said.

His sacrifice touched her deeper than anything he could have done. She took a bold step toward him.

She didn't get to take another before Stryker swept her into his arms, holding her close. He lowered his head and kissed her with such possession that he stole her breath away. She returned his passion, giving of herself completely in that one kiss.

Several long moments later, he eased back. Looking down into her dark blue eyes, he asked the question in his heart. "Could you ever love me, Jacey?"

"No," she answered honestly. "Not could. Do. I've loved you since—"

"Since when?" he demanded.

"I think since I stepped down off the train and looked into your beautiful eyes."

"Men don't have beautiful eyes."

"You do," she corrected. Cocking her head, she waited.

"What?" he asked warily.

She swallowed down her trepidation and raised her chin. His lips twitched at the act.

"Getting ready to defy me?" he teased.

She shook her head, then asked the question she couldn't hold back. "And me? Do you love me?" The last words were said in a whisper.

"More than life," he answered solemnly.

"Stryker," she said in soft invitation.

"Marry me, Jacey?"

She laughed. "I already did."

"This time for real."

Her laughter fled, and she stared into his eyes. "Yes, oh, yes!"

"Look out, lady, I may never let you go," he warned, his voice deep with love as he swept her into his arms.

"Never is a long time," she teased. Her eyes sparkled with love for him.

"Not long enough." He nuzzled her neck with his lips.

"Then always," she whispered.

"And forever."

He took her lips again in a kiss to seal their love and their future together.

For always and forever.

Epilogue

Jacey adjusted the lace wedding veil over the blond curls of her twin sister with shaky hands. She stepped back and surveyed Jeanette with a wide smile. Light blue eyes met sapphire ones.

"Almost ready?" Jacey asked.

Stepping back carefully, Jacey smoothed her hand down the bodice of her own white wedding gown and smiled in pure joy. She rested her hand on her waist, savoring the moment.

Unable to resist a quick look, she tiptoed over to the door so as not to disturb Jeanette in front of the mirror and opened the door a crack to peer out into the church. Searching, she spotted him immediately.

Stryker stood at the front of the church, waiting for her. He glanced her way, and she knew he saw her by the smile on his face. She waved at him, and he tipped his dark hat to her with a wicked grin, not paying a bit of attention to the people sitting in the pews watching.

Her wedding, Jacey wanted to shout the news this time.

This time was different from the first. It was to be a double wedding with her remarrying Stryker, and Jeanette marrying Brett. It would be the first double wedding in the history of Braddock. The entire town had turned out, except for Madeline Raines, who had fled town one night.

Stryker winked again, and Jacey giggled, then stepped back out of sight. The one thing that mattered was different at this wedding. This time she was marrying for love.

Same dress.

Same strand of pearls.

Same wonderful bridegroom.

She laid her hand back over her waist and smiled at the one additional difference in her. Their child would be at this marriage of love.

"Will you shut the door?" Jeanette scolded her. "It's bad luck to see the bridegroom before the wedding."

Jacey looked over her shoulder at the near replica of herself in an almost identical white gown.

"Don't worry, my bridegroom saw me quite well this morning," Jacey teased.

"Well, mine hasn't, so shut the door," Jeanette insisted.

A pair of giggles outside alerted them to Rosalyn and Linda's entry.

"Ready?" Rosalyn asked.

"That's a foolish question," Linda said with a laugh. "Of course they're ready."

Jacey fingered the strand of pearls at her neck, their gift to her, and hugged both women.

Rosalyn winked at Linda, and asked, "Can we pick 'em?"

"Yup," Linda answered without a pause. "Getting both our boys married off good."

At Jacey's surprised look, Rosalyn explained, "We picked your answer to the ad."

Jacey's mouth dropped open. "But that was Jeanette."

"No matter," Linda dismissed the correction. "We got two brides for the price of one."

A knock at the door signaled Uncle Harvey's arrival. He peeked inside and beamed. "Shall we go, girls? Your bridegrooms are waiting." He held out both arms.

Jacey walked down the aisle on one side of her uncle, with her twin on the other. However, she only had eyes for her handsome bridegroom standing at the front of the church. She scarcely noticed when Uncle Harvey placed Jeanette's hand in Brett's.

As she laid her hand in Stryker's, she gazed up at him. The love she saw shining from his eyes nearly brought her to tears. She blinked several times.

Stryker leaned forward to whisper, "If you faint again, I'll have to carry you off. Again."

Jacey felt the heat of a blush spread over her cheeks. She lightly elbowed him as the preacher began the ceremony.

The words flowed over Jacey this time, happiness enveloping her. She inched closer to Stryker, wanting his nearness. He held her hand tightly, as if he were afraid she would flee. The thought brought a smile to her lips. He slipped his other arm around her, likely as not creating a scandal in the town, but she didn't care.

"You may kiss the bride, Brett," the preacher said.

Turning to Stryker, he prompted, "You may kiss the bride again, Stryker."

And Stryker proceeded to do just that. He lowered his mouth over hers, claiming her lips in a devastating kiss of love, of surrender, of possession.

Jacey thought she might truly faint.

Laughing, Stryker lifted her up into his arms to hold her close to his chest. She could hear the rapid beat of his heart. Turning, he carried her from the church.

A round of applause followed them out the door.

Outside, Stryker lowered his head, and whispered, "Wife."

"Husband," Jacey murmured against his lips.

They sealed their real marriage in a kiss that nearly stole both their breaths away, proclaiming their love.

For always and forever.

Put a Little Romance in Your Life With
Rosanne Bittner

DATE DUE
DATE DE RETOUR